The *Light* Will Come

The Light Will Come

Brenda Dalton Clemens

WESTBOW
PRESS®
A DIVISION OF THOMAS NELSON
& ZONDERVAN

Copyright © 2018 Brenda Dalton Clemens.

All rights reserved. No part of this book may be used or reproduced by any means, graphic, electronic, or mechanical, including photocopying, recording, taping or by any information storage retrieval system without the written permission of the author except in the case of brief quotations embodied in critical articles and reviews.

WestBow Press books may be ordered through booksellers or by contacting:

WestBow Press
A Division of Thomas Nelson & Zondervan
1663 Liberty Drive
Bloomington, IN 47403
www.westbowpress.com
1 (866) 928-1240

Because of the dynamic nature of the Internet, any web addresses or links contained in this book may have changed since publication and may no longer be valid. The views expressed in this work are solely those of the author and do not necessarily reflect the views of the publisher, and the publisher hereby disclaims any responsibility for them.

Any people depicted in stock imagery provided by Getty Images are models, and such images are being used for illustrative purposes only. Certain stock imagery © Getty Images.

THE HOLY BIBLE, NEW INTERNATIONAL VERSION®, NIV® Copyright © 1973, 1978, 1984, 2011 by Biblica, Inc.® Used by permission. All rights reserved worldwide.

This is a work of fiction. All of the characters, names, incidents, organizations, and dialogue in this novel are either the products of the author's imagination or are used fictitiously.

ISBN: 978-1-9736-2567-4 (sc)
ISBN: 978-1-9736-2566-7 (hc)
ISBN: 978-1-9736-2568-1 (e)

Library of Congress Control Number: 2018904378

Print information available on the last page.

WestBow Press rev. date: 5/22/2018

Acknowledgements

In the spring of 2009, I was in a Sunday school class taught by Irene Tomlinson. Her lesson was on one of Paul's epistles written while he was imprisoned in Rome. During the course of the class, she wondered what happened to the soldiers who were Paul's guards, and if he had an impact on them.

I went home that day and told my husband Bobby that I wanted to write a short story about an imaginary Roman soldier assigned to guard Paul. Bobby was very supportive, and even though he was ill with leukemia, he took an active interest in my little project. He suggested I use some of his Latin books which contained useful information about ancient Rome, and we talked about some of the material that I found about daily life during the time of Paul. After completing a lot of research, I began my story and completed a couple of handwritten pages. Bobby became much sicker, and I put my story aside. Sadly, Bobby died in October of 2009. As the weeks and months passed, life was very difficult, and writing was far from my mind. My only sibling, Helen, was battling bone cancer and my dear friend Carole Sneed's brain cancer returned. Carole died a short time after Bobby. My sister Helen had no children. Her husband died of cancer in 2008, and I had the responsibility of her care and taking her for chemotherapy.

In the summer of 2010, I found the research that I had put away. I had a decision to make. Should I dump the material in the trash or pick it up and begin to write again? I felt led to continue, so a year after I began the research, I started writing again. It was good therapy for me and took my mind off Helen's illness and my loneliness. During that summer I wrote Part I. My beloved granddaughter Jessie Clemens spent a lot of time with me that summer and did the preliminary typing of my "short story" (which I now called a novella)! Both my sister and my best friend Dr. Carolyn Huff liked my novella enough that they encouraged me to write more. My sister insisted that Part I hadn't ended the story, and she wanted to know what happened to Paulus and Livia. I wrote about fifteen pages more, and then my sister suddenly died in October, 2010. Again, I put my writing aside and became consumed with the emotional and business details of her death. The loss of my husband and my only close blood relative in less than a year left me reeling. Without the support and love of my stepchildren, grandchildren, friends, and my faith in God, I believe I would have given up. In the spring of 2011, during some lonely evenings, I again began to write. I completed Part II that summer. My friendship with the husband of my friend Carole grew. We talked a lot and shared our deepest feelings. He read Parts I and II and was also very complimentary.

To the surprise of everyone, Lowell Sneed and I married on November 5, 2011. Again I put my project away, but finally around Easter of 2012, I completed the last of Part III. Both my friend Carolyn and Lowell were there encouraging me as I completed the longest "short story" ever written! I want to add a special thank you to my grandson Robert Clemens IV for helping me get the final draft to the publisher.

I pray that the words I have written will give praise and glory to my Lord and Savior Jesus Christ and do honor to His name.

Brenda Dalton Clemens

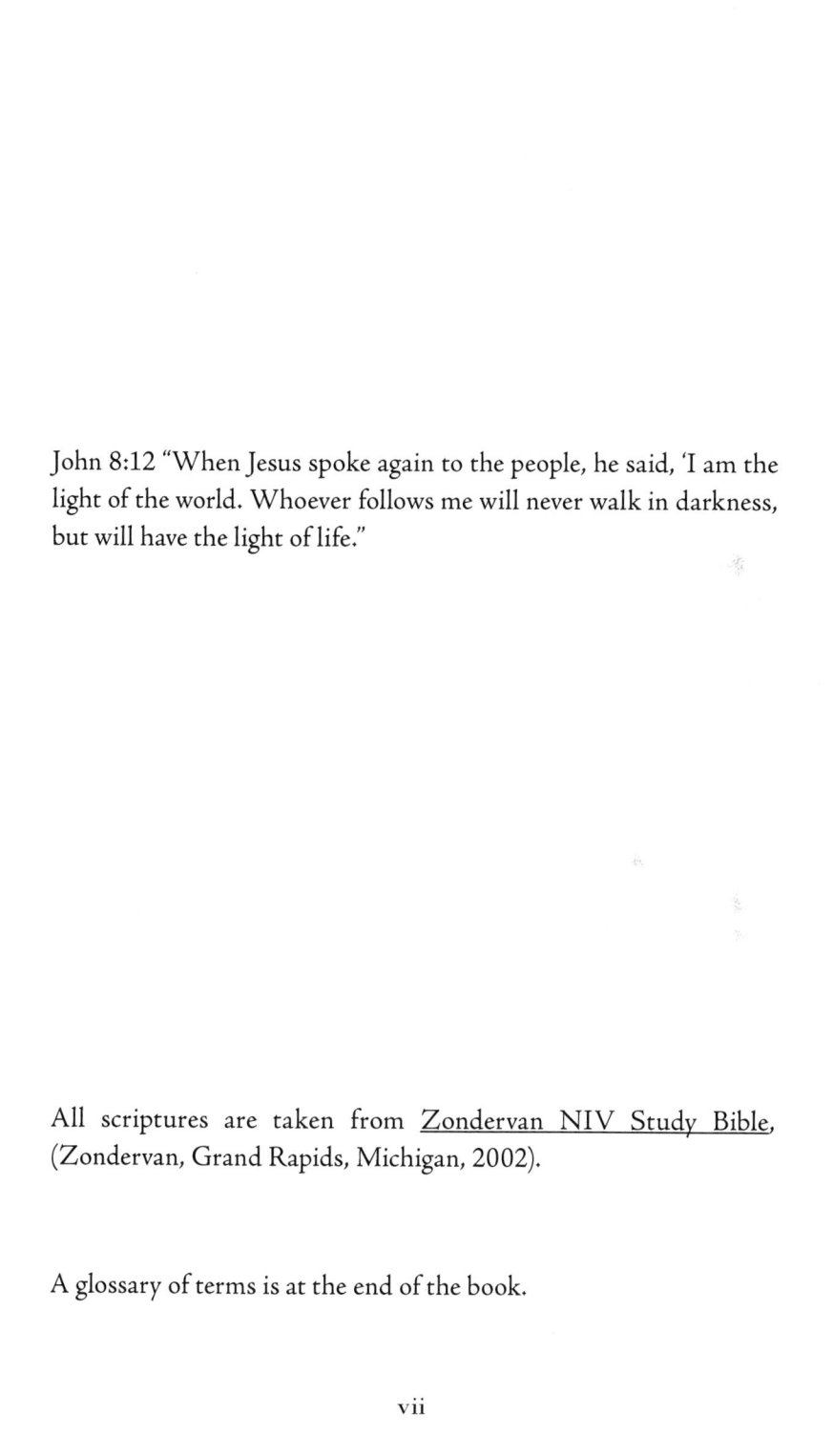

John 8:12 "When Jesus spoke again to the people, he said, 'I am the light of the world. Whoever follows me will never walk in darkness, but will have the light of life."

All scriptures are taken from <u>Zondervan NIV Study Bible</u>, (Zondervan, Grand Rapids, Michigan, 2002).

A glossary of terms is at the end of the book.

Part One

Chapter 1

The sun was shining on an early autumn day in Rome, but the morning rains had left the air so humid that it seemed as if a soggy, woolen tunic had formed a ceiling under the sun and sky. Paulus walked down the Esquiline Hill where his father's villa was located and then tramped on down the narrow streets where one of the largest *insulae* of Rome was located. The sounds and smells of the various shops (from fish markets to spice stalls) on the ground floor of the *insulae* attacked the senses of most of the people in the streets. Paulus, however, was barely aware of the weather or the activities in his surroundings. His thoughts were only of his own circumstances – the humiliation of the past few days causing a simmering anger to burn within him.

"I should be with the other soldiers in my *maniple* — off fighting the barbarians. When we had our games, I always outran and outfought my friends, and my *gladius* was greatly feared as we trained! I should not be here! Me, the nephew of a Roman senator and the son of a courageous warrior – now reduced to this!" Paulus muttered to himself as he walked along the wet Roman streets.

Two little boys were wrestling and playing in one of the side streets as Paulus hurried on his way. They stopped their play, watching the angry soldier talking to himself. Paulus glanced at the boys as they resumed their wrestling match. He remembered when he and his friend Marius used to do the same, and he always beat Marius. "But now, Marius is the leader of 200 men, off on an adventure, and I'm stuck in Rome," thought Paulus.

To be honest, Paulus had to admit his troubles were his own fault. He got into a fight at the public baths several days ago over some comments about his sister Livia. One of the loud-mouthed soldiers commented on his sister not being married. Another soldier laughed and said she was too ugly and boring for anyone to ever want her. Paulus had demanded an apology. The man then said that even with the family's money for a dowry, no man would want her "horseface" in his bed. Paulus hit him. He had always had a quick temper, and he adored his kind, quick-witted sister Livia. It was just his luck that their captain saw the blow and wanted to know the cause. By then a crowd had gathered, and Paulus did not want to repeat the things said about his beloved sister. Paulus was so enraged that he refused to explain to his superior and as punishment, he was pulled from his *maniple* and here he was. He knew he was fortunate not to have further punishment, but, due to his father's precarious health and the family's prominence, he was simply assigned a new duty in Rome.

Paulus was 22 years old. He was a tall, handsome man with a good mind. His father had insisted that he have an excellent education, and his Greek tutor was determined that Paulus become proficient in many disciplines. He had been a good pupil, but what he dreamed of was glory on the battlefield. He preferred adventures in far-off lands to the study of Greek philosophers and Roman conquests. He wanted to be in campaigns, not learn of them. Now due to his quick temper, he was given a boring assignment to guard one prisoner!

The house where the prisoner was staying was on the edge of town. While it was a rather long walk from his father's villa, he knew the exercise would help him clear his mind of anger. He had been warned by his captain not to get in any more trouble, so he had to follow his orders very carefully.

After the brisk walk, Paulus found himself at the entrance to an unimposing house. Taking a deep breath, he walked into the courtyard. Still unable to calm his anger, he thought to himself, "Me, the best soldier in my training class – a guard for a Jew! A Jew called Paul. I suppose the captain thought it amusing that our names are the same."

Paulus knew very little about Jews. There were lots of them in Rome, but they kept to themselves. He supposed this Jew must be a very dangerous man to require guards, and he must have influence with someone to not be in a prison cell. Paulus walked inside and saw his charge – Paul.

He could not believe he had been pulled from his *maniple* to guard this, this dull-looking Jew. The Jew was a small man of ordinary countenance, and not in the least impressive. He wore a simple, ordinary robe, typical of all Jews that Paulus had seen. When Paulus walked closer to the Jew, he expected his prisoner to cower in fear. Instead, Paul casually greeted him with a nod and resumed his conversation with another Jew. Paulus had been told that he was an imposing man. He was much taller and stronger than most of his friends. In fact, he had to have his *sagum* remade because it wasn't at all large enough. With the anger that he knew must show on his face, he expected the Jewish prisoner to be intimidated by his appearance. However, it was evident that he was so involved with his discussion that he barely noted the changing of the guards.

Paulus looked toward an older soldier called Silvius who had been guarding the Jew for some weeks. Having arrived before Paulus, Silvius had posted himself to the left of the door leading to the courtyard. Paulus asked where he should stand, and Silvius directed him to the right where another guard was just leaving. Unfortunately, his assigned place was very near the Jew.

"I can't believe this! If the Jew had been a more important man, I might not find this job so demeaning. But he's nobody and is probably not aware of my family's importance," Paulus thought to himself. "I'll certainly not talk to him; there is nothing I can learn from a Jew."

As the hours passed Paulus was surprised to learn that the prisoner spoke several languages. He had a lot of visitors, all of whom spoke to the Jew with deference. As the evening hours approached, three men came who were obviously in some distress. Since they spoke to Paul in Greek (a language Paulus learned early in his studies), he found himself listening to their conversation.

"My dear brother, I know it is not what you want. But you have to return. It is the right thing," said Paul.

"But he may be killed!" cried one of the other men.

Paulus' attention was now completely caught by the conversation.

"We have cried and prayed about this for days now. It is God's will. You must return," said Paul.

Paulus strained to hear more, but since the visitors spoke so softly, he could make out little of their responses. Then to his surprise, all of them knelt with their arms around each other, and they began to pray to their god. It was truly embarrassing. He shook his head and looked to Silvius, who seemed not to be surprised. Grown men crying and praying loudly! It was so unseemly that Paulus had to look away. After their lengthy prayers and a lot of tears, one of the visitors, that they called Onesimus, rose from his knees. With a look that was almost beatific, he said to Paul, "Dear Sir, you are my father, my master, my counselor, and my brother. I trust God's desire to be in your words."

Onesimus spoke with eloquence. He said something strange about God revealing himself in the person of someone named Jesus Christ. ("He must be some prophet the Jews had," thought Paulus). It was hard to hear all of the conversation, but Paulus found himself listening. Maybe it was the boredom of standing guard, but he found their fervor oddly compelling. Silvius appeared to be uninvolved, but Paulus couldn't ignore the men. These men (two Jews and two Greeks) were of no importance, but they were so assured and confident that some decision was their god's will.

After a few more tears, the visitors left. Paul knelt again and began praying. Shortly thereafter, another man entered. He carried papyrus, and it was obvious that a letter was to be written. Paulus thought to himself that the letter would have to be written quickly, as the oil in the lamp was disappearing fast and soon there would be little light.

Paul walked around the room dictating a letter to someone named Philemon. The scribe had to wait for Paul's words as Paul became emotional and had to stop. Paulus was curious as to the nature of a letter that would cause such grief. Paul suddenly stopped dictating his message and turned to the soldiers and said, "My fellow Romans, I pray that you never have to cut a friend from your bosom as I must today."

He turned back to the scribe and continued the letter. Paulus was listening with interest now but pretended to be disinterested. He caught pieces of Paul's words, "Onesimus…became my son while I was in chains, but I am sending him — who is my very heart — back to you… Perhaps the reason he was separated from you for a little while was that you might have him back for good—no longer as a slave, but better than a slave, as a dear brother."(Philemon:10-16)

Paulus was shocked. The man who had been there earlier was obviously a runaway slave and Paul was sending him back to his master. Paulus wondered if he should report this to his superiors. It seemed that Paul was sending him back to face the consequences from his master, Philemon. It was too bad for Onesimus. He seemed a very learned man. But Philemon could have him branded on his forehead or even executed if he wished. Paulus decided he didn't need to be involved with these Jews, but in truth the emotions of the men touched him, even as he tried to ignore them.

Just as Paulus was pondering these events, the replacement guard arrived. There was only a single guard on duty for the night. They exchanged greetings, and Paul and the scribe bade them farewell and nodded a greeting to the new guard Lucien.

Walking hurriedly back through the darkening city, Paulus found it hard to forget the events of the day.

"Was the earlier visitor to the prisoner a runaway slave?" Paulus asked Silvius.

Silvius shrugged and replied, "The thin Greek has been here most of the time I've been on guard duty and that has been several weeks. They seem to me to be friends. He has a lot of visitors and they come and go often."

"I'm surprised that he is allowed such access to visitors."

"Well, he's a Roman citizen."

"I see. So that's why he addressed us as 'my fellow Romans'. I thought it strange," said Paulus.

Silvius continued, "They say he was born in Tarsus and is very well educated. I know he has traveled everywhere. It's odd. You know he's here because some of the Jews wanted him arrested, don't you?"

"What? I thought he had broken one of our Roman laws," replied Paulus.

"No. It's something to do with a man called Christ or Jesus Christ. We executed him a while ago, and the Jews were in favor of it. But some people now say he was a god," Silvius said.

As they came to where their paths home separated, they said farewell, and Paulus continued his walk home. When he arrived home, he saw Livia seated on a bench by the pool in the courtyard. By the moonlight, he couldn't tell if she were alone.

"Could she have a lover, and we not know about him? He better not come here," thought Paulus. He felt his familiar temper flare as he walked quickly to where she sat.

"What are you doing out here? It's almost dark."

"Oh, I couldn't sleep, so I came out here to look at the stars and think for a while. Paulus, do you believe in our gods?" asked Livia.

"What a foolish question! We have been taught about all of the gods and their powers. Our shrine to our household gods is just to your left. Our Emperor himself is one of our gods also."

"Well, do you pray to them?"

"I'm a busy man. I don't have time for long prayers. I'll leave them to men like that Jew I'm guarding. He seems to spend half his time praying!"

"What gods do these Jews have? Do they have special Jewish household gods?"

"How should I know? I've only been guarding him for one day, and I've never had any interest in learning about Jews!" Paulus replied with some gruffness. For some reason, he could never dismiss Livia. His other two sisters — yes. They were interested only in their families, their new tunics, and the gossip that flowed throughout the Roman Empire. Their silly chatter annoyed him. He was glad they had moved with their husbands to far north of the city.

"I heard them speak about Jehovah a time or two. I got the idea he must be their chief god like our Jupiter. They seemed to mention a Jesus in their prayers. He must be another god or a prophet or something. I didn't listen very closely," said Paulus (not telling the complete truth). Paulus wasn't really lying. He wasn't interested in their prayers, but he was somewhat intrigued by the prisoner's lack of concern for his situation.

Paulus was tired from his new job and he needed to sleep before he had to return tomorrow to that same dingy house. "It is so unfair, my training and talents are being wasted! I wonder what my friends are doing in the campaign," he thought.

Turning to Livia, he said it was time for both of them to go to bed.

Chapter 2

The next morning, Paulus rose later than usual due to the guard duty lasting into the late evening. His father and Livia had already left the house. His father undoubtedly had had his slaves carry him by sedan chair to the forum for some business. After the injury to his hip and side during a battle five years earlier, his father had trouble walking and was often in great pain. Atticus, his father, was somewhat ashamed of his injury. He had prided himself on his skills of horsemanship. However, it had not been an injury of the enemy that had caused him to be lame, but instead it was a careless fall from his horse as he led his *cohort* against a minor rebellion. Since no wheeled traffic is allowed in the city from sunrise until mid-afternoon, slaves carrying sedan chairs are really the only means of transportation other than walking. Paulus' father felt it somehow beneath his dignity to have to use them, so he usually received callers at home. Paulus was a bit disappointed that he couldn't talk to his father about his prisoner, but there would be another time.

Since none of his family was home, Paulus was eager to leave the house. A slave girl served him some fresh bread from the bakery. After eating a couple of figs and some bread dipped in olive oil and honey, Paulus prepared to leave for the day. As he walked through the atrium, he passed the small shrine to their household gods. He paused for a moment, but felt no urge to pray as the Jew had done.

Paulus wondered if the Jew had a shrine for his god. If so, he hadn't seen it, but there were a couple of chests in the house where a shrine could be hidden.

It was a clear and breezy day. The air was free of the city smells that had been so oppressive last evening. As Paulus walked to the public baths, his mind unbiddingly returned to the Jewish prisoner.

"I wonder why we have him in prison if he simply broke some Jewish law," thought Paulus.

Of course Paulus could have asked the prisoner, but he decided the less he had to do with any Jew the better. He certainly didn't feel inclined to begin a conversation with him.

Even though Paulus' house had a bath, he preferred the camaraderie of the public baths. His favorite baths were at the Campus Martius, where he had trained for so many hours. But now that he was living at home rather than at the barracks, he chose the baths nearest his house. These baths had a big gymnasium and several training rooms, where Paulus could exercise and practice some of the skills needed for battle. On arriving at the baths, Paulus headed to his favorite training room. He paid little attention to the jugglers entertaining the crowds along the colonnade or the musicians performing in the gardens. Since the pools for the baths were not open until noon, many people came early and spent their time reading in the library, watching the entertainers, or making business deals in the rooms around the baths. Paulus, however, was focused on one thing only — maintaining his superior talents as a Roman warrior.

"After all, just because I have to be a guard for some Jew is no reason to let my body get weak and undisciplined," reasoned Paulus.

After his exercise, he rested in one of the gardens outside the pools. As he sat in the shade, he wondered where Livia had gone that morning. Since most young women of her age were already married, she didn't have a lot in common with her old friends. But they did have cousins who lived nearby, and she probably went to visit them. Unfortunately, she didn't enjoy the sewing and weaving that were considered the proper duties of a well-bred Roman lady. Since the death of their mother, she spent most of her time overseeing the slaves and servants. Paulus knew she was too lenient with them, but she was so gentle and kind that giving orders was hard for her.

"By Jupiter, I find giving orders a lot easier than taking them!" mused Paulus.

The baths finally open, Paulus had both a hot and cold bath and then a massage. He wanted to go to the chariot races, but he was afraid he didn't have time. After all, he had to return home, eat a bite and then go to that house again this afternoon. Still feeling the unfairness of his duty, he returned home.

When he arrived, no one was there to greet him except the slaves. Unable to get any sympathy from his family, he bitterly complained to himself, "Sure, they are off enjoying the day, while I have to guard a Jewish nobody."

In a bad mood for a second day, he set off to guard his prisoner Paul. Upon arrival at the house, he greeted Silvius, who appeared to have been there for some time. "Apparently, he has nothing better to do than spend extra time in this unpleasant house," thought Paulus.

The prisoner and a man he recognized as the scribe from the night before nodded a greeting to him. As he resumed his post from the previous day, he saw that they were still working on the same letter from yesterday. For a time, he didn't listen to their conversation, but soon he found himself caught up in the words of the letter.

"No, no, I want to write part of it, by my own hand!" Paul told the scribe.

"But, why?" questioned the scribe.

"I want Philemon to know how much pain I'm feeling over this letter. If it is written in part by my hand, I feel it might be stronger," replied Paul.

He finally closed the letter with greetings from several people. Paul read aloud the final words, "The grace of the Lord Jesus Christ be with your spirit."(Philemon:25)

The scribe then rolled the papyrus and they knelt in prayer. They prayed for a long time. Paulus wondered who this Jesus Christ was.

He had heard the name mentioned the day before, but it meant nothing to him.

While they were praying, the same men from yesterday returned. They greeted each other warmly. Paul then gave the papyrus to one of the men whom he called Tychicus. The thin Greek Onesimus (that Paulus believed to be the runaway slave) knelt at Paul's feet, and the Jew placed his hands on the Greek's head and gave some kind of tearful blessing. Onesimus slowly rose and with a triumphant look on his face walked out the door.

The room was silent for a short time, and then Paul finally spoke, "I pray that I am not sending him to his death."

"I have faith that our brother Philemon will treat him well for your sake," replied the other man named Timothy.

"Even if he dies, he will no longer be a slave, but a son in Christ's kingdom," said Paul.

Paulus couldn't understand this strange dialogue, "Where was this kingdom and how could some slave become a son in it?" he wondered.

The rest of the afternoon passed quickly. There were several visitors, including a couple of Romans. Why these noble citizens would be interested in visiting a Jewish prisoner was strange to Paulus. One of the visitors was an old Jew who carried a scroll with him. Paul opened the scroll and read it with tears running down his cheek. It apparently was an ancient text called the *Torah*. As Paul lovingly touched the words on the papyrus, it was obvious that he knew the text by heart. He often closed his eyes while reading passages from the writings. After a time the old man left with the scroll.

Preparing to retire for the night, he looked at Silvius and Paulus and said,

"My good fellows, the comfort of those ancient words is like a blanket for a chilled soul. May God one day give you such a peaceful joy."

Paulus appeared stoic on hearing Paul's words, as did Silvius. However, the peace that the prisoner seemed to have was certainly interesting. When their replacement arrived, Paulus and Silvius again walked into the city together. Paulus wanted to discuss what he had heard that evening, but he didn't really want Silvius to think he was overly interested in the Jew. Silvius told Paulus he had to hurry home to his family. It was his son's 21st birthday and they were having a late feast in his honor. They then said their farewells, and Paulus went along to his home in deep thought.

When he arrived, he found Livia in the same place in the courtyard where she had been last evening.

"Here you are again! It's too late for you to be out here in the courtyard. What if someone passed by and saw you? It's, it's just unseemly, by Jupiter!" complained Paulus.

"Oh, brother dear, I was hidden behind one of the tall plants, and I was very quiet," Livia replied sweetly.

As he looked at her in the moonlight, Paulus decided that she was not "horsefaced." It was true that she was very tall for a woman, and she often seemed to slouch to appear smaller. Now though, seated with her hair hanging loosely over her simple white tunic, she seemed to be a lovely, unspoiled pool of calmness.

Even though he was tired, Paulus sat by her on the bench and asked her, "What is troubling you so much that it costs you your sleep, dear Livia?"

"Oh, I've just been thinking of our mother and how much I miss her. Do you still think of her? I know it's been five years, but sometimes when I sit here in the quiet darkness, I think I can almost feel her. It's almost like I have a peaceful joy during those times."

Paulus reacted to her comment with shock. He remembered that the Jew had used almost the exact same words when talking about the text he had read.

"What's wrong?" asked Livia as she noticed his stunned silence.

For a minute he thought about claiming that there was nothing the matter, but this was his dear Livia. Maybe he should tell her.

"Oh, it's just that your words reminded me of what my prisoner said this evening – something about peaceful joy," said Paulus.

"Was he remembering his mother as well?"

"No," chuckled Paulus, "he was overcome with joy over some old Jewish text. It was about a Jew called Abraham and a covenant he had with his god. There were a lot of other people mentioned, but I can't remember their names. Oh, and their main god Jehovah was always interfering in their lives," said Paulus.

"What do you think of the Jew?"

"Well, he certainly has a lot of visitors, and they seem to really respect him. I found out today that he is in prison because of some sort of religious dispute. I know our Emperor wouldn't like there to be unrest, so I suppose if he is detaining him for a trial, the Jew must have caused problems. Oh, and he is a Roman citizen," said Paulus.

"He's what?" cried Livia.

"A Roman citizen. That's why he gets such good treatment, and he even rents the house where I keep guard. Today, there were two Romans who visited him—men of obvious wealth. I've never seen anyone quite like this Jew. He gets very emotional when he talks to others about this Jesus Christ. It bothers me and I turn my head sometimes."

"Oh, Paulus, I want to meet him!" cried Livia.

"Are you completely crazy?" replied Paulus. "He's a prisoner and I'm his guard."

"It's just that you never seem to be interested in people unless they are in the military. Mostly you talk about chariot races, your training exercises, or your favorite horse. Now, you're talking about Jewish texts and joy. You just have me wondering if this prisoner is maybe influencing your thinking."

Paulus was horrified. "I am not being influenced by some Jewish nobody. I'm tired, and I am going to bed."

After Paulus stormed away, Livia thought to herself, "I'm going to see this man. I don't care what Paulus says, but I certainly won't mention it to father. I know he would forbid it."

Since the death of their mother, the marriages of her sisters, and Paulus' military training, Livia had spent a lot of time alone with their father, Atticus. They had read, talked about philosophy, and discussed history and religion. Atticus had found Livia an excellent listener with a sharp mind. It was perhaps his fault that she was more interested in intellectual pursuits than in the typical activities of young women her age. This was one of the reasons Livia had few suitors and seemed to find most young men of her age boring and childish. Her obvious disdain for the young Roman friends of Paulus was probably the cause for their taunts at the public baths. Paulus had never told her the reason for his being removed from his *maniple*. She only knew he had been in a fight, and since his quick temper was well-known, she accepted his assignment simply as a punishment for the fight.

Chapter 3

The following day Paulus got up, dressed, ate a quick breakfast and went out into the atrium. He wasn't surprised to find his father Atticus and Livia sitting on a bench near the fountain in a deep discussion. He knew they often talked and read together in the morning. Of course, normally he would be off with the other soldiers training or having fun. But that was before he had been forced to guard that Jew. Livia had told Paulus that their father greatly enjoyed their little debates, and it was the one time he seemed somewhat animated and not so depressed over his condition.

Paulus walked over to where they sat and joined them. It was another nice day and he smiled at them as he sat down on a nearby bench.

"Don't let me bother you," said Paulus, "Continue your discussion. Who knows? I might even enjoy adding my thoughts," he added, hoping to please his father.

"Do join us," cried Livia. "Father has been telling me some things he knows about the Jews."

Paulus' expression clouded immediately. The last thing he wanted to discuss this morning was a foreign religion.

Livia continued, "Paulus, did you know they only have one god – Jehovah? Imagine no *numina*, no temples devoted to various gods, and not even any household gods. It must be awful!"

Atticus answered for Paulus by saying, "They do seem a strange and often reclusive people. I've had little personal contact with them, but my friend Valerius was assigned to a *maniple* in Jerusalem several years ago. You know Jerusalem is their holy city. He says he will never forget what happened while he was stationed there."

"What happened?" Livia asked.

"Oh, it was an ordinary execution, a couple of thieves and a Jewish rebel called Jesus. It was during their holiday called Passover. There were thousands of pilgrims in the city. Valerius said there was deep unrest in the city over this rebel."

"Did the rebel have a large army ready to fight us?" asked Paulus with sudden interest, remembering Paul's speaking his name several times.

"Hardly that," replied Atticus. "According to Valerius, his followers were all simple fishermen, farmers, or tradesmen. They were no threat to Rome. It was the Jews who wanted him dead."

"What! I thought he was a Jewish leader?" said Paulus.

"No, he had crowds of Jewish followers, but the Jewish leaders hated him. Apparently, he broke a lot of their strict rules. Some of the soldiers even claimed they had seen him heal people and do amazing miracles. Valerius didn't believe any of these ridiculous claims, and he wasn't at the execution. But he said it sure was a strange few days."

"How so?" asked Paulus.

"Well, for one thing there was a sudden darkening of the sky and then some of the Jewish leaders went into panic because some kind of veil in their holy temple split down the middle. There was trembling in the earth and everybody was very nervous – including Valerius."

"No wonder he couldn't forget that experience," said Livia. "Was the execution one of those horrible crucifixions?"

"Yes, but you know they are necessary to keep our Empire safe," answered Atticus. "Valerius had more to say about that week. Several days before the execution, there had been a big procession or parade or something with Jesus riding through the crowd on a donkey. The crowds were waving palm branches at him and shouting 'Hosanna', and Valerius' commander was afraid there would be violence. The people seemed to love him so. But at his crucifixion, there were only a few followers, mostly women."

"So it was over. I don't see why Valerius would have considered it important." Paulus said.

"That's not quite all the story. It seems that a couple of days after the death, the body disappeared. Our soldiers were on guard, but Jesus' body seemed to vanish. They were told to not let anyone near the tomb, but somehow someone stole the body. His followers claimed something crazy. They said that he rose from the grave, alive again. Of course, that is nonsense. But Valerius was in the group assigned to look for the body. They searched everywhere, but they found nothing, just his grave clothes. You know those cowardly followers who didn't even go to the crucifixion? They were now singing, laughing, and praying all over the city! They kept saying 'He is Risen! He is Risen!'"

"How come I never heard about this odd story? I know lots of men who are old veterans, and I have never heard this even mentioned," said Paulus.

"Valerius told me because I'm his good friend, and he trusts me. All the Roman soldiers who were there that week were ordered not to talk about the body's disappearance. They knew it would amount to nothing if not discussed," said Atticus.

"Well, I find this story fascinating. Father, I'd like to talk to Valerius about this," Livia said.

"I hardly think that would be proper and it isn't possible anyway. He is posted in Cappadocia now – far from Rome," replied Atticus. "Why are you so interested in all this, Livia?"

"Oh, I don't know. I've just heard Paulus talk about his Jewish prisoner. He seems to know about this Jesus Christ. Father, I know it is blasphemy, but sometimes I have doubts about all our gods. They don't seem real to me," said Livia. "You know I've studied the religions of Egypt and of North Africa. This is just a new one that I would like to study. That's all."

Paulus watched his sister carefully, not revealing her request to visit Paul from last night. He knew their father would strictly forbid it and would be angry at both of them for such a request (at her for asking such an outrageous thing and at him for getting her interested in Jews).

Livia got up and smiled sweetly at her brother and left Paulus and Atticus alone.

"Your sister is an unusual woman," Atticus remarked. "I'm not sure I've done the right thing by encouraging her to become a seeker of truth. She should be planning a wedding or choosing a new color of tunic or asking for jewels. Instead, she is asking about Jews. By the way, is this prisoner Paul very troublesome?"

"Not really. He has a lot of visitors. That makes guarding him a little difficult. But he is courteous and kind to Silvius and me. He's a very learned man and what is strange is his serenity in his situation. I am a little intrigued by his lack of fear," replied Paulus.

"Just remember he is a Jew. They are an odd group, and we have as little contact with them as possible," said Atticus.

"But most of his visitors are Greeks and Romans," said Paulus.

"Are you serious? Now that is surprising. You must tell me more about this later. My legs are hurting, and I must lie on my couch for a while. I hope your day is pleasurable."

He rose slowly and hobbled to an interior room. Paulus watched him with a sad heart. Atticus had been one of the finest soldiers in all of Rome, and now his world was reduced to his household and infrequent visits to the Forum.

Paulus got up and made his way into the city.

Chapter 4

Paulus went to his favorite public baths, as usual. Today, however, he decided to forego the calisthenics and simply have cold, warm, and hot baths. After bathing, he stopped at a *taberna* and ate a quick meal of olives, eggs, cheese, and bread. Feeling invigorated by the baths and food, he decided to make his way to the arena to see some chariot racing.

When he arrived at the arena, he was disappointed to find no one he knew near the entrance, but he knew he would still enjoy the races. Paulus liked watching the parade and the pageantry of the chariot races. The opening ceremony was usually a performance worthy of the theater — the presiding magistrate riding in a triumphal chariot leading the way, then the priests carrying images of the gods, and finally the musicians marching and playing their instruments. While watching the competing charioteers was exciting, what Paulus enjoyed most was seeing the horses. They were always magnificent steeds of various breeds. Paulus had developed his love for horses at an early age. His family had a country villa on a farm near Ostia, and his father taught him to ride as a child. He spent many wonderful days enjoying the freedom of riding through the fields. Unfortunately, since his mother's death and his father's injury, he had only been back to the farm one time. He really missed those carefree days. Paulus watched two races, cheering for the charioteers wearing the Blues of the senate. Noting that time was quickly passing, he returned home to prepare for another day of guarding the Jew.

When he arrived at the house a bit early, he was again surprised to find Silvius already on duty and the other guards gone. Paul was alone for a change and seemed to be so deep into meditation that he didn't even appear to notice Paulus' arrival. There was one bizarre scene shortly after his arrival. A young man came tearing into the room and ran toward Silvius. Paulus prepared to draw his *gladius*, but Silvius quickly held up his hand and introduced the man to Paulus.

"Paulus, this is my impetuous son Tatius. He seems to have some family business to discuss with me."

They whispered briefly. Then Tatius nodded at Paulus and quickly left. Paulus wondered what that was about. Even Paul opened his eyes to observe the commotion.

Later that afternoon, several people came to talk to Paul about a service of worship that was to occur the next day at the house. They were quietly planning the different activities. Paulus took little note of the plans, but after Paul retired for the night he asked Silvius if this type of thing was permitted. Silvius said yes, and that it had occurred every week and sometimes twice a week since he had been guarding Paul. The afternoon passed quickly and Paulus and Silvius began their journey home. Paulus commented to Silvius about his son, secretly thinking that Silvius would share with him the family drama that had caused Tatius to rush into the house.

"He's a tall, strong-looking fellow. Is he in training to be a soldier like you?" asked Paulus.

"Oh, no," replied Silvius. "His three older brothers are soldiers, but Tatius is a scholar. He speaks several languages, writes treatises on philosophy, and can never read enough. Someday, he may decide on a career, but for now he is a sponge – soaking up knowledge."

Paulus chuckled, "It sounds a dull life to me, but he sounds a bit like my sister Livia."

"A woman scholar?" said Silvius. "Now that's something you don't often find. It's a pity they can't share their ideas with each other.

Tatius is very advanced, you should hear him debate. He completely overwhelms me when he gets into a topic."

"You should hear my sister with my father. Just this morning she was pressing my father about his knowledge about Jews and about somebody named Jesus."

Silvius didn't comment, but instead said he needed to hurry home. Paulus assumed he had to attend to the family crisis that had precipitated Tatius' bursting into the house that evening.

When Paulus arrived home everyone was in bed. Since he had been in the sun at the races and had then stood for long hours on guard, he was very tired and immediately retired for the night.

Chapter 5

The next morning Paulus again got up rather late. One of the slaves served him breakfast, and he started toward the atrium. Livia, who had been in the courtyard, saw him and cautioned him about disturbing their father. She said he had had a bad night. His hip and legs were really hurting him, and he had told the slaves to have no one disturb him this morning so that he could rest.

Paulus and Livia talked for a time about their father's poor health. With their mother gone, neither could bear the thought of Atticus dying. Trying to change the subject from their sad thoughts, Livia asked Paulus,

"Did anything new happen with the Jew last night?"

"Not really. He and some visitors made plans for some kind of worship ceremony this afternoon. I didn't pay much attention to their conversation."

"Oh, I would love to see it. Are they going to make sacrifices and burn incense?" cried Livia.

"I doubt it, after all they are meeting in a house and not in the Temple of Apollo!" said Paulus.

"Don't be sarcastic! Be sure and notice what they do. I wonder if they'll talk about that man Jesus that Valerius discussed."

"I will listen if it is at all interesting. Oh, by the way, I met Silvius' son last night."

"Who is Silvius?"

"The other guard on duty with me. It was a bit odd. His son came tearing into the house, and I almost attacked him. But apparently he had some urgent family matter to tell his father."

"What was the problem?" asked Livia.

"He never told me," said Paulus. "You would probably like him."

"Why is that?"

"First of all, he is very tall — even taller than you!" teased Paulus.

Hitting him playfully with her *palla* (shawl), Livia replied, "His being a giant is not enough to make him interesting."

"Oh, he's not a giant," said Paulus, "and the reason I thought you would like him is because he is a very fine scholar, according to his father."

"Well, I, myself, am far more intrigued by these mysterious Jews than some giant."

"I give up. He isn't a giant! Just go weave something or bring me something good to eat," Paulus ordered good-naturedly.

"No," replied Livia. "I must hide myself, the giant might come here," she said with a laugh.

With a smile, Paulus left the house and began his usual routine. He went to one of the larger public baths, hoping to find a friend, but again he saw no one that he knew. He did some training exercises, ran the track several times and then had his baths. Afterwards he ate in one of the shops by the gymnasium. Noting the library was vacant at the bath, he decided to enter and check some of the Roman histories for information about Jews. If anyone were to enter that he knew, he could say he was studying old battles. Two old gentlemen followed him into the library, but they took no note of him. Paulus sat on one of the couches and looked for information about the Jews and in particular the Jew, Jesus Christ. He found nothing about this Jesus, but he did find that there had been some serious rebellions by the Jews – in particular there were the Maccabean revolts against the Greeks. Since the takeover of Palestine by the Roman Empire, there had been many small problems and disturbances; however, there was no mention of the events described by Valerius.

"Oh well, I don't know why I am wasting my time on this silly pursuit. I need to return home and prepare for a fascinating evening of Jewish worship!" thought Paulus with disgust.

Chapter 6

Time passed quickly for Paulus, and he soon found himself on his way to the Jew's house once again. Upon arrival, he was surprised to see a lot of activity. Silvius was already there as usual, and the other guard that Paulus was replacing, left as he saw Paulus approaching.

"What's happening?" he asked Silvius. "I thought their ceremony wasn't until later."

"They're bringing food for a meal and moving furniture in order to make room for the people," explained Silvius.

"Where's the Jew Paul?" asked Paulus.

"He's in the back, praying."

After about an hour, people began to arrive. There were a few Jews (he could tell because they were speaking Aramaic), several Greeks, and many Romans. What was more surprising was that many women were also present. Many brought food, and they obviously intended to stay for the service.

Paulus had thought this was to be a worship ceremony, not a feast, but there was certainly a lot of food. The people talked, and seemed to be enjoying themselves. Paulus and Silvius were offered food. Paulus declined, but to his surprise, Silvius took several things and ate them with relish. Paulus thought this a violation of conduct for a soldier, but Silvius had been a guard for some time. Maybe it was permitted.

With the meal completed, the ceremony began. Paul stood and began to speak to the group. He took a loaf of bread in his hands and said something crazy that sounded like, "This is my body. Take and eat." Paulus quickly looked to see if the Jew had a dead body that they were going to share! It was only bread. He saw Paul pass the bread and each person broke off a piece and ate it, while Paul said something like, "Do this in remembrance of me." He then took a goblet of wine and said, "This is my blood." They passed the goblet and everyone took a sip. Paulus felt sick. "Were these people pretending to drink blood and eat human flesh?" Paulus thought.

Paulus had begun to have some admiration for these friends of Paul, but this service was shocking and very disturbing. After they ate the bits of bread and sipped the wine, they began singing. Paulus supposed these were songs of praise to their god. He was familiar with such hymns, since the Romans had excellent praise songs to their gods as well.

The crowd increased and Paulus was jostled several times, but Paulus controlled his angry impulse to strike the offenders. Paul began to speak and it was obvious that everyone wanted to be as near to him as possible. He spoke in Greek with occasional phrases in Aramaic that Paulus couldn't understand. The oration was long and concerned this Jesus Christ. He seemed to be saying that Jesus was the Son of God. (This didn't seem strange. Jupiter had several sons.) Then Paul said that he loved all people so very much that he died for them – to save them. Paul told how he was on the road to Damascus and a light from heaven blinded him. He claimed Jesus spoke to him. (Paulus thought, "That cannot be. He's dead. Valerius told us about his execution.") He told how several days later his eyes were opened, and he knew then that Jesus Christ was the Son of the Living God. There was a lot more, but he didn't try to listen to it all.

Becoming somewhat bored, Paulus turned to watch the people. To his great surprise, at the back of the crowd he saw Tatius (Silvius' son). He would not have spotted him except for his towering over the other people. Paulus looked at Silvius. Silvius was looking at Paul, with a complete lack of emotion. He apparently had not spotted his son. The oration finished, and Paul said to the crowd, "He is Risen." They returned with, "He is Risen indeed." Then Paul said the same thing again, and the crowd gave the same response. Paulus looked at Tatius. He was joining the crowd with the same, "He is Risen indeed."

It was getting late, and the people began to leave. Paulus looked, but Tatius was no longer in the courtyard. After everyone had gone, Paul said he was retiring for the night. It was evident that the ceremony, oration, and crowds had made the Jew very tired. The replacement guard soon arrived, and Silvius and Paulus left for home.

When they were a short distance from the house, Paulus told Silvius, "I saw Tatius in the crowd tonight."

Silvius replied, "I'm not surprised. He is a seeker of truth. His inner thoughts are very deep and he studies all the time."

"But he repeated the, 'He is Risen indeed' with the others."

"Well, I suppose he must believe it."

"Aren't you going to do something about his actions?" asked Paulus.

Silvius just smiled and said, "I'm very tired, and what I'm going to do is hurry home to my bed."

Paulus began to wonder about Silvius. "Was he a secret follower of this Jesus Christ?" he thought to himself. When he got home, he was disappointed no one was still awake. He had wanted to talk, but he decided it could wait until the next morning. He slept poorly. He kept seeing the glowing faces of the people as they listened to Paul. Also, once he woke from a nightmare about people drinking blood and eating human flesh.

"Oh, I wish I were with my *maniple*," he muttered. "It's not fair."

Chapter 7

*D*ue to his restless night, Paulus rose early the next morning. Finding no one in the atrium, he went outside to the garden. There, he found Livia picking flowers.

"Where is father?" asked Paulus.

"Uncle Cornelius came by in a mule cart just before dawn, while wheeled travel was still allowed. He said there was some business at the Forum that father would want to hear," replied Livia.

"But he was ill yesterday!"

"I know, but perhaps seeing other people will make him feel better."

"Come into the atrium with me, and I'll tell you about last night."

"Yes! Yes! I'll put the flowers in some water and be there in a moment." Livia said.

He had wanted to tell his father about the ceremony, but since he wasn't there, he decided to talk with Livia. She was a great listener and had been eager (too eager!) to learn about the Jew. Paulus recounted the events of the ceremony while Livia listened with acute interest. She only reacted one time, and that was when he told about the words spoken during the bread and wine ritual.

After describing the entire service, he regretted telling her about it, since her interest was now even more piqued.

"Is that all you can remember?" pressed Livia.

"Yes. Oh, one more thing, I saw Silvius' son Tatius there."

"Oh, the giant," said Livia. "He was probably just curious like I am."

"He is not a giant," replied Paulus with amusement. "I think it's more than a passing interest for him. He repeated the chant 'He is risen' with the crowd."

"Maybe I'll meet this giant someday and quiz him about what he knows," Livia said playfully.

Paulus picked up some fruit from the table and left for his usual day in the city. Livia pondered what he had told her and determined that she would find a way to meet this extraordinary man named Paul.

Chapter 8

Paulus returned home that afternoon to find a surprising visitor in the atrium with Livia. He couldn't believe it. There sat Tatius on a bench talking with Livia!

"What are you doing here?" demanded Paulus roughly.

His face reddening, Tatius rose quickly and explained, "My father is ill and will not be on guard tonight. He talked to his captain, and the captain gave permission for his absence. Since there would be only one guard present he wanted you to know in advance why he was absent."

"Oh, I see," replied Paulus with some discomfort over his angry greeting.

Tatius continued his explanation, "I've been waiting for your return. Your gracious sister offered me some apple juice and has been entertaining me until you come home."

Livia blushed and said, "It's a warm day, and Tatius walked quite a distance. I thought he might need a refreshing drink. Would you like some juice as well?" asked Livia as she reached for the pitcher.

"No, I'm not thirsty. Thank you, Tatius, for coming here to alert me to the change in the situation."

"It was my pleasure," replied Tatius. He bade farewell to Paulus, and as he got to the door, he turned and said to Livia, "Thank you for listening to my stories. My father and mother say I talk too much. Good-bye."

After he was gone, Paulus turned to Livia and said, "So you met the giant!"

"He is not a giant!" Livia said. "He is a lot taller than me, however, oh, and you as well."

This remark didn't please Paulus. He was proud of his superior height. "Well, he certainly isn't as strong as I am. His shoulders look very weak."

"Perhaps you are right. But did you know he is only 21 years old, and he has already studied in Athens? His grandmother is Greek, so he has relatives in Athens. He's traveled everywhere! He spent almost three months in Thessalonica. I've always wanted to go there. He's been to Corinth, Ephesus, Crete, and ..."

"How did you learn so much so quickly? Has he been here long?" Paulus asked with some suspicion as well as a bit of jealousy. "She never listened to my stories about games, competitions, and my military training with such enthusiasm," he thought.

"Oh, he was here only a short time, but I asked him lots of questions. He's very smart and has studied with some of the greatest Greek tutors. His father didn't have to pay for it either. His teacher here in Rome knew he loved to learn, and he sent letters to his friends in several centers of learning asking them to teach Tatius. They did so, and he has only been home in Rome for a few months," said Livia.

Paulus watched her as she was talking about Tatius with so much animation. Her usual pale complexion was rosy, her eyes were flashing, and her posture was erect as she presented her case. "If my friends saw her now," thought Paulus, "they would be enchanted by her happy excitement and certainly not think her a 'horseface'."

"What did he say about the Jewish ceremony last night?" asked Paulus.

"Oh, I didn't mention it. I wasn't sure if you would want me to let him know you had seen him there," replied Livia.

"That's probably good. I must prepare for my 'solo' duty tonight," he said with a defeatist attitude.

A short time later, he started on his journey to the Jew's house. As he walked, he thought about Livia. His father had not negotiated a marriage contract for her when she was young, as he had for his other two daughters. They were betrothed at fourteen. Livia, however, showed little interest in their friends' sons, and his father found it comforting to have her at home. They talked a lot, and she had been in charge of the household slaves and servants since their mother's death. His father knew Paulus would be away in the service of the Empire for long periods of time (at least, he was supposed to be away!), and he didn't want to be alone.

Chapter 9

When Paulus arrived at the house, the other guards he was replacing were outside waiting for him. He asked them if there were problems, surprised at their obvious eagerness to leave. They assured him all was well; however, since Silvius always came early, they were used to leaving early. Paulus said farewell to them, and they left.

Walking into the house, Paulus was surprised to find no visitors there. Paul wasn't on his knees praying, nor was he dictating letters. Instead he had pulled his chains to a couch and was lying motionless on it. Paulus watched the Jew for several minutes. Fearing he was ill or even dead, he walked over to him and said sharply, "Jew, are you alive?"

Paul opened his eyes and looked at Paulus with a gaze so penetrating that Paulus almost gasped.

"Yes," Paul said, "I'm alive – alive in Christ."

Paulus was uncertain how to reply. He had had no personal interchange with the prisoner, and he wanted to keep it that way.

"I don't know about being alive in Christ, I just want to make sure you are alive in Rome!" said Paulus, feeling that his response was somewhat clever.

Paul then said, "I'll not be alive in Rome for many years. I fear

Rome will grow tired of us soon. I only regret I'll not be able to preach the good news to the whole world."

"What on earth is this good news that's so important?" demanded Paulus.

"A part of it you heard the other night. He is Risen, and there is so much more. But you aren't ready to hear it yet. I pray, young Paulus, yes I know your name, that your heart and eyes will be opened to the light very soon," said Paul. He then rose from the couch and knelt to pray.

Paulus backed away and went to his guard post very disturbed by this short conversation with Paul.

While Paul was praying, three visitors entered, obviously talking among themselves about some serious problem. On hearing them, Paul ceased praying and welcomed them all with an embrace. A man, whom Paul addressed as Epaphras, began talking about some type of problem at a church in Colosse. Paulus didn't listen very closely because he couldn't stop thinking about Paul's comment that he wasn't able to hear the news yet. "How foolish," thought Paulus, "I hear quite well!"

Paulus heard the men say that they would return tomorrow with a scribe. He knew that would mean another letter-writing session.

Listening once more, Paulus heard Epaphras say, "My people in Colosse need your guidance, dear brother. I pray that the Holy Spirit will direct your words. Farewell, God has placed us in your hands."

They left, and Paul turned and said to Paulus, "Sometimes I fear that I will not be strong enough to help all these dear children. I must pray and work harder."

Paulus started not to reply, but since no one else was present, he replied, "How can they expect you to help? You are a Roman prisoner! You are not a god!"

Paul smiled, "Such passion! I would expect no less from the Livian family. A noble name you carry, young Paulus."

"What do you know of my family?" Paulus demanded sharply.

"Oh, I have known who you were from the day you first arrived here. My grandfather told me about the great Livian family – its power and influence. He found your great-grandfather to be a man of honor and wisdom."

"I don't believe this. My great-grandfather had no contact with Jews! He was an officer during the time of our great Julius Caesar!" yelled Paulus.

"Be calm, young Paulus. I have told the truth. I and my family come from Tarsus. Have they never told you of the earthquake that happened near Tarsus? Many soldiers were crushed to death, but a few were rescued. My grandfather and his cousins spent days digging through the rubble for bodies and injured men. Your great-grandfather was the last soldier pulled out alive. It was during a harsh winter, and my family cared for the wounded for weeks before help came from Rome."

"Jews saved my great-grandfather? How come my father never told me this story?" asked Paulus.

"That I do not know," replied Paul. "But my grandfather was given Roman citizenship for his efforts. He often spoke with feeling about the officer who was your great-grandfather. He said 'Cornelius Livius is a Roman with wisdom like our Solomon.'"

Paulus stumbled and almost fell. He righted himself, and began thinking, "Could it be true?" He turned to ask Paul more questions. Paul, however, was again on his knees praying for the Colossians. After his prayers, he went to bed without further comment to Paulus. For Paulus, the afternoon passed very slowly and when his replacement arrived, he rushed out into the city eager to go home and talk to his father.

When he arrived home, the entire household was asleep. Paulus considered waking his father, but he knew he needed rest after spending the day at the Roman Forum.

Chapter 10

After another restless night, Paulus rose the next morning determined to talk to his father. Going into the atrium, he met Livia and two of the female slaves.

"Where are you going?" asked Paulus.

"We are going to Uncle Cornelius' house. I'm going to take them some of our fig preserves, and I'll spend some time with my cousins," replied Livia.

"But you usually find them annoying. You say they only talk of fashions and jewelry or which soldier smiled at them. And they are so much younger than you, Livia," Paulus said.

"Do you not want me to go? Did something happen with the Jew?" Livia asked eagerly.

Paulus wanted her to stay, but he could see they were loaded with gifts, ready to leave. So he said, "No, go ahead. There's no problem. We'll talk later." They said their farewells and Paulus went in search of his father.

He asked one of the slaves if he had left, and he was told that he was still in his bedroom. Paulus went to his room, knocked on the portal, and his father told him to enter.

Paulus was shocked to see his father still in bed. He looked very tired.

"Are you sick, Father?" Paulus asked with concern.

"No, my son, it's just that yesterday was very difficult for me. The ride in the mule cart was rough, the business at the Forum was disturbing, and we didn't return until late," said Atticus. "Do you have a problem?"

"Well, not exactly. But I must talk with you," said Paulus.

"Give me a few minutes to dress," Atticus said, "and I'll join you in the atrium."

Paulus went into the atrium, ate some bread, and drank a glass of wine. Shortly afterward, his father hobbled into the room and sat down on a couch.

Paulus could wait no longer, and he quickly told him the tale Paul had recounted about the earthquake in Tarsus and his great-grandfather's rescue. Atticus listened very carefully and was astonished at the story.

"It isn't true, is it?" demanded Paulus.

"I'm not sure," replied Atticus. "But I'll tell you what I do know. Your great-grandfather was injured in an earthquake. It was somewhere in Cilicia, and of course, Tarsus is a city there."

"Did he mention anything about being rescued by a Jew?"

"No, but he stayed there for some weeks. There were many others hurt and several were killed."

"Why do I know nothing of this?"

"It was a long time ago. My grandfather returned home with no lingering injury, unlike mine," Atticus said bitterly. "Of course, he died before you were born, so you would not have heard anything about it from him."

"But could his rescuer have been the Jewish prisoner's grandfather?" insisted Paulus.

"I don't know," replied Atticus. "Why is it so important?"

"I must know!"

"Your Uncle Cornelius would know more than I about it. You can speak with him. It's interesting that your concerns involve Jews," Atticus said.

"What do you mean?"

"You know I was at the Forum yesterday with your Uncle Cornelius?"

Paulus nodded.

"Well, the debate was about what should be done with the Jewish sect that seems to be following this Jesus Christ that we crucified," said Atticus. "They are refusing to worship our Emperor Nero. They won't accept him as a god, and there are other serious concerns."

"What are they?" asked Paulus.

"Some of our Roman citizens are even following this Jesus! There are groups all over Macedonia and Galatia. They call themselves 'churches'. Do you know who started most of these 'churches'? Your prisoner, Paul! Many want them completely wiped out. They have even infiltrated the palace! Your uncle doesn't believe this is a good approach. For some reason, he has always seemed to be tolerant toward Jews. But I'm not sure this new group (some have called them Christians) should be even called Jews. After all, many are Greeks, Romans, and even Egyptians! Many of the senators consider them dangerous. It's said that our Emperor has suggested that they be thrown into an arena with the lions or covered with tar and lit with fire!"

Paulus was horrified. This talk was something he would have associated with people like the barbarians of Germania. He had listened to the "Christians" talk. Obviously they were a deluded group, but they never talked about rebellion. They prayed, talked about love, and forgiveness, and seemed to be completely peaceful.

Atticus continued, "I don't know what is going to happen, but be careful when you are guarding Paul. There are people who would kill him today if he weren't a Roman citizen. You could be hurt if they attack him. Also, tell me if you see any Romans of importance visiting the Jew."

Paulus started to mention Tatius' attendance at the ceremony, but he felt it a betrayal, somehow. Anyway, perhaps Tatius was just a curious observer. Paulus noticed his father beginning to tire so he wished him a good day and left for his usual day in the city.

Chapter 11

As Paulus was walking to the public baths, he suddenly decided to go to the Forum instead, in order to talk to his Uncle Cornelius. It was a good distance away, but since he wasn't going to exercise at the baths, he knew the walk would be good for him, and it would give him time to think as well. Paulus knew that Cornelius was named after his great-grandfather, but was he likely to know more than his father about the earthquake? After all he was the youngest brother. He walked on with determination to find some answers.

When he arrived at the Forum, he had to push his way through the crowds of people. The area teemed with life—reflecting every class of society. Inside the Forum were patrician senators, bankers, lawyers, soldiers, shoppers, prostitutes, and pickpockets. As he made his way to the *Curia* where the Roman Senate met, he passed by many of Rome's most famous temples and monuments. Paulus' mind was so focused on what Paul had told him that he scarcely noticed the ancient Temple of Castor or the gleaming columns of the Temple of Divus Julius. Passing through the colonnade of the Basilica Aemilia, he finally came to the *Curia*. Just as he arrived, he saw his uncle, walking from the building. He looked every bit the statesman in his toga edged in purple (only worn by Roman Senators). Paulus hurried to him and after a quick greeting, asked if he had time to speak with him. Cornelius told him that he was free to talk for a short time. They found a bench in the shade, and Paulus began "Sir, I am disturbed by some information that I have heard and want your help."

Cornelius was pleased that Paulus was seeking his counsel. Paulus had always been so caught up with the military that he never seemed to have much interest in philosophy or politics. These topics were the focus of Cornelius' life. Since Cornelius had no son, he had hoped to one day guide Paulus into politics.

"How may I assist you, my nephew?"

"Sir, my father seems to think you might know more facts about your grandfather Cornelius than he knows. I would like to know some information about him."

"What would you like to know? Of course, I was only a lad when he died, but I spent a lot of time with him. Your father, uncles, and grandfather were all away with the army. Since I was at home, and perhaps because I'm named after him, he taught me a lot. Oh, he had great stories!"

"What do you know about his being in an earthquake in Cilicia?" asked Paulus.

"Well, I know that he and many of his men were injured in the earthquake. Several men died there. Your great-grandfather was seriously injured but recovered completely."

"I learned that from Father. Do you know who rescued him? That's what I'm interested in knowing."

Somewhat puzzled by this question, Cornelius said, "Yes, it was a family in Cilicia that lived in Tarsus. They were Jews. Grandfather said they dug for hours freeing him from the rubble. He stayed with the family for a long time until he was able to return to Rome."

"Do you know the name of these Jews?" Paulus asked sharply.

"No," Cornelius replied, "but they were very devout. They had a hard time having someone they considered a heathen (and maybe even unclean, according to them) in their home. However, they saved his life. Grandfather learned a lot about their religion while he was with them. One interesting thing he told me was about something called the *shema*. They put it on their doorposts and even tied it around their wrists."

"Was it a secret plot?" Paulus asked with disbelief.

"Oh, no," chuckled Cornelius. "It was merely an instruction from their god. Let me see if I remember it. It was something like 'Love the Lord your God with all of your heart, soul, and mind.' I think that was it. Grandfather remembered it because they said it so often in his presence. Oh, there was something else. They had a lot of laws in a sacred book called the *Torah*."

Not being particularly interested in all this religious information, Paulus interrupted his uncle with another question. "Could these Jews have been granted Roman citizenship because of their actions?"

"Now that you ask, I believe they were granted citizenship. Why are you so concerned about this, Paulus? It was a long time ago."

"I think it possible that the Jew Paul that I'm guarding may be the grandson of this family."

Cornelius was stunned. He knew of Paulus' assignment but had no particular interest in the prisoner. "Isn't he one of those cult members who follow this Jesus Christ?"

"Yes, he is. He told me the earthquake story last evening. It has disturbed me greatly."

"I understand. I suppose one of the reasons I have argued against eradication of this Jewish sect is because of Grandfather's feelings. After his experience, he respected Jews. He felt their moral laws were even superior to ours. If not for my position, I would really like to talk to this Paul. Now, I must return to my duties. Please keep me informed if you learn anything else of interest from the Jew. One more thing Paulus, you might find some information in your great uncle Titus Livy's writings about this event. He is after all our greatest Roman historian," Cornelius said proudly.

"Thank you sir, and farewell," said Paulus.

Paulus was in no mood for chariot races or entertainment. So he walked home in deep thought.

Chapter 12

Upon arriving at home, he found his father asleep. Apparently the previous day at the Forum had been very hard for him. Since Paulus had not gone to the baths today, he washed away the grime from his long walk in the tiny family bath. Returning to the atrium, he received another surprise. Livia and her maids were just returning from visiting Cornelius' daughters.

"What happened to you?" Paulus demanded on seeing Livia.

"What do you mean?" replied Livia with a blush.

"You know what I mean," said Paulus.

"Well, my cousins have just been helping me a little with my hair."

"Ha," answered Paulus, "hair is not all, by any means."

"Do you not think I look better?" Livia asked shyly.

Not wanting to hurt her, he replied, "I suppose so. But you look like a woman – not my dear Livia."

"I am a woman!" Livia said hotly.

Livia was wearing a brightly colored *stola* over her *tunica*. She also wore a *palla* over her shoulders. Unlike her usual simple shawl, this *palla* was trimmed in lace. What shocked Paulus more was her hair and face. Her long hair was dressed in curls with a ribbon at the top! And, she had edged her eyes with charcoal, and her lips were colored a light red. In truth, she looked very elegant and quite pretty. But for Paulus, this new Livia was hard to accept.

"I suppose you are hoping to see the giant again," Paulus said with sarcasm.

"No, I just want to look better! Why are you in such a bad mood? Is it something concerning the Jew?"

"It's a very disturbing story. Do you have time to listen or must you go and try on some jewelry?"

Sitting down on a bench, Livia restrained her impulse to reply with anger and said simply, "Tell me about it, Paulus."

Paulus told her what Paul had said, what his father had said, and finally what his uncle had told him. Livia was very interested. She stopped his telling of the story several times with questions. Finally, she asked him, "What are you going to say to the Jew tonight? Are you going to accept that his story is true? Will he want special favors from you now? Would they pull you from this duty if they knew the story? Could I meet him? Paulus, do you—"

"Stop! Stop! How can you ask so many questions? Go put chalk on your cheeks or something. I don't know what I'll say or do!" Paulus stormed away to his bedroom. He had to get ready to go on duty at the Jew's house in a couple of hours.

Chapter 13

After what seemed to Paulus a very short time of rest, he started on his journey to his guard duty. It had begun a slow drizzle, and this certainly didn't help his mood. He wasn't sure what he would say about what he had learned. "Maybe Paul will not mention it again," thought Paulus. Even so, Paulus' curiosity would be too great not to seek more information.

When he arrived, he found the other guards gone and Silvius on duty again. He looked pale, and when Paulus greeted him, he responded with a voice barely above a whisper.

"You should not be here. You are still sick," said Paulus.

"I didn't want to cause you any difficulty by not being here," Silvius whispered.

"There were no problems. You know there is little danger here."

"You never know," whispered Silvius.

Paulus finally took note of Paul. He was poring over several sheets of papyrus. A scribe stood nearby.

Paul nodded a greeting to Paulus and resumed his walking, pulling his chains with him. There were three other men with him. One who was frequently present was a man Paul called Mark. Another was the man who came yesterday called Epaphras. He brought some kind of news to Paul about followers of this Jesus Christ at Colosse. The third man was the one to whom Paul gave the letter for Philemon a few days ago. Paulus listened with more interest today.

"I'm not sure I've said enough. I want it to be clear," said Paul to the others. "This is the most important thing there is in the world, you know."

Paul seemed somewhat agitated as he waited for their response.

"You have spoken well," said Epaphras. "My people have great faith in your wisdom."

"It's not my wisdom," said Paul. "It's the Holy Spirit, the spirit of Christ, the Living God, speaking through me. They must continue in the faith no matter what happens. After all, they have the joy of the Living Lord."

"They must know what I have said is essential. These parts of the letter are so important. 'Christ in you, the hope of glory,'(Colossians 1:27) and 'You have been given fullness in Christ, who is the head over every power and authority.'"(Colossians 2:10)

As Paul continued, Paulus found himself drawn in by the fervor of Paul's words. The scribe began writing again as Paul dictated more.

Paul continued, "'My purpose is that they may be encouraged in heart and united in love…and in Christ, in whom are hidden all the mighty, untapped treasures of wisdom and knowledge.'"(Colossians 2:2-3)

More casually, no longer dictating, Paul said, "They must realize they don't need the restrictions of the old laws. They are new people in Christ."

Dictating to the scribe again, Paul said, "'Here there is no Greek or Jew, circumcised or uncircumcised, barbarian, Scythian, slave or free, but Christ is all, and is in all.'"(Col. 3:11)

When Paul spoke, he was no longer the unimposing old man Paulus had first seen. He spoke with authority and great passion. Most of the letter to the Colossians had already been dictated, and Paulus found himself wishing he had heard it all. It was oddly compelling. As they finished, Paul asked (as he had in the letter to Philemon) to write a final greeting in his own hand. He read it aloud as he wrote, "'Remember my chains. Grace be with you. Paul.'"(Col.4:18)

The scribe then rolled the sheets of papyrus, and tied and sealed the thread around them. Paul turned to Tychicus and said, "You must tell your dear people about my circumstances and ask for their prayers. Epaphras is to remain here with me, but he will return to them in time. He's been a wonderful witness and will minister to them and the other churches in Laodicea and Hierapolis again very soon." He then handed the letter to Tychicus.

"I am very sorry you had to wait to leave, but I had to send this letter to the Colossians. Thank you for delivering both letters on the same journey."

"We will depart in the morning with your letters and personal messages. You know he is coming to say another short farewell to you again this evening," said Tychicus.

While they were speaking, a man suddenly rushed into the room. It was the slave Onesimus! He ran and fell at Paul's feet once more. With great emotion, he said, "I wish one final farewell before we leave tomorrow. God has given me such a peace now, and my only sorrow is leaving you. I would have gladly been your brother or your slave forever."

With tears in his eyes, Paul embraced Onesimus and Tychicus. He prayed with them briefly and then they left, with the letters in hand. Soon after, Epaphras, Mark, and the scribe departed. Paul sat on the couch, overcome with exhaustion and emotion.

Paulus, who had become completely involved in the events of the evening, turned to look at Silvius to see if he were paying attention to what had just occurred. Paulus was surprised by what he saw. Silvius was leaning against the wall, his eyes closed, his face ashen, and his breathing very ragged. His *gladius* was lying on the floor!

Paulus called his name, and he opened his eyes slowly. Then he started shaking violently and slid to the floor. Paulus was greatly alarmed. "Does he have some kind of plague?" thought Paulus. He went toward him with some fear.

Suddenly he heard a commanding voice say, "Bring him over here. My chains prevent me from going to him." It was the prisoner speaking.

Paulus hesitated, but Silvius was now an unconscious mass on the floor. He didn't know what to do!

"Bring him to me. You know I'm unarmed," Paul said.

Silvius was not as big or strong as Paulus, but he was too heavy for Paulus to carry. So laying his *gladius* aside, he dragged Silvius to Paul's couch. Then to Paulus' horror, Paul placed his hands on Silvius' chest and prayed a simple prayer,

"Dear Father, if it be your will, please heal our dear Silvius. In the name of Jesus Christ, Amen."

In just a moment, Silvius opened his eyes and asked what had happened. He looked at Paulus and Paul. No one said a word. He stood up slowly and asked Paulus to get him some water. Paulus found a pitcher and poured him a partial cup of water. Silvius drank, smiled, and then said, "It's strange, but for some reason, I feel a lot better."

Paulus noticed Silvius' voice was much stronger and the color was returning to his face. He reached to his side and asked, "Where's my *gladius*?"

Paulus pointed to the floor, and Silvius went and picked up his *gladius*. Still standing near Paul, Paulus watched to see what would happen next. Paul smiled and said simply, "Thank you Jesus."

Thankfully, their shift was almost complete. Paulus was so disturbed by the events of that afternoon that he could find no words to say to Silvius or Paul. When their replacement came, Paulus nodded farewell to Paul and left with Silvius.

Outside the house, Paulus asked Silvius if he needed help getting home. Silvius replied, "No, I'm feeling much better." Paulus considered telling Silvius what had happened to him, but he didn't know what to say. "Had Paul healed him?" thought Paulus. He knew even thinking such things could be serious or even dangerous. So he simply told Silvius he was glad he was better, and they went to their own homes.

Chapter 14

The next day, when Paulus entered the atrium, he was surprised to find his father and Livia arguing about something. Paulus didn't really want to talk about last night, and he had been relieved to find everyone in bed when he came home last evening. Now he was sure they would ask questions that he didn't want to answer. But instead, his father quickly started on a new subject.

"You are finally up. Eat something quickly and then escort Livia to the large market near the Circus Maximus. She has some shopping that she wishes to do."

"But I was planning to go to the baths, do some exercise, and perhaps see a race," said Paulus with annoyance.

The last thing he wanted was to follow Livia into shops and also have to answer her persistent questions.

Turning to Paulus, Livia said, "I've told Father that I've gone to the market and shops many times with only my servants. He seems to think he isn't doing his duty by me because he can't go with me. Tell him, Paulus," she insisted, "I'll be fine."

Paulus looked at Livia then and quickly realized why his father was concerned. This was not the old Livia with her unkempt hair hanging over her dull, grey *stola*, nor was this the girl with a *palla* tied over her slumped shoulders. He thought, "She's stunning! No wonder Father is concerned."

"I'll take her," said Paulus angrily, "but I can't stay all day."

"Oh, thank you, thank you! You are too kind!" Livia said mockingly. "I'm a poor, simple female, who must have a male leader," she continued as she hurried out the door.

"What happened to my sweet Livia?" asked Paulus.

His father chuckled as he watched them walk away toward town.

"Ah, yes," he thought, "this dear child has her eyes on a young man."

Chapter 15

*A*s Paulus was walking Livia to the shops, a soldier that he had met a few times stopped to speak to him. They talked about the campaigns that their *cohorts* were in at the moment. The soldier had had a minor injury and was to join his *maniple* soon.

"Paulus," he said, glancing at Livia, "who is this lovely creature you are escorting?"

"She's not a creature! She's my sister. Farewell to you," replied Paulus hotly.

The soldier left, and Livia turned to Paulus and said, "You were very rude. He was just being friendly."

"Friendly, hah! You were flirting with him. He's a notorious womanizer. What has come over you?" asked Paulus.

Livia glared at him and did not respond.

After passing wine stores, oil merchants, meat markets, barber shops, pharmacies, and many other shops, they finally arrived at one of the large shoe stalls. Paulus then went into several shops and stalls with her, following her with a look of hopeless martyrdom. Seeing his look of misery, Livia said,

"Oh, go on to your games. I'll be fine."

"No, I must stay. Father expects it of me," replied Paulus.

He was getting in an increasingly bad mood. Finally, Livia said, "My maids' arms are full, and we are almost finished. I only want to get some pastries as a special treat for dinner, and then we'll hurry home. You are very near your baths. Go! We'll manage now."

Paulus hesitated, but his feet were tired, and he had to stand guard again tonight. If he walked her home and then back to the baths, he would have no time to bathe and relax. He walked her to the bakery, made her promise to pull her *palla* around her head, and reluctantly left her pondering which pastries to choose for the evening meal. They normally ate fruit and cheese for dessert, but Livia felt this shopping day was a special occasion. Atticus had insisted that he wanted her to buy whatever pleased her. She never requested things, and he was pleased with her new interest in fashion. She had bought jewelry, silk, shoes, lace, and several types of toiletries. "And tonight," Livia decided, "we'll have something rich for dinner!" Livia finally made her selections. Since her servants' arms were filled with her other purchases, Livia had to carry the sweets. They were stacked loosely, and she knew she had to walk carefully. Looking at her desserts, she walked to the door, paying little attention to anything else. Suddenly, a man rushed into the shop and ran into Livia. Her pastries went everywhere – on her face, into her hair, on the front of her *stola*. She shrieked, and then looked into the face of the man with whom she had collided. It was Tatius! He immediately began to apologize, "I'm so sorry. I'm forever rushing into people. I'm afraid I don't seem to be able to think and walk at the same time. I've just come from the book store I told you about, and my mind was on one of the books I saw."

"It's not your fault. I was only looking at my sweets. Oh, I've ruined your tunic," cried Livia, seeing the red juice stain on his chest. "I'm so sorry."

"Don't apologize. I am going to buy you more pastries. This time I'll carry them home for you, and that way you won't have to worry about my running into you again," he said with a laugh. "It won't be any trouble. I know where you live, remember?"

Livia finally agreed, and they walked home, with Tatius carefully holding the new sweets. Livia was unsure how her father would react to Tatius' presence, but she wanted to talk to Tatius, so she decided it was worth a scolding.

They talked about the beautiful weather that day, the lovely view of the hills all around, the flowers they passed on the way, and the Emperor's new villa up in the hills. Livia wanted to ask him some questions, but she was enjoying the walk so much she just let herself be happy for the moment.

When they arrived at Livia's house, Livia explained what had happened and then introduced Tatius to her father. Atticus remembered Paulus' mentioning that Silvius had a son who was a scholar. He seemed a nice young man. Obviously, Paulus hadn't stayed with Livia after all!

On impulse, Atticus asked, "Would you like to dine with us this evening? You're wearing part of our dessert, after all," he said with a laugh. "Dinner won't be ready for some time, but you can use our bath to remove our pastries."

Blushing, Tatius said, "I would like that, but I don't want to cause too much work for your servants."

"It's no bother. They wouldn't mind preparing for a guest. Livia, go tell them there'll be one more for dinner. Oh, and you probably should make yourself look a little less like a pastry shop as well!"

Livia left and went into the back rooms.

"My Livia is a dear treasure," said Atticus. "She has a mind any scholar would want, and more importantly, her heart is uncommonly kind."

"I don't know her well, of course, but I can see why anyone would be drawn to her. If I may say so, she is so lovely that I'm amazed she isn't married," said Tatius.

"That's my fault. I'm afraid I have selfishly kept her near me as a companion. Of course, many men do not want a wife with a sharp mind."

"Oh, but that's one of the things I find so lovely about her. She's, she's like a fresh drink of spring water. She renews your spirit!"

Atticus looked at him carefully. Then he said, "If she wishes you to call on her, you have my permission."

"That's more than I could ever have dreamed of from the moment I met her."

When Livia returned, Atticus rose and asked to be excused. He said that he needed to rest before dinner.

Livia sat on a bench near the fountain in the *impluvium*. Tatius rose and asked if he might join her. They watched the sunlight as it played on the pool. Both too shy to speak for a while, Tatius finally said, "Your father thinks you are very special."

"Oh, all fathers think that of their daughters," replied Livia.

"But I think this father is probably right."

Livia blushed. Tatius reached over and gently wiped away some of the pastry still on her cheek. She turned to him and looked into his eyes and caught her breath.

Tatius rose suddenly and rushed over to a different bench. (It was obvious that Tatius was forever rushing to different places!)

"Why are you moving? The sun is more pleasant over here," said Livia, flirting for the first time in her life.

Tatius knew he should remain on a different bench. If not, he knew he would not be able to stop himself from kissing her. Her father could return at any time, and servants were walking about, and he had to maintain control. He finally said, "To be so near you makes me too aware of your beauty."

No one had ever called Livia beautiful except her father. With a boldness she didn't know she had, she said, "I would like it very much if you would spend time with me. I don't know if my father would approve, but I would enjoy talking to you."

Tatius was silent for a moment. "This is the daughter of a Roman aristocrat, and her father has great wealth. I have nothing except my studies, and most importantly she doesn't know that I'm a Christian," thought Tatius.

Livia was growing ashamed of her daring comment. Tatius didn't speak for a while, obviously in deep thought. Then he rose from his bench and joined her again. He then said,

"Livia, I would consider becoming your suitor the greatest award that I have ever received in my life."

He took her hand and gently kissed her fingertips. With a smile, he said,

"I must see if there is any of the first dessert left on your fingers."

With a last loving look, he brought her hand to his throat where she could feel the rapid beating of his heart. Then he rose and asked where he could wash for dinner.

When Tatius returned, Atticus was just hobbling into the atrium. He asked if they had had a pleasant chat.

By the look on their faces, Atticus knew that his days of having Livia to himself were probably gone.

"Perhaps you've debated politics or philosophy?" he inquired.

"No, we just talked about things in general. Father, you could tell Tatius about some of your military campaigns," suggested Livia.

Intending to tell only a few stories, Atticus found himself talking at length to this erudite young man. Livia hadn't seen her father so animated in a long time. While they were discussing battles and politics, Livia was replaying in her mind the feel of Tatius' gentle caress.

Suddenly Paulus came hurrying into the house. He had spent too long at the races, and he didn't want to be late for his guard duty. Seeing Tatius talking to his father, he thought that Silvius must be ill again. "So much for Paul's prayers for healing!" he thought.

"I suppose your father is ill again?" asked Paulus.

"Oh, no," said Tatius, "he seems almost completely well. He told me this morning that he couldn't believe how fast he started to improve. It was almost like a miracle."

"Obviously, Silvius remembered nothing about last night," thought Paulus. "Only Paul and I know."

Atticus then explained that he had invited Tatius to dinner, after he (not Paulus!) had escorted Livia home. Paulus wasn't sure Livia's meeting Tatius was a coincidence, but at least Livia got to see her "giant" again.

"I mustn't be late," said Paulus. "Enjoy your dinner, and I'm glad your father is still well." He quickly dressed in his military gear, got his *gladius* ready, and left for Paul's house.

The dinner was very pleasant, with everyone talking. Atticus, Livia, and Tatius were able to discuss many things – literature, philosophy, history. At the close of the meal, Tatius thanked Atticus and Livia and said he would see them soon.

Atticus watched them say farewell. It was very formal, but their eyes told a story all their own.

Chapter 16

Paulus arrived at the prisoner's house to find Silvius there, early as usual. The other guards were already gone. Silvius bore little resemblance to the man who was so ill yesterday. He smiled at Paulus and gave him a hearty greeting. Paulus was in somewhat of a quandary. Should he mention the prayer for healing that Paul had made (and its subsequent result!)? He decided to wait until later when they had more privacy.

Today, Paul had several visitors with him, and it was apparent that they were making plans for another worship ceremony. Paulus was glad that he was going to be gone for five days; therefore, he would not have to witness another of their "blood and flesh" ceremonies. While at the public baths this afternoon, he had been approached by one of the garrison commanders, who had a position of authority at the Campus Martius. Knowing the status of Paulus' family and his current situation as guard for a prisoner, he invited Paulus to represent his *cohort* at the Equus October Festival of Mars. Paulus had accepted with pride and gratitude. The commander said that he would make arrangements for a replacement guard and for his transportation to the Campus Martius.

Paulus was thinking about how much he was going to enjoy the celebrations, feasts, and especially the races at the festival, when Paul suddenly walked toward them and said,

"My fellow Romans, I pray that you will pardon the turmoil of so many guests this evening. We are making plans in case I am no longer here."

"Are you to be released soon?" asked Paulus eagerly. He immediately thought that maybe after the Festival of Mars, he could be assigned to a new *maniple*. Then he could go fight the barbarians where his talents could be used!

"No, I doubt that will happen," said Paul. "No, we have news of disturbing punishments for my fellow believers in Christ. On the way into the city this morning, my dear brother Luke saw several 'Christ followers' hanging by the roadside. There was a tribunal, apparently, that sentenced them to death. There were even two women – both young believers. We are making plans for the churches in case I too am soon executed. If not for my Roman citizenship, I'm sure I would have been killed already."

Paulus didn't know what to think. A few days ago, he would not have cared, but recently he had become more accepting of these Jews and their deluded ideas. Besides, it seems the Livian family owed a lot to the ancestors of this Jew from Tarsus. Paulus looked at Silvius, who was usually so stoic and impassive. His chin was quivering and tears were running down his face. Silvius said nothing, but Paulus' instinct told him immediately, "He is a believer!"

Paul said, "I pray that the Lord Jesus Christ will be with you both, and that his salvation will come to your hearts." Then he returned to the men who were talking hurriedly as if there was little time. A few of the men had papyrus on which they were making notes, others were praying quietly, and a couple of the men were watching the door fearfully.

Silvius and Paulus remained silent throughout the evening. Several men came to talk with Paul. There were women who appeared as well. Paul greeted them as "sisters in Christ's kingdom." Finally as evening approached, the stream of visitors diminished, and Paul was alone with Silvius and Paulus. Paul fell on his couch with his chains clanging, and his fatigue was apparent to them both. He drank a few sips of water, lay down, and was soon fast asleep.

When their shift was complete and their replacement had arrived, both Silvius and Paulus looked at Paul and wondered, "Is this the last time we will see him alive?"

As they walked out into the street, Paulus could stand it no longer. He blurted out to Silvius, "He prayed for you and you got well, you know!"

"I suspected as much," replied Silvius calmly.

"You're one of them, aren't you?" demanded Paulus.

Silvius stopped walking for a moment, and Paulus paused as well. Knowing his admission was dangerous, Silvius, nevertheless, drew a deep breath and then answered, "By the grace of the living Lord, yes I am."

Even though Paulus had had some suspicions about Tatius and even Silvius (Why was he always there so early?), his admission was still a shock.

"What must I do? What will happen to you if I tell our superiors? What will become of your family? What do I tell Livia? She likes your Tatius," said Paulus. He knew he was babbling, but he couldn't seem to stop himself.

Silvius said gently, "Do what you must. As Paul often says, 'For to me, to live is Christ and to die is gain.'(Philippians 1:21) I must go home and speak with my family now. Goodnight, my son." Silvius turned and started on his journey home. Paulus remained in the same spot for a moment, and then he too headed toward home. After all, he had to leave before dawn for the Festival of Mars.

Muttering to himself, Paulus complained, "I should be preparing for five days of great entertainment, but now I know a terrible secret. I don't know what to do. Why is my fun always spoiled?" When he arrived home, everyone was asleep. It was just as well. He wasn't quite ready to talk to Livia or his father about this latest development.

Chapter 17

Paulus rose before dawn the next day. He had been in such a rush yesterday that he hadn't mentioned anything to his family about his going to the Festival. He decided to wake one of the servants, tell him about his plans, and have him inform the family when they awoke. Though not very hungry, he ate some cheese and bread and drank a little wine. If it hadn't been for the disturbing events of the previous night, he would have been very happy. He was excited to be part of the celebration. The commander had said that he could choose one of the finest horses for his ride in the procession, and he loved horses! There would be parades, games, music, races, feasts and lots of festivities. More importantly, he would be with military men again!

Paulus had never been to this celebration, held at the Campus Martius, located just outside the city. Of course, he had seen the altar erected to Mars and the Temple of Mars while in military training. However, he had never visited the magnificent Pantheon, built during the time of Emperor Augustus. All the talk about their god at the prisoner's house made Paulus want to see the temple for all the Roman gods. He doubted these Christians would ever have anything as glorious as this temple! Paulus had heard about several activities during the Festival that should be impressive — including the mock battle staged by some of the surrounding residents, and the Salian priests, dressed in their unusual costumes, leaping and dancing in the streets. These events should be interesting, but most of all, Paulus just wanted to be away from all these followers of this Jesus Christ. He decided to tell no one about Silvius and to make no decisions about what he had learned last evening until his return from the Festival.

A mule cart arrived just before dawn, and Paulus was on his way to the great Equus October Festival of Mars.

When Atticus and Livia got up, the servant told them about Paulus' honorary duty for the next five days.

"I hope Paulus is prepared for the ending of the Equus celebration there," said Atticus.

"Why? What happens?" asked Livia.

"He can explain, when he returns," said Atticus, not wanting to get into a lengthy discussion of a ceremony that he disliked immensely. "What are your plans for today, Livia?"

Livia blushed. "Tatius asked if he could call on us this morning, and I answered yes for both of us," said Livia.

"I doubt he is interested in calling on both of us!" said Atticus with a chuckle. "I like him. That would be fine with me. Go get ready, dear one, while I rest here in the morning sun."

A couple of hours later, Tatius arrived at the Livian family home. Livia was wearing a new pale pink *stola*, and over it she had draped a pink *palla* on which she had sewn white lace. The pale pink of her *stola* and *palla* showed her glossy black hair to great advantage. Atticus noted that she was wearing a simple pearl necklace above her *bulla* (a locket containing an amulet to ward away evil spirits). The pearls were one of her purchases yesterday. While not obvious to a casual observer, Livia had used a few cosmetics also. Atticus thought her the most exquisite young woman in all of Rome! "Of course, I might be a little bit biased," he thought with a chuckle.

They greeted Tatius warmly and asked if he would like some juice or wine to drink. Tatius said that some juice would be appreciated. Atticus excused himself very soon, claiming he needed more rest.

Tatius and Livia sat on two chairs at a small table that Livia had had the servants move to the atrium. She had carefully arranged red and white roses from the garden in a vase on the table. The table itself was inlaid with mosaics of a seascape with splashing dolphins. Looking at Livia across the table, Tatius said, "Even these roses pale when compared to your loveliness."

Livia blushed and said, "Thank you. Let's drink some of the fresh juice the servants have brought." As they drank their juice, they began talking about some of their studies. They debated some of Seneca's ideas, talked about the views of Socrates, discussed Roman Literature, and analyzed the dramas they had seen at the theaters. Livia was surprised to learn that Tatius even had an interest in horticulture. In Greece, he had stayed with a man who was in charge of the most beautiful gardens in Athens. "I can't believe Tatius is also a nature lover," thought Livia. "Even my father doesn't share my love for plants and flowers."

Time passed quickly, as Tatius and Livia laughed and talked. Atticus came to the door of his bedroom and watched the happy couple for a short while. They were so involved with their conversation that they didn't even know he was there. His joy for them was tinged with a touch of sadness — partly because it brought back the memories of those wonderful days with Livia's mother and partly because he knew Livia was leaving him behind.

Tatius finally realized he had stayed for a long time, and he rose to leave. Atticus had returned to his room, so Tatius only said farewell to Livia. Telling her he had some matters he needed to address the next day, he then asked if he could call on her the day after tomorrow. She readily agreed, and he left with a smile. The day had passed with both young people leaving some of their thoughts unsaid. Livia didn't want to interrupt their happy conversation by asking why he was at the ceremony at the Jew's house, and Tatius had fully intended to tell Livia that they should not see each other again. He knew that her father would never permit her to marry a "Christ follower", but he enjoyed her company so much that he decided a short delay in revealing he was a Christian would not matter. He did keep his emotions under control and had no physical contact with her.

After Tatius left, Livia rehearsed all the conversations they had shared. She found him so very interesting and exciting. Secretly, she wished he had kissed her fingers again or at least touched her. "I'm a shameless woman!" thought Livia. Somewhat overcome with such disturbing emotions, Livia thought, "If only my mother were still alive, I could tell her my feelings. Oh, I think I love him!"

The rest of that day and the next day passed slowly for Livia and Atticus. They both missed Paulus, and neither seemed to be able to talk to each other.

Chapter 18

The day for Tatius' next visit finally arrived. Livia rose early, ate, and then began getting ready for his call. Today she chose to wear the other new *palla* that she had bought. It was a lovely shade of blue. She decided to not prepare her hair in curls as was fashionable, but instead, she tied it back with a lace ribbon and then let it cascade down her back.

Growing nervous from waiting, she asked her favorite servant Philippa if her appearance was acceptable. Philippa assured her she was lovely. While arranging roses in a vase for the table, Livia recalled Tatius' compliment that compared her to such flowers. She could barely contain her impatience to see him again!

At last Tatius arrived. Atticus was feeling ill and had asked Livia not to disturb him, so Livia was the only one who welcomed Tatius. Livia noticed immediately that Tatius seemed much more quiet and subdued than on previous visits. "Is something wrong?" asked Livia, suddenly wondering if she had misjudged his interest in her. After all, she had little experience dealing with suitors.

"Not exactly," Tatius replied, turning to look at her. "Oh! When I look into your eyes, I don't know what I'm to do!" said Tatius with emotion. "It's just that, Livia, there are things about me that you don't know."

This frightened Livia a bit. "But Tatius is only 21 years old," she thought. "He couldn't have done many bad things."

Tatius suddenly stood and said, "Could we go somewhere and talk privately – away from everyone?" asked Tatius.

"There's a shade tree at the back of our garden. It has a bench under it. No one could hear us nor see us easily," said Livia.

"Did he want to propose marriage?" wondered Livia. "This is too soon and Father would have to make a contract first."

They walked through the kitchen area into the garden. Finding the bench under the shade tree, they sat down.

Livia could tell by the serious look on Tatius' face that he had something important to tell her.

"Tell me Tatius! I must know," cried Livia with impatience.

"You remember I told you about all my travels to Athens, Ephesus, and many other places?"

Livia nodded.

Tatius took a deep breath and said, "Well, there was another place where I spent a long time when I was nineteen. It was Corinth. I made friends there, and they introduced me to…"

Livia interrupted him while blushing, "Oh, I've heard about the wild activities at Corinth. I've heard about the Temple of Aphrodite and the women where men uh…Oh, Tatius, it was long ago, and I can forgive you!"

Tatius chuckled. "Livia, I never visited the Temple nor any brothels while in Corinth. I was studying very hard with a great philosopher. My grandmother lives in Corinth, and I stayed with her and met some of her friends."

"So what is this 'great' secret? Don't tease me so. Tell me," pleaded Livia.

"My grandmother's friends introduced me to some searchers of truth who had become believers in Jesus Christ. Livia, I am a Christian! I am a follower of Jesus of Nazareth. I am sure he is the Son of God. 'For God so loved the world that he gave his one and only Son, that whoever believes in Him shall not perish, but have eternal life,'"(John 3:16) said Tatius with passion. "This is my secret! And oh, what joy it has given me."

Livia was stunned. She sat in complete silence, not moving a muscle. Finally she said, "But Tatius, he was crucified – by us! How can you believe in him?"

"Oh, but He is Risen," said Tatius. "You know I studied at many places, with many scholars. I was searching for answers, Livia. I found them in this Jew called Jesus."

Seeing how disturbed Livia had become, Tatius rose to leave, but she caught his hand and pulled him back to the bench.

"Why did you tell me this today?" asked Livia with confusion.

Tatius looked at her and said, "There are two reasons. First of all, my father admitted he was a Christian to Paulus last evening. I knew it would not be long before Paulus told you. But more importantly, I don't want to hurt you. I should not have shown my feelings for you. Forgive me, dear one."

"Oh Tatius, I think I'm already in love with you! Please don't leave. No man has ever touched my heart and mind until I met you," said Livia.

"You don't understand. Don't think my heart isn't involved. I can barely restrain myself from touching you! But you don't know the dangers involved."

Livia reached up and gently caressed his cheek. "Oh, I'm not afraid. Your secret will not leave these lips."

Tatius, looking at her lips, suddenly pulled her to him and kissed her gently. Realizing he should not have touched her, he jumped up quickly and said he must go.

Before Livia could stop him, he rushed back through the house and out the door.

Chapter 19

For the next few days, while Paulus was attending the Festival of Mars, Livia was left with uncertain feelings. Atticus noticed that she was much more silent than usual, but being the father of three girls, he had found it prudent not to try to understand the "mysterious" moods of his daughters. Since Tatius had not returned, he did venture one question,

"Is something wrong with you and Tatius? He hasn't behaved improperly toward you, has he?"

"No, Father. He's a good man," answered Livia, obviously not inclined to discuss Tatius or anything else.

Atticus did notice her standing and looking at the shrine to their household gods for a long time. Another time he saw her with her eyes closed, toying with her *bulla*. However, he knew his vivacious daughter would return to him before long.

On the third day, Livia approached her father around noon and asked that a servant be sent to Tatius with a message that it was urgent that she speak with him. Her father agreed, and the servant went on his way. Atticus was very curious, but being a patient man he knew Livia would confide in him in time.

In less than an hour, Tatius came rushing into the atrium (yes, Tatius was always rushing!). Seeing Livia and her father, he cried, "What's happened? Has Paulus had an accident? Are you unwell?"

"No, I'm sorry if I caused you alarm. It's just very important that I speak to you. Father, would it be permitted for Tatius and me to stroll in the city this afternoon? I promise to be home before dusk," said Livia.

This was a highly unusual request, and Atticus hesitated. Tatius said, "I'm an honorable man, sir. I will neither cause nor permit any harm to come to your daughter."

Atticus believed him and said simply, "Take your cloak, dear one, you must not become chilled."

Livia put on her cloak, and they began walking. When they were a short distance from the house, Livia said, "Tatius, tell me about Corinth."

He told her about the house church where he first was introduced to this new doctrine. The "church" had been established by the Jewish prisoner Paul that his father and Paulus were guarding. In fact, Paul had actually lived in Corinth for over a year. He told her how he had searched for answers in the great Greek philosophies, but he had found none. He continued with the simple sermon preached to him by the people in Corinth, and how he came over time to believe in this one God and his son Jesus Christ.

Tatius was speaking with such intensity and Livia was listening so closely that they were almost run over by a mule cart. Just in time, Tatius pulled Livia and himself to the roadside.

"I wonder if we were almost killed by vestal virgins or some royal wives!" said Tatius, knowing these two groups were the only ones permitted to use wheeled vehicles in the daytime.

Livia smiled and then said, "I want to meet him – the prisoner Paul!"

Tatius stopped walking and said, "I'm not sure that is safe for you. You'll be recognized, and I promised your father you would be safe."

"Isn't your father on duty in a short time, and isn't he alone since Paulus is away?" asked Livia.

"Uh, yes," replied Tatius.

"Well, we can sit in the park for a while and then I shall pull my *palla* over my head and face and we can go!" said Livia with determination.

"This is certainly a woman who knows her mind and is used to her own way," thought Tatius.

"I'll agree to it, but you must be watchful for any of your friends," said Tatius.

They sat for over an hour, while Livia asked many questions. "But Tatius, why do you think this Jewish God Jehovah is superior to our Jupiter? Are our gods not real to us just as this Jehovah and Jesus are real to these Christians? I don't see the difference."

"How do you worship Jupiter, Livia? Do you pray to him often each day? Does he speak to you in your thoughts?" asked Tatius.

"I go to the temples of several gods on their festival days, and the priests do our praying and sacrifices for us!" answered Livia.

"But what about you and these gods? Do you talk to them? Do they fill your life with such a joy that you feel you must tell the whole world about them?" asked Tatius.

"Well no, not really," replied Livia.

"I know all the stories about the Roman gods, Livia. Frankly, they seem to be portrayed as if they were 'bad people,' only they have more power. They are selfish, jealous, lustful, violent, exploitative and often cruel. I don't want a god like that to worship." Looking around to make sure they were completely alone, Tatius continued, "And what about our Emperor being worshiped as a god? You've heard the stories about what happens in the palace. Emperor Nero is no god!"

Livia gasped to hear Paulus make such comments. "If we reject our gods Paulus, they won't continue to help us in our wars and keep us rich!"

Tatius replied with eloquence and passion. "I'm not very interested in wealth or treasures here on earth Livia. In Corinth, they often quoted these words of Jesus, 'Do not store up for yourselves treasures on earth, where moth and rust destroy, and where thieves break in and steal. But store up for yourselves treasures in heaven…For where your treasure is, there your heart will be also.'"(Matthew 6:19-21)

The Light Will Come

Disappointment over Livia's comments showed in Tatius' face. Livia quickly said, "Oh Tatius, I don't care if I'm rich or not. It's just that I'm so confused about everything." In truth, Livia, though born into a wealthy family, had never been a materialistic person. Of course, she had had little interaction with people of a different class—with the exception of the slaves and servants in her own household.

With her eyes filling with tears, Livia stood and said that it was time for them to go see Paul. It was obvious to Livia that Tatius was deeply committed to this new religion. He had replied with such eloquence and passion that she knew his fervor was unlikely to disappear.

When they arrived at the nondescript house, Livia took a deep breath, and they entered. Tatius immediately introduced her to his surprised father. Then he took her to where Paul was reclining on a couch. Livia was shocked. As had her brother, she expected someone of a more impressive appearance. She averted her eyes from the chains, as he rose to greet them. Paul nodded in greeting to her and warmly embraced Tatius.

"So you are another of the Livian family. I see you too would give honor to your ancestors. How may I be of service to you, my child?" asked Paul.

Livia didn't understand what he meant by "our ancestors".

"What do you mean by talking of my ancestors?" Livia asked curtly.

"Did your brother not tell you? No, I see by your confusion that he did not. It's not at all important. Why are you here, child? I'm a prisoner. I doubt your father would approve of your presence here," said Paul.

"I have questions, and Tatius seems to think you know all the answers," replied Livia.

Chuckling, Paul said, "I don't know all the answers and will not until I am in the Kingdom of Heaven with my Lord. But perhaps I can answer a few of your questions. After all, I have nowhere else I must be!" said Paul lightheartedly. "What questions do you have, my child?"

Livia was surprised at the beauty of his speech. His Latin was perfect, and yet he was a Jew from Tarsus!

"Well," began Livia, "I can't understand how anyone could believe in just one god. I don't know how I would live without my household gods, and I am very fond of the Goddess Minerva!"

"Ah yes, the goddess of wisdom. Will you sit for a moment while I tell you a story?" asked Paul.

Livia sat down and Paul began, "There was a time when I was trying to kill the followers of Christ that I now call my brothers. But then you see, I was on the Road to Damascus, and a light shone down from heaven and I heard a voice saying, 'Saul! Saul! Why do you persecute me?'(Acts 9:4) And I..." Paul continued the story of his conversion, his call to preach the good news, and how his life had changed.

Tatius watched Livia, and it was obvious that she was completely captivated by his words. Livia interrupted and said, "My father's friend Valerius was in Jerusalem when this Jesus Christ was crucified. He said that some of the man's followers stole the body! Why do you insist that he rose from being dead?"

With a gentle smile, Paul said, "No one took his body. His main followers cowered in fear at his execution. They returned to their routines—thinking that their belief that he was the Messiah promised to the Jews had been wrong. But when some of the women went to the tomb, His grave clothes were there, but He was not. Then He appeared to many of his disciples, teaching them more about the kingdom of God. He came to me on that road to Damascus, and now, He is my life! You see, I had searched for answers to the mysteries of life since my childhood. I now have found my answers — not in philosophies, but in a Man. And even though I'm here in chains, I am free and at peace. What joy fills my heart because of Him! He is my Savior and Redeemer!" said Paul with an expression of sheer bliss on his face.

Tatius watched as Livia's face began to change from doubt to belief. Paul told her many things that Jesus had said to his followers, and she drank in the words with amazement. She then reached her hand toward Paul and said, "Sir," (This to a Jewish prisoner!) "I think I too need a Redeemer. I, I know I long for joy in my life. Show me how to be a follower. Please, I must know how today!" said Livia.

Paul took her hand, and they knelt on the cold, hard floor. Paul prayed for some time, and then told her how to pray as well. She did so. Finally Livia rose and ran to Tatius, tears streaming down her face. Both Silvius and Tatius had been praying silently. They too were crying, as was Paul. Anyone entering the house at that moment would have thought there had been a death. But one look on Livia's face told a completely different story.

"Go, my children, you need to go home. God's grace be upon you," said Paul.

As they were leaving, two men entered. Livia pulled her *palla* down over her face and they were gone. Tatius thought to himself, "How fortunate we were to find Paul alone! Then again, maybe it was all God's plan."

Chapter 20

When they had come to a small garden not far from Livia's house, Tatius said they must stop and talk for a while. Livia thought they had been "talking" ever since they had left Paul's house. But Tatius guided her to a bench and began what was a very sober and serious discussion.

"What are you going to tell your father and your brother?" asked Tatius.

"Oh, Tatius, let's not talk about this just yet. I am so full of joy!" said Livia.

"I'm afraid we must. You know your father will probably no longer permit me to call on you when you tell him your news. In fact, I suspect he will forbid any contact between us," said Tatius.

"I doubt that. He wants me to be happy."

"And then, there's your brother," said Tatius, "he has a quick temper. How will he react? You know, Livia, this kind of commitment can cause great family problems. I know because it has caused difficulties in my family. The day I first met Paulus, I had come to tell my father that my brother Flavius had just returned from battle in Britannia. He had been away for many months, and when my mother told him we had become "Christ followers", he became furious. He said we were being unpatriotic and threatened to have our father removed from the military. He has calmed down now, but he is not a believer. You never know how even those who love you will react to the news."

"Are you afraid?" asked Livia with some disappointment.

"No, I truly am not afraid for myself. But I've been a Christian for two years, and I know what can happen, even to us Romans. I fear your family's prominence will not be enough to shelter you. And Livia, there's more news you should hear. I'm leaving for about ten days. I knew…"

"What? Oh, you can't! I need you. Please don't leave me now!" cried Livia.

"I must. Let me explain. Before I even met you, Paul asked me to make a journey for him to some churches a good distance from Rome. He was sent some money for them from several Greek churches. These brothers and sisters in Northern Italia are almost destitute. Many have lost their ability to earn a living because they will not bow and pray to our Emperor as a god. Tychicus could have gone, but he has gone to Colosse on a mission with letters from Paul. Tychicus, like me, has travelled much throughout the Empire. I am never questioned about my travels. Maybe it's my age or that I just look harmless – even if some might consider me a giant!" said Tatius.

Livia smiled as she remembered all the "giant" talk between Paulus and her.

"I must go, my dearest. People there need help."

Tatius continued, "I had planned to travel as an emissary of Paul for as long as he needed me. I have been learning so much from him since I arrived in Rome, and Paul has always said it is best not to marry in order to devote all to the Lord Jesus. But now that I've met you, I can't bear to even think of life without you. When I return, I'll talk to Paul about us. But first of all, there is your family to consider."

Livia heard all he had to say, but one phrase she rehearsed in her mind several times. He had said that he couldn't bear to live without her. "Oh," thought Livia, "I have found a Savior, and then he has given me someone who loves me. I know that no day of my life will ever be as wonderful as today!" Tears again flowed down Livia's cheeks.

"We must return. Your father will be worried," said Tatius.

They stood up, and Tatius reached up and wiped the tears from her cheeks. They looked at each other for a short time and went to Livia's home.

Chapter 21

When they arrived, Atticus was sitting in the atrium with a look of obvious concern. Before he could say anything, Livia ran to him and said, "Tatius is leaving for several days, and we had a lot to discuss, Father."

"Farewell again!" Livia said to Tatius, and he knew she wished to be alone with her father. Tatius said farewell to them with some hesitation, and then he went out the door.

"Oh my dear father, it has been quite an afternoon," said Livia.

Atticus, with a gleam in his eye, said, "Yes, I think I remember vaguely what being in love is like."

"You do want me to be happy, don't you?" asked Livia.

"Yes dear. My health is not good, and I want you to be well-cared for in the event of my death. I have always worried that Paulus, though he loves you dearly, would be too focused on himself and his career to properly see after you," said Atticus.

"I don't need anybody to see after me!" said Livia with a bit of petulance. Realizing how silly and prideful she sounded, she quickly said, "I know you worry about me, but I don't think your death will be for a long time."

Atticus was silent. Livia had no idea of the increasing pain he was having in his side. The doctors were of no help. Obviously, there were internal injuries from the fall that were growing worse with time. Atticus smiled and said, "Well, tell me why you are glowing my dear!"

Until this moment, Livia had thought that telling her father about her experience in Paul's house wouldn't be difficult, but now that the time had arrived, she was at a loss for words.

"Well, does Tatius care for you, Livia?"

"Yes Father, I'm sure he does."

"I see no problem then. I will draw up the contract at once. Is this not your wish, my dearest?"

"Yes, Father."

"Tatius comes from a fine, old military family. While I don't know them personally, they have an honorable reputation. I'm sure the dowry will be acceptable, and since you are both well-acquainted, I see no problems."

"But you will," said Livia.

"I will what?"

"See problems. Oh Father, I can bear this no longer. Father, Tatius is a Christian, and I have become a believer this evening. I have never felt more at peace. It's as if my whole being is flooded with a kind of peaceful joy."

Atticus almost collapsed on the nearest bench. "Livia *Tertia*, don't be foolish. You are not a Jew. You know nothing of those 'Christ followers.' You…"

Fearing that her father was going to faint, Livia took his arm and steadied him.

"Lean on me, Father, and I'll take you to your couch."

Atticus did as Livia ordered. He lay down on the couch, but he appeared to be very shaken.

"Oh, Father, I'm sorry my news has caused you such distress," said Livia.

Regaining some of his strength, Atticus shook his head and said, "This is impossible. You know nothing of these people. We are Romans! We rule the whole world, and you want to follow some ragtag Jews who believe this crucified Jesus is alive! I told you what

Valerius said. He was there, Livia! We crucified him! I can't believe you could be so easily led into such nonsense, just because you are in love with that, that Tatius! Your brother will go mad when he hears this! Remember he guards this, this Jew. Leave me now. I want to rest."

Livia slowly walked away to her room. Her most perfect day was gone. Crying softly, she began to pray as Paul had taught her. As she prayed, her resolve increased, and by the time night came, she was at peace. "Yes," she thought, "I am a Roman. I am a Roman Christian." and she went to sleep.

Chapter 22

The next morning Paulus returned from the Festival to find Livia alone in the atrium. Instead of greeting him with her usual high spirits, she simply said, "It's good to have you home, Paulus. Father and I have missed you."

Paulus wondered what had happened to his lively sister with her hundreds of questions and her teasing.

"Are you ill, Livia?" asked Paulus.

"No, Paulus," she replied.

While this odd interchange was happening, Atticus hobbled into the room with more difficulty than usual.

"Welcome home, my son," said Atticus.

"I'm very glad to be home," Paulus was suddenly aware of the frailty of his father. "Had he been so preoccupied with his own affairs that he hadn't noticed this decline?" Paulus wondered.

"Father, are you unwell?" asked Paulus.

"Not more than usual." Atticus looked at Livia but did not speak to her. "Paulus, tell us about your days at the Festival of Mars. Were the races spectacular?"

"Well, it began quite grandly. Different groups of soldiers marched in a procession at the Temple of Mars. The *Pontifex Maximus* burned incense and dedicated all victories to Mars. The first days, I was really happy to be there. But toward the end, everything changed."

"What changed?" asked Atticus, even though he could guess the problem.

"The last day began with Salian priests dancing and singing. They were actually amusing in their strange armor. Then the chariot races began. What magnificent steeds were in those races! You know what came next, don't you Father?"

"Yes son. I was afraid it would disturb you," answered Atticus.

Livia spoke finally and said, "Well, I don't know what happened."

Paulus then recounted how after the race, the right-handed horse of the winning pair of horses was sacrificed to the god Mars. The horse's tail was cut off and rushed to *Regia* to have blood drip on the altar there. The head was severed, and there was a mock battle over whether the Sacravienses or the residents of Subura would get the bloody head. "What a waste of such a magnificent creature! I found no more joy in the celebrations after that," said Paulus.

Atticus, like Paulus, had a great love for horses. Although Atticus had never attended the Equus October, he knew about the horse sacrifice.

"I understand, Paulus, but at least it gave you time with your fellow soldiers before you must return to guarding that Jew," said Atticus, while looking at Livia.

Paulus nodded. What he would not tell his father was that he found Paul and his visitors to be more interesting in some ways than his fellow soldiers. They were so, so loud and pompous. All they wanted to do was drink, talk about how many barbarians they were going to kill, and brag about the women they had had. Paulus thought, "What is wrong with me? It just isn't fair. I am a strong, young soldier. Why am I not happy?"

Interrupting Paulus' musings, Atticus said with sarcasm, "Livia has some news I'm sure you will find interesting. Tell him Livia! Perhaps he will share in your newfound joy!"

Livia had never been the object of her father's scorn before, and tears started down her cheeks.

"Well, must I tell him?" Atticus asked sharply.

"No, Father. I will tell him. Paulus," Livia said softly, "I have become a believer in Christ. I am a Christian."

Much to Atticus' surprise, Paulus did not show his usual quick temper. He turned to her weeping face and asked calmly, "When, and how?"

Livia began an account of the events from Tatius' confession of his belief to her visit to Paul. (Here Paulus gasped!) Then she related in detail what occurred at the prisoner's house and what her feelings were now. Paulus never interrupted her but just listened. During the telling of the story, Atticus rose and slowly hobbled to his room.

When Livia finished, Paulus took her hands and said, "You know these Christians are being tried and hanged, do you not? Rumor has it that our Emperor may begin sending them into the arenas with the lions soon. Have you heard that as well?"

"Yes, Paulus, Tatius told me," said Livia.

"But dearest Livia, you are a member of the great Livian family. Can you turn away and leave Rome and us so easily?"

"I don't do this easily, Paulus. But I have found what I've been seeking. I know little of what I am to do or where I will be, but I have found a reason for living. I love you, Paulus."

With tears streaming down her face, she went to her room, leaving Paulus standing in a silent room.

Chapter 23

After such an emotional homecoming, Paulus decided he needed to relax and forget his morning. He hoped that a visit to the public baths would wash away his confused feelings over the celebration at the Festival of Mars as well as his worries about his beloved Livia.

While Paulus was at the baths, Atticus stayed in his room. Livia went about her household duties – giving orders to the servants, checking on the flowers in the garden and sewing a torn tunic. Livia hoped that Paulus would return that afternoon with enough time for her to talk more with him before he left for his guard duty. However, perhaps by design, Paulus returned with just enough time to get his *gladius* and say farewell. Atticus remained in his room.

Livia knew she was going to have to be prepared for a solitary life for a few days. In her heart she prayed that with Tatius' return she would have some hope for the future. But for now she would have to be content with remembering some of the words that Paul quoted from Jesus while he was on earth. He said, "I tell you the truth, whoever hears my word and believes Him who sent me has eternal life and will not be condemned; he has crossed over from death to life."(John 5:24) One quote she remembered very clearly, "Now is your time of grief, but I will see you again and you will rejoice, and no one will take away your joy."(John 16:22) Paul said these were words that Jesus said to his disciples, but tonight she thought, "He was talking to me!" Livia thought about remaining up until Paulus returned, but the emotional stress of the day was too much. She needed rest, and perhaps tomorrow would be better.

When Paulus arrived at the Jew's house that afternoon, he was prepared to express his strong disapproval over Livia's visit to Paul. He knew Livia was a determined girl, and if Tatius had not brought her to Paul, she probably would have come alone! But Paulus needed a scapegoat for his feelings of confusion about the Festival as well as Livia's sudden conversion. He was prepared to vent his frustration immediately. However, when he entered, he found Silvius, Paul, Mark and three or four other men on their knees praying. Taken aback by seeing this situation (especially seeing Silvius not at his usual spot), Paulus walked to his usual place and waited. After some time, they stood up. Silvius and Paul nodded to Paulus in a greeting, and Paulus saw that both had been crying.

"Remember he is in the Lord's hands. I know it looks bad, but we must trust. Our faith must not waver even unto death," said Paul to the others.

Paulus desperately wanted to know what had happened, but he certainly would not ask.

"Rumor has it that more are to be killed besides those set afire at the Campus Martius. Should we warn our people to flee or should we give our lives as our Savior did? Tell us what to do, dear brother," said one of the men.

Paul said, "I must pray now, and I'll give you an answer tomorrow. As for me, I know my time of death is drawing near. Silvius, I know Tatius was to be on the road where the rampaging soldiers killed many of our fellow believers, but perhaps he escaped unharmed."

Containing himself no longer, Paulus said, "We Roman soldiers do not go on rampages!"

"You are right, my son. I fear Emperor Nero gave the orders for the troops to rid the Empire of us Christians. I doubt the soldiers acted without orders."

Paulus couldn't believe this news. He had left the Campus Martius very early this morning, and there had been no executions at the time of his departure.

"When is this supposed to have happened?" demanded Paulus.

"I don't know exactly," answered the unknown man. "But I saw several bodies on my way into the city. They were burned."

"When did Tatius leave?" Paulus asked Silvius.

"Yesterday," answered Silvius. "He was going north along the Tiber."

"If what you say is true, he made it through the Campus Martius area before any of this occurred. I left there early this morning and all was calm."

Silvius showed signs of some relief. Paulus didn't understand why Tatius would be in danger. After all, he was a Roman and there was no brand on his forehead saying he was a Christian. Then it suddenly struck him why they so feared for Tatius. Both Paulus and Atticus knew the secret about Tatius and his family. These men feared the Livian family had already alerted the Roman authorities.

"I need to fast and pray alone, my dear brothers. Go home and do likewise," Paul said to the men. Of course, being "alone" meant being with Silvius and Paulus. Before going to his couch, Paul turned to Paulus and said, "I met your charming sister yesterday. My Lord Jesus entered her life here beside my chains. His grace is free to you when you are ready to receive it. Good night, son."

Paulus could think of nothing to say. His earlier anger was forgotten. He knew he should be furious at being called "son" by this Jew. But seeing the sorrow on Paul's face over the deaths of his fellow believers and the worry he had over Tatius, he thought that his views could be told at another time. Silence led them to the end of their time on duty. When their replacement came, Silvius and Paulus went into the street with somber thoughts. Neither man wanted a conversation, so they went their separate ways.

When Paulus arrived home, he looked for Livia. Learning from the little servant Philippa that she was in bed, he retired for the night with a deep sense of sadness. So many things were not right: his father's health, the ending to his Festival of Mars celebration, Livia's announcement that she is a Christian, and the executions of these "Christ followers" near the Campus Martius. He knew that the lives of the Livian family were never going to be the same.

Chapter 24

The next five days passed with a monotonous routine. Paulus would rise and find his father or Livia (sometimes both) in the atrium. Neither would be speaking. Paulus tried to make conversation with them, but both seemed lost in their own thoughts and not inclined to talk.

Paulus found it easier to be away. He spent much time in the city at the baths, at the racetrack, at the theater, and, of course, at the house of the Jew. He mentioned nothing about the deaths of the Christians to Livia.

On the fifth day after her conversion announcement, Livia was sitting on a bench in the garden, when she was startled by her father walking slowly toward her. He said abruptly, "He may be already dead, you know."

With surprise that he was speaking to her, Livia asked, "Who may be dead?"

"Tatius," said her father with some gentleness.

"Oh no! Please no!" cried Livia, "Father, why do you say that?"

"Close to a hundred were executed at the Campus Martius a few days ago. All were these 'Christians' and several were Romans, according to word sent to me by Cornelius. You'll surely not continue this charade if he is gone, will you?" asked Atticus.

Crying softly, Livia paused (and prayed) before answering. Then she said quietly, "I love Tatius, Father, but even if he is dead, I will remain a follower of Jesus Christ until I too am dead!"

Atticus saw it in her eyes. This decision was not going to change. He had lost his Livia to a crucified Jew. He walked back inside the house with his head bowed and a heart overcome with grief.

Livia had told neither her father nor Paulus about Tatius' trip to the north. Neither had asked why he had not called on her. She assumed they thought he would know he was not welcome.

After her father left, Livia was surprised to see her maid Philippa approaching her cautiously. (Philippa was not a slave. She and her brother Alexander had been in service to the Livian family since the death of their father. Livia's family liked them and paid them a wage greater than necessary.)

"Yes, Philippa, do you need something?" asked Livia.

"No, miss. I want to tell you something if you please," said Philippa. "I have a message from Paul. Alexander and I are Christians. We go to the ceremonies each week at one of the homes of our Greek friends. Twice, we have met Paul! Last night, Paul asked me to give you a message."

Philippa paused to gather her courage. Livia insisted, "Tell me. Tell me!"

"I don't understand it all, but he said to tell you that Tatius was not among the bodies, and he said to tell you this was the prayer Jesus taught his disciples,

> 'Our Father, who art in heaven
> Hallowed be thy name.
> Thy kingdom come,
> Thy will be done,
> On earth as it is in heaven.
> Give us this day our daily bread.
> Forgive us our debts,
> As we forgive our debtors.
> And lead us not into temptation,
> But deliver us from evil.'(Matthew 6:9)

Oh, and he says God loves you this very day."

Livia was stunned that Paul would have time to think about her.

"Was there anything else?" Livia asked eagerly.

"No, miss, but would you mind if my mother and Alexander prayed for you tonight?" asked Philippa.

"I would be so very grateful, if you did. Thank you," said Livia with tears in her eyes.

Philippa hurried away, and Livia felt her peaceful joy rising once more.

Chapter 25

That afternoon when Paulus returned, he found Livia in the garden singing.

"Well, now this is the sister I've not seen lately!" said Paulus. "Where's Father?"

"In his room as usual. He doesn't want to be near me, and I think his health is much worse. I wish he would talk to me. Will you run from me today as well?" asked Livia.

"No, I don't think I will. I've missed you, *little* sister," said Paulus teasingly.

"And I you *big* brother!" she answered. "I don't want to argue, though. Could we just talk?"

"Yes Livia. Are you sure of your decision to become a follower of this Jewish sect called Christians?"

"Yes Paulus."

"I thought so. I understand more than you might think possible."

"Oh, Paulus, are you a believer too?"

"No, but I am listening to Paul more than at first. Don't tell Father." Making sure Atticus was not nearby, Paulus said, "I never thought I would say this, but I want you to be happy. It appears your 'giant' is a fine man, and I will not object to him even if he is a Christian. However, I am worried about your safety. Please be careful, sweet Livia."

Paulus then did something completely uncommon for him. He bent and kissed her on the forehead. Paulus ate quickly, dressed for his guard duty, and began the familiar walk to Paul's house.

Chapter 26

Three more days passed and little changed in the Livian household. Atticus had softened somewhat in that he now spoke to Livia with civility. They even talked about trivial household matters. However, there were no longer any happy spirited discussions of philosophy, politics or religion that they had once so enjoyed.

Livia could hardly contain her secret that Tatius would return in a couple of days. She knew not to mention it, but in her heart she felt that if he could, he would come to her again very soon. In the afternoon, Livia was seated in her favorite spot in the garden – the place where she and Tatius once sat. Suddenly she felt a pebble fall near her feet. She looked up, and another pebble came over the wall. When a third arrived, she knew someone was giving her a signal. She couldn't see over the wall, but she picked up the last pebble and threw it back over the wall. Another small pebble flew over the wall. Enough was enough! She walked with purpose through the back rooms into the atrium and out the front door. She didn't care if her father saw her. Just outside the door, she saw him – Tatius with his arms waving and rushing around the side of the house toward her. She shook her head at him. He nodded as if he understood – no words needed. In hushed tones, he said,

"I may be in danger. It is a long story, and I don't have time to tell you about it. Tonight, Livia, I must leave tonight!" he said hurriedly.

"There will be no other chance. Do you love me enough to come with me?"

"Yes Tatius, I love you with all my being. How shall we meet?" she asked with no hesitation.

"Tonight after Paulus returns and is asleep, I'll be waiting just outside your door. Leave very quietly and bring only a few things. I'll explain more to you later. Hurry back inside now. No one must see you."

When Livia went back into the atrium, she saw Paulus and her father coming from their rooms. They were engaged in a discussion about Emperor Nero's new edicts and paid little attention to her. She listened as they talked about the increased violence.

"They won't bow to him as a god, Father, even if they all are killed."

"I think our Emperor should leave them alone, but what difference would it make if they just pretend he is a god? After all, we doubt our Emperor is the son of Jupiter ourselves, but we bow to him."

"They won't do it. They only worship one God, Jehovah."

"What about this Jesus? Isn't he a god too?" asked Atticus.

"It's complicated. They say that their God is three in one – something about..." seeing Livia for the first time they broke off their discussion.

"Well, I must go see after my prisoner," said Paulus. "I'll see you later."

Livia suddenly rushed to Paulus and hugged him saying, "I love you, big brother. Please be careful."

Paulus chuckled, "I have my *gladius*. Don't worry." Paulus was sure that Livia had heard their talk about violence and was worried about him. He was touched by her concern. He truly loved her.

Atticus, thinking she was worried about Paulus, said somewhat kindly, "He'll be fine. He's not a Christian."

"I know, Father." Livia then, taking a chance that Atticus would not rebuff her, kissed her father on the cheek. She then said, "You have been a wonderful father to Paulus and me."

With tears in her eyes, she went to her room and began preparing to leave. She put her oldest *tunica* in a cloth bag, along with an extra *palla*. She looked lovingly for a moment at her new clothes, cosmetics, and jewelry, but she knew she could not take them. Dressing in another of her older tunics with its matching *stola*, she decided at the last minute to take her new pearls that she had bought on her shopping trip with Paulus. She hesitated about taking them, but they could be sold if there was need, and her father had wanted her to have them. With her cloak over her arm, she then waited until Paulus' return from guard duty.

While Livia waited, she looked at the house where she had lived all her life. It was hard to leave it, but nothing was as hard as leaving her father and Paulus. She truly doubted that she would ever see them again.

"Dear Jesus, please give me strength," she prayed.

After leaving Paul's house that night, Paulus walked home with a sense of foreboding and uneasiness. Perhaps it was due to all of the stories of death and executions told by the Christians. The violence had intensified, and Paulus knew Paul would not be spared for long. His father's health was also a concern. He was definitely getting weaker. Tomorrow, maybe Livia and he could convince their father to see a new doctor. For whatever reasons, Paulus wanted to hurry to the safety of the familiar and secure surroundings of his home. After arriving home, he went immediately to bed.

Hearing Paulus' return, Livia waited until she was sure he was asleep, and then she quietly left her room. As a final break from the old ways, Livia placed her *bulla* on her new pink *palla* in the center of her bed. Tiptoeing out the door, she gave a final glance at the shrine to the *lares* (household gods) and then prayed silently to Jehovah for protection.

Tatius was waiting.

Part Two

Chapter 1

Paulus got up early on that October morning, and as he walked into the atrium he could feel a touch of coolness in the autumn air.

"Ah," he thought, "it's going to be a good day. I don't know why I had such a feeling of gloom last evening, but it's probably because of all the dreary people at Paul's house. I've had about enough of this religious stuff! Today, I'm going to have a day of relaxation and amusement. I may go to see some races or, who knows, I might even visit some of our 'pleasure houses'!"

More hungry than usual, Paulus went to find some food, and as he passed one of the servants going to the kitchen, he asked, "Is my sister up yet?"

"I haven't seen her sir," replied the servant.

"Hmm," he thought, "it's unusual for Livia to sleep so late."

After eating a hearty breakfast of eggs, cheese, bread with honey, and then drinking two glasses of milk, he felt invigorated and ready for a relaxing and entertaining day.

Before going into the city, Paulus wanted to talk to Livia about their father's health, and he thought that this morning would be a good time for such a conversation.

Since Livia had been spending a lot of time in the garden recently, Paulus decided to see if she were there. But she wasn't in the garden.

"That's strange. Livia is always up. Could she be sick?" wondered Paulus.

Going back into the atrium, he walked to her room and tapped on her door. When she didn't answer, he opened the door and walked inside. There on her bed was her new pink *palla* and on it lay her *bulla*! With a sadness he could not believe, he reached for the *bulla*, held it in his hands for a moment (as if he could still feel her warmth on it), and he knew. He knew Livia had walked away from their world.

Ever since learning about Livia's becoming a Christian, Paulus had worried that she would leave the family, but in truth, he never expected her to go without an explanation or a farewell. He knew his father's coldness to her had put up barriers that were very hurtful to her, but he felt that his own relationship with Livia was still one of affection and trust.

"Why didn't she tell me she was leaving?" thought Paulus. Then he realized what a conflict such a confession would have been for him. After all, a Roman father had complete control of his children by law, and if he had kept such a secret from his father, it would have caused a terrible situation for Paulus.

Questions rushed at him immediately.

"Where could she go?"

"Was she with Tatius?"

"How am I going to tell Father?"

"What will he do?"

"Will the news kill him?"

Returning to the atrium, he sat down on a bench near the *impluvium* to think. As he pondered what to do, he noticed the servants and slaves standing in the far corner of the room. He knew they were waiting for orders, and Livia was not there to direct them. Suddenly realizing they might have seen or heard something, he motioned for them to come closer.

"Have any of you seen my sister this morning?" he asked.

Some said, "No sir," some shook their heads, and some (not understanding Latin) stared at him blankly.

"Did any of you see my sister last evening?"

Philippa, a young Greek servant, who was one of Livia's favorite maids, finally spoke and said, "Sir, I saw her in her room a short while before dusk. My brother Alexander and I always leave in time to get home before dark, and I usually check to see if she needs anything before leaving. Last evening, I went into her room and found her sitting on her bed crying."

"Did she say why she was crying?" demanded Paulus harshly.

"No sir. I asked her if she were sick, but she just smiled at me and said I had served her well. She then bade me farewell, and I left," said Philippa.

Shyly, her brother Alexander, who worked in the garden, said, "She hasn't worked with the flowers this morning."

Of course, Paulus had assumed that already. He then questioned the others about last night. No one had seen or heard anything. Paulus had no idea when she had gone. Asking one final question, "Did she dine with my father last evening?"

One of the kitchen slaves, hardly more than a boy, said, "Sir, I took your father some food to his room. Your sister ate a while before him. They haven't eaten together for several days."

This remark caused Paulus renewed pain, and he then knew the rift between his father and Livia had become very deep. Thanking them (something very unusual for him!) for their help, he dismissed all of them except Philippa. He then asked her if she could direct the other servants and slaves as to their tasks today. With a smile, she said, "Sir, I will act as Miss Livia would wish and consider it my blessed gift to her."

"What a strange response! What a strange girl!" thought Paulus. She seemed to have no fear of him, unlike the others. He had known her and her brother Alexander for many years but had paid little attention to them. After all, they were servants. For the first time, he noted how tiny Philippa was and that she was extremely pretty.

"Oh well, I must make some decisions and not let myself be distracted by some Greek servant!"

Paulus knew he had to wake his father and tell him about Livia. If he waited until his father got up, Paulus knew he would be blamed for doing nothing. So he tapped on his father's door. Atticus asked with annoyance,

"Who is it? I do not want to be disturbed!"

"I'm afraid I must talk to you Father. Livia is gone," said Paulus.

"What do you mean 'Livia is gone?'" asked Atticus.

"I'm sorry Father. Please come out and we will talk," said Paulus.

Atticus, in obvious pain, walked slowly into the atrium. "Let me help you Father," said Paulus. Paulus led him to a couch and then brought him some bread and wine. Atticus refused the food and demanded to know what had happened. Paulus told him that Livia was not in the house, and then he told him about the *bulla*. They both knew Livia had left it to tell them she was leaving her old life behind.

"Has she run away with that Christian Tatius?" demanded Atticus.

"I don't know, Father. I'm not even sure he is alive. There was a..."

"I know, I know. Cornelius told me. But where else could she go? Surely, she wouldn't go to that Jew's house. After all, you guard him, and if you hadn't gotten her interested in that Jew, this wouldn't have happened."

Paulus knew his father was just angry and trying to find someone to blame. In truth, Atticus had encouraged the friendship between Tatius and Livia – until he found out about Livia's becoming a "Christ follower". Paulus didn't try to argue with his father because it was obvious that Atticus was in very poor condition.

"Father, let me go to the *insula* where Tatius' parents live. Perhaps they know something," said Paulus.

"They are probably just as upset about Tatius' new religion as we are about Livia's, but go see what you can learn from them," said Atticus.

Paulus didn't want his father to know that Tatius' parents were Christians and especially that he had known that fact for days.

"Are you well enough for me to leave you?" asked Paulus.

"Of course. Go now, and I'm going to send word by one of the servants to Cornelius that I need to see him. He may have some ideas about what to do."

Chapter 2

*A*s Livia was climbing into the boat, she looked back at the last views of her homeland and couldn't keep from crying silently. She knew her decision to leave with Tatius would affect many lives. Tatius and she had prayed together for much of the night, and she had a calmer assurance that this was her new God Jehovah's will for her, but she was still sad. Tatius saw her tears, and, not knowing what to say or how to comfort her, simply gave her his hand and steadied her.

As Livia made her way (with Tatius' assistance) to the deck of the ship, she went over in her mind the events of the last few hours. When she met Tatius outside her house, he had hurried her into the street and then down the Esquiline Hill. At the foot of the hill, outside a *taberna*, a mule cart and driver were waiting for them. They climbed into the cart and began traveling through the city. Tatius had cautioned her to say nothing while they were in the cart, so she was very quiet.

By the time they were in the mule cart, it was nighttime. With no street lights, it was dangerous to be on the streets after dark. However, it was a bright, moon-lit night, and the lamps in the *insulae* gave enough light for the skilled mule-cart driver to navigate through the streets. After what seemed to Livia like a very long time, they were on the outskirts of the city. When they finally stopped, Tatius helped her from the cart, paid the driver, and began leading her down a dark road into the countryside. When the mule cart was out of sight, Tatius asked, "Livia, my dearest, how are you?"

"Well, that was a most uncomfortable ride. I think the mules must dislike their duties *almost* as much as I dislike their transport. I'm fine, Tatius, but where are we going? Surely, we aren't going to spend the night on this lonely road or in the high grass alongside it!"

"We're going just over this little hill, and then you'll see a house where we will be welcomed," Tatius said.

As Tatius said, when they were on the hill, a lamp could be seen in a tiny house just ahead. "Let's hurry Livia," said Tatius. "We need rest and we aren't safe on the road in the dark."

Gasping for breath from running, Livia, with her cloth bag, and Tatius, with a bundle under his arm, arrived at the door of the cottage. Tatius tapped on the door, and an old man opened it and welcomed them inside. As they entered the dark little house with its one lamp burning, Livia saw an old woman putting food on a table. She smiled shyly and spoke to the old man in a language Livia didn't understand. Tatius turned to her and explained that they were Jews, and she spoke only Aramaic. Much to Livia's surprise, Tatius spoke to them in Aramaic – apparently thanking them for their hospitality. The old woman smiled and motioned them to a table where she had wine, fruit, cheese, bread, and fish prepared for them. Livia had eaten a little at home, but she had been too nervous to eat much. Tatius told her she had to eat. It was their custom.

Before eating, Tatius bowed his head and gave thanks for the food, and then said "Amen." The old couple repeated the "Amen" as well.

The room where they ate was apparently an atrium, dining room, reception area, and kitchen combined. Livia had never been in a house that was so poorly furnished. There was one couch near the door, a table, a lamp, two chairs, a large chest, and a brazier for cooking in the far corner. The old couple said something, which Livia assumed was a good night to them, and went into a tiny room which was obviously their bedroom.

Tatius said, "They have a little farmland, but they are in such poor health, they can't cultivate it. They have one son, but he lives in Jerusalem. Before his eyesight failed, Isaac, the old man, was a Jewish scribe who worked for several rabbis. They have been Christians for some time now, and I have visited them on more than one occasion. (What Tatius did not tell Livia was that he had used part of the money he had made tutoring to buy them much needed food and supplies.) They are a blessing to me each time I see them."

"Will we be safe staying with them?" questioned Livia with uncertainty.

"Oh, we're only here until dawn and then we are on the road again. This time we will be making our way to Ostia," said Tatius.

"Ostia? Tatius, we have a villa there. It has many rooms. Could we not stay there?" asked Livia with a hopeful look. She didn't want to remain in a tiny house such as this one, when their country villa was unoccupied.

"Livia, I fear that would be most unwise. Your father's servants would undoubtedly notify him, and I don't believe that is my Savior's plan for us," Tatius said gently.

"Well, tell me His plan! I'm ready to know it now!" said Livia, too tired to care if she sounded petulant.

"I don't know all His plans, but I do know He wants me to go to Gaul. A new friend of mine has arranged passage for us tomorrow afternoon. It is the only time we could go, since the ship won't sail from here again until next spring."

"I've never been on a ship. I find the thought of sailing a bit frightening but exciting," she said with enthusiasm.

With a chuckle, Tatius said, "I'm not sure this will be a comfortable time for you. It's a cargo ship with a few passengers. I just pray the winds are strong, but not too strong, and that we make landfall with no problems."

As they moved to the couch and sat down, Livia turned to Tatius and said, "I've been patient, but I must know why we had to leave so quickly. My father said you might be dead!"

"It's only by God's mercy and providence that I am alive."

With his arm around her, he told her the story of his trip.

"When I left Rome I followed the Tiber past the Campus Martius where the Equus October celebration was just ending. On the road, I met some troops who knew my father and one of my brothers. Thinking nothing of it, I stopped to chat and told them I was going north for a few days.

"Their captain then laughingly said to me, 'If you see any Christians on the way, send them to us.'"

"Before I could think, I asked, 'Why would I do that? Have they ever caused Rome any problems?'"

"Looking at me very suspiciously, he then said, 'Are you trying to question our authority over these, these secretive Christian rebels?'"

"Realizing that several others had joined them and that there could be problems, I told them I had no doubts about their authority and that I was a loyal Roman citizen. I then bade them farewell and hurried on my way. Walking as rapidly as I could, I reached a small inn where I spent the night."

"The next morning, as I was leaving to continue my journey, a man came into the inn telling how soldiers had killed three families and all their slaves and servants because they were Christians. I was horrified! It seems they were stopping people traveling on the road I traveled and asking them to bow and worship the Emperor. There was a caravan of Greek families just leaving the city who were stopped by the soldiers. They apparently had been in the city with their slaves to get building supplies. When asked to bow to Emperor Nero and honor him as a god, one man said, 'Only Christ is my Lord and Redeemer. He is the son of the only God Jehovah, and to Him alone will I ever bow.' The soldiers killed them all. They knew me and my family, and the captain's questioning of my loyalty surely caused the soldiers to be curious about my travels. I was afraid that I had become a danger to all those I loved. Since they knew us, I feared they might come to my home. And, Livia, my father, mother, and one brother are all Christians. They would all have refused to worship the Emperor and would have been put to death. After that, I knew I could not go home to live. You know Livia, if asked by the soldiers to worship our Emperor, I, too, would have refused and would have been killed as well."

"Did our Emperor order them to execute anyone who didn't bow?" asked Livia, trembling.

"I'm not sure. Perhaps the captain that I met (who obviously hated Christians) gave the orders. But I'm sure he had been given the idea from someone high in authority. Anyway, when I returned, I slipped into the city by a completely different route. On the road, I met only one person— another Christian. He told me that his brother was captain of a ship leaving for Gaul tomorrow. In my heart, I felt God telling me I was to be on that ship. Oh Livia, I know this has been very rushed, but I feel that it is our one chance to spend our lives serving our Lord Jesus Christ together."

Tatius and Livia slept a little, while sitting on the old man's couch, but just before dawn, Tatius woke Livia and told her to get ready to leave. They both hurriedly prepared themselves for departure – eating some leftovers, doing their toilette, and gathering their meager belongings. Another mule cart arrived, driven by a friend of the Jewish couple. The old couple gave them a little bag of food, kissed each of them on the forehead, and gave them God's blessing. They rode the mule cart to Ostia, and now they were on a ship going to a place neither had ever seen.

As Livia returned from her musings to the ship and Tatius, she felt it was almost like a dream. She thought, "Yesterday morning I was sitting in my lovely garden, and now I am on a cargo ship sailing into the unknown." For just a moment, she was afraid and then she saw the sunlight reflecting on the water. Its rays changed the water into sparkling jewels of light. Looking out over the water at the seagulls fishing, she heard Tatius praying very softly by her side.

Her emotions suddenly calmed, and her peaceful joy returned. Livia felt she had been changed like the water by the rays of the sunlight. She knew with more certainty now that God had chosen her, and she would not fail Him.

Chapter 3

As Paulus climbed the steps of the *insula* to Silvius' apartment, he tried to prepare what he would say. If he wanted to gain information, he knew he should not be threatening. After all, he wasn't completely sure Livia was with Tatius. For that matter he didn't know if Tatius was even alive.

When he arrived at the fourth floor (where he was told by a downstairs shopkeeper that Silvius lived), he was a bit startled by the condition of the hallway. He had assumed that Silvius' family lived in a nice building. However, if the hall was any indication of the apartment, Silvius must live in a place as dingy and drab as the Jew's rented house. Arriving at the door, Paulus heard angry voices talking within. After a moment's hesitation, he knocked loudly on the door saying, "Silvius, it is Paulus. Could I speak with you, please?"

The voices quieted, and the door opened immediately. Silvius was there and asked him to enter. He introduced his wife Herminia and sons Flavius and Titus to Paulus. It was obvious that Flavius was angry over something.

"Please excuse my interruption, but I have a very serious matter to discuss with you," said Paulus.

With alarm, Herminia asked, "Has something happened to Tatius?"

"No, no, madam. It's my sister Livia. She has gone, and she left her *bulla* behind."

"Oh, I see," said Herminia, and then remembering her duties as a hostess, invited Paulus to be seated, and went to get some refreshments from the kitchen.

Paulus continued, "I won't bother you for long, but I must ask. Has Livia gone somewhere with Tatius?"

Before Silvius could answer, Flavius angrily said, "I am ashamed that I must call Tatius my brother. He has just returned from a secret trip for that Jew Paul, and now he has probably left again on some special mission for his precious Jewish god and these Christians!"

"Silence, Flavius!" said Silvius with authority. "You will respect us and our beliefs in this house. Paulus, I'm sorry for my son's outburst. Please be seated, and we will talk."

Paulus sat on a long couch. As Silvius' wife gave him wine to drink and some bread with honey, Paulus noted that the apartment was nothing like the hall. While not large like their villa, it was beautifully decorated with embroidered hangings and unusual tiles. Noticing Paulus' glances at the furnishings and decorations, Silvius said, "My wife is part Greek and has brought a sense of style from her background. Most of the things you see are her work. She is very talented," said Silvius with pride.

Silvius continued, "I don't know where your sister is, Paulus. As for Tatius, he returned to us yesterday. He had taken a trip north, as you know, and we had heard nothing from him for several days. He only stayed here a short while and then said he had to leave us again. He didn't mention your sister, but he simply said he knew where God wanted him to be. He cried and told us how much he loved us, but when we questioned him about his destination, he said that it was better if we didn't know where he was going. I don't know where he has gone or with whom."

"Didn't you try to stop him?" asked Paulus.

"Oh, I would never interfere in the work for God's kingdom," said Silvius.

"There you go again — talking about kingdoms! No wonder our Emperor despises Christians. There is only one kingdom – the Glorious Empire of Rome!" said Flavius.

Titus spoke for the first time, "My brother does not share our beliefs, and he fears we will be in danger soon."

Paulus remarked on the differences in Silvius' children. Flavius was short and stocky with a ruddy complexion, and his facial features were similar to Silvius. Titus looked like an older version of Tatius. He was tall, as was Tatius and his mother, and he had a quiet dignity about him, much like his father Silvius.

It was evident that Flavius was not a "Christ follower" and was unhappy with the other members of his family.

"It's not just the dangers caused by these deluded ideas," said Flavius. "My military career could be hurt by your god! I came here from Britannia with special reports to our Emperor himself. My wound will be healed shortly (Flavius had a wound on his arm from a lance), and I shall soon return to Britannia. I was in line for advancement in rank. What if they hear my family has become Christians? Not only would I be the laughing stock of my *cohort*, but I would have little chance to further my career!"

"Flavius, Paulus has not come here to hear about your career or our family quarrels. He wants to find his sister." Turning to Paulus now, Silvius said, "We know nothing of her whereabouts, nor that of Tatius. Perhaps they are together. I do not know, but we will pray for the safety of them both. I will see you this afternoon at Paul's house."

After bidding farewell to Silvius and his family, Paulus returned home with no new information about Livia. He was certain that Silvius had told him the truth.

Chapter 4

When Paulus arrived home, he saw that his Uncle Cornelius was already there. Entering the atrium, he found Cornelius and his father in a heated discussion.

"No Atticus! You **can not** go. You are barely able to stand!" said Cornelius.

"I'm going," said Atticus.

Paulus walked over to the couch where his father Atticus was reclining. He greeted his uncle politely and then said to both of them, "Silvius does not know where Livia has gone, and his son Tatius has left as well. He saw Tatius briefly yesterday, but he only said he was leaving and refused to say to where. It seems likely to me that they are together, even though he mentioned nothing to his family about Livia." Paulus decided not to reveal anything of Silvius' family and their religious differences. He felt a sense of loyalty to Silvius, and their problems had nothing to do with Livia.

"That settles it then," said Atticus. "I am going to see the prisoner Paul. This new religion of this Jew has caused Livia to lose her common sense — that and her infatuation with Tatius."

It was obvious to Paulus that his Uncle Cornelius had been trying to dissuade his father from such an action. It was also evident that Atticus was in severe pain, and that his pain and the grief over Livia's abandonment of the family had clouded his judgment. Usually the most sensible and calm of men, Atticus now was querulous and unreasonable.

"Father, you will make yourself more ill, and there is no need for you to go see the Jew. I'll be on duty in a short while, and I can find out if he knows anything about Livia," said Paulus.

"No. I'm going to go. He'll not lie to me. Cornelius has come here by *lectica*, and we can go to the Jew's house in the same way!" said Atticus.

Cornelius had apparently been trying for some time to persuade Atticus that it would make him sicker to go see Paul. Trying a new argument, he asked, "Do you think it wise for us to be seen at a Christian's lodging after the recent troubles?"

Pausing for a moment and actually considering his brother's position, Atticus said, "You are probably right, Cornelius. I have little time left alive, and I don't think there would be any problems with my going. But I'm not sure it would be a good idea for a Roman Senator to be in a prisoner's house. You must understand though, I have to find my Livia!"

Hearing his father say that he thought he would die soon caused Paulus great pain. His father was the person he held most dear in the world. Seeing that there was little use in arguing with his father, Paulus said, "If you feel you must go, I'll walk beside the *lectica*, and then I can stay for my guard duty."

"Atticus, I'll go also. I have some curiosity about this Paul. I'll go with you in the *lectica*, and since Paulus must stay at the Jew's house, I'll see you home and in bed after our visit. I still think it unwise, but perhaps the gods have ordained it."

Paulus was startled by Cornelius' last comment. He sounded somewhat like Paul's friends, except they had only one god.

Chapter 5

*I*n a short while, they began the journey to Paul's house. Paulus walked beside the slaves who carried his father and Uncle Cornelius in the *lectica*. It was a slow walk. People had to be cleared for the group to pass. They attracted attention and some scorn as the slaves jostled several people in the crowd with the long poles that jutted from the *lectica*. Paulus was relieved when they finally arrived at the Jew's house.

Paulus walked in and as usual Silvius was at his position, with the other guards already gone. His father and uncle strode in with an air of both authority and a touch of belligerence. Paul was seated on a couch talking to his usual scribe, with another man called Timothy standing nearby.

Atticus began, "We have questions for you, Jew. We are men of authority who will permit no lies from you. Do you understand?"

Paul smiled and said with the utmost graciousness, "Sirs, I will tell no untruths to any man and certainly not to two outstanding Roman gentlemen." (Paul could see by Cornelius' toga that he was a Roman Senator.) "May I introduce myself? I am Paul – a servant of Jesus Christ, and this is my brother in the Lord, Timothy, and finally our most excellent scribe, Ezra."

Cornelius was somewhat ashamed of his brother's rudeness, so he began the visit by saying to Paul and his friends, "We are not here to cause you problems, but to find out if you can tell us where our dear Livia might be. I am her uncle and this (pointing to Atticus) is the father of both Livia and Paulus."

Paul began, "Perhaps you will not believe me, but I have not seen her since the day she received the joy of God's grace and salvation. She was…"

To the horror of both Paulus and Cornelius, Atticus interrupted Paul and demanded, "You know where Tatius is, and that is surely where Livia will be found!"

While Atticus was talking, the scribe began rolling up the papyrus on which he had been writing. Thinking the writings might be some information that Paul was hiding, Atticus demanded the scribe bring it to him. The scribe meekly gave the scroll to Atticus. Atticus then handed the scroll to Cornelius and said, "Cornelius, read to us about the plots these Christians are hiding!"

By this time Atticus had almost fallen twice. Timothy picked up a chair and placed it near him, and he finally sat. Paulus had never seen his father like this. He had always been such a kind man. Even after his accident, he had suffered the pain with a quiet acceptance. Now he looked as if he were near death, and he spoke with agitation and harshness. Cornelius unrolled the scroll and saw the salutation.

"It's a letter to the people in Ephesus, Atticus. It doesn't seem to mention Livia or Tatius," said Cornelius as he looked over the scroll.

"I'll assure you sirs, it has nothing to do with your daughter or Silvius' son," said Paul, pointing to the guard who stood near the door. Both Silvius and Paulus had remained completely silent, while the drama before them unfolded.

Again Atticus commanded, "Cornelius, read more from the scroll. Perhaps there are secrets in other parts of it!" Cornelius was not accustomed to receiving orders, but he knew Atticus was not himself.

Cornelius began reading:

"For it is by grace you have been saved, through faith – and this not from yourselves, it is the gift of God – not by works, so that no one can boast."(Ephesians 2:8-9)

"Oh, that's just religious gibberish. Read from some other parts. Their plots are probably hidden later," Atticus said.

Cornelius began reading different parts of the letter.

"As a prisoner for the Lord, then, I urge you to live a life worthy of the calling you have received. Be completely humble and gentle; be patient, bearing with one another in love. Make every effort to keep the unity of the Spirit through the bond of peace."(Ephesians 4:1-3)

"Atticus, I believe this is mostly a letter of philosophical advice about how to be a good person. It's a rather humble letter in parts. Listen to this, 'Pray also for me, that whenever I open my mouth, words may be given me so that I will fearlessly make known the mystery of the gospel, for which I am an ambassador in chains. Pray that I may declare it fearlessly, as I should.'"(Ephesians 6:19-20)

Paulus watched Paul as Cornelius read. While Timothy seemed a bit frightened, Paul on the other hand, was the calmest and most assured person in the room. He stood perfectly still with his chains at his feet. His eyes were closed, and Paulus knew that he was praying. After scanning the rest of the letter, Cornelius rolled up the papyrus and gave it back to the scribe.

Gently Cornelius said, "Atticus, there are no secret plots in this letter, nor does it mention Tatius or Livia. We came to ask questions. Let me talk to the prisoner and perhaps he will be of help."

Atticus was now in such an emotional and physical state that he no longer seemed ready to challenge Paul.

Paulus spoke for the first time. Turning to Paul from his guard position, he asked calmly,

"Has Tatius been here?"

"Yes, he was here yesterday. We talked and prayed for a while. He had already made plans to leave, but I do not know where he was going nor with whom. He has traveled for me as my emissary, but he said God had now revealed what his new destination would be. He said it was safer if he told no one of his plans."

"But what about my sister Livia? Did he not speak of her?" asked Paulus.

"No, son, he did not. However, several days ago, before he went on the journey north at my request, he told me that he loved her, and he felt God had brought her into his life. We prayed that Livia and he would know God's plans for them, and then yesterday, he came to say farewell. I doubt we will ever see each other again until at the Throne of God," said Paul.

Atticus stirred and said, "Where is this throne you are talking about? Do you think there is any throne which can overthrow our Empire?" he asked mockingly.

Paul answered calmly, "Sir, I have always preached that 'Everyone must submit himself to the governing authorities… The authorities that exist have been established by God.' (Romans 13:1) The throne I'm talking about is the one I'm going to see when I shed these chains and meet my Savior. Sir, this will be when I die. Fear not that I shall rebel against Rome. No, I am simply compelled to preach the message of peace and joy that can only come with the good news of Jesus Christ. 'I am not ashamed of the gospel, because it is the power of God for the salvation of everyone who believes…'" (Romans 1:16)

Paul spoke with such passion and fervor that no one interrupted him. His countenance had an otherworldly radiance that silenced even Atticus. Paulus watched the Jew and felt himself drawn to his words in a way that he had not experienced in all the many days he had listened to him. While he wasn't ready to accept this new God as yet, he was beginning to listen.

After Paul finished responding to Atticus' question, he said to him quietly. "I see you are suffering, sir. If you wish, I could pray for your healing."

Atticus, who had been silent throughout Paul's comments, reacted with anger.

"I do not want or need prayers from a Jewish prisoner! Cornelius, I think I should leave now. I don't think we will get any information about Livia from him. Paulus, be alert to any news you hear from the Jew's visitors about her."

Remembering how Silvius had miraculously recovered after Paul's prayer, Paulus was sorry his father had refused his prayers. Atticus rose slowly and with the help of Cornelius and Paulus walked to the *lectica*. As Cornelius and Atticus were leaving, Cornelius turned to Paul and said, "Perhaps I shall return and discuss our grandparents with you in the future."

"It would be my great honor," said Paul. Atticus glared at his brother as they began the journey to Atticus' house.

After they were gone, Paul said to Paulus, "My son, I'm truly sorry for the loss you must be feeling. I can only console you by saying that God will travel with your sister wherever she may go. I must rest for a while and pray for these two dear young souls now." Paul dragged his chains to his couch and reclined.

The remainder of Paulus' guard time passed slowly. Visitors came to the house as usual, and Paul counseled some, prayed with others, and in general comforted them all. When the replacement guard came for Silvius and Paulus, Paulus actually dreaded going home. He didn't know in what kind of condition his father would be, and the light of their household, Livia, would not be there.

Chapter 6

The light of the morning sun made the Mediterranean Sea look like undulating waves of turquoise. There was wind enough for the sails and just enough clouds to keep the sun from being oppressive. The whitecaps on the water, as the ship made its way north, contrasted with the bright blue to make a perfect picture for a seascape.

Livia sat on the rough bench and watched the water known to the Romans as *Mare Nostrum* (our sea). Tatius was busy working with their supplies and helping the three other passengers do the same. She knew that she could be of no help. For her entire life, slaves or servants had done all the work of the household (except in the garden where Livia had spent much time planting and taking care of flowers). Now she felt as if she were in a dream with every bit of her old life being washed away as the land disappeared from view. In some ways it was a lovely reverie. She tried to find something in her past with which to compare the water. It looked somewhat like the blue bolts of silk she had seen in the shops, and if she closed her eyes, she could image the whitecaps as shiny pearls lying on the silk. But when she opened her eyes, she realized it was a poor comparison. The sea was so vast, so blue, so soothing in its rhythmic folds. As she looked at the blue sky with its puffs of clouds and then at the water, she felt the majesty of nature. Tatius said that the Lord God Jehovah could sometimes be heard in the voices of his servants (such as Paul), sometimes He spoke in a quiet, inner voice to those who listened for Him, and sometimes as you looked at the beauty of His world you had an overwhelming sense of His presence. Livia felt at that moment God was speaking to her in the beauty of the sea. Livia prayed, "Dear God, I don't know the proper prayers of your people the Jews or even the prayers of the new Christians, but I want to be your servant now as I sail on this beautiful water and forevermore." Then as she remembered to close with an "Amen", she added, "Oh yes Lord, and Amen."

While Livia was having her moments of contemplation and prayer, Tatius was surveying the provisions he had at hand for the voyage. The way the drama of their journey had unfolded had been so unbelievable that Tatius knew God was directing it all. Meeting the brother of the ship's captain on his return to Rome was the first of many "coincidences"! When he arrived at the outskirts of the city, he decided to stop and say farewell to the old Jewish couple. They suggested the stopover for the night at their little farm and told Tatius that they had a Christian neighbor who took a mule cart to Ostia two or three times a week when he went to pick up fresh fruits and vegetables for the stall run by his family near the Forum. On his return trips, he was always loaded with goods, but on the way there, he would have room for two people. During Tatius' visit with the couple, the old man talked to his neighbor, and the arrangements were made.

As Tatius was pondering the miraculous circumstances of their being on the ship, Livia came to where he was working and asked, "Why are you working so much? Come and enjoy the beautiful day."

"Livia, these are our supplies for the next few days. You know we had to bring our own supplies – including food and a tent," said Tatius. "I'm trying to set up the tent and get our provisions inside." Livia suddenly realized that she knew nothing about how they would live on the ship or afterwards, for that matter.

"This is our tent, my dear, where we will eat, sleep, and basically live. The huge jars you see are filled with our water for the trip.

Those bundles contain our bedding, our meager food supplies, and the large pot is for… you know. After we use it, we throw our uh… waste overboard." Tatius had become quite red over this last explanation.

"Tatius, where did you get these things?"

"I'll explain as soon as I finish tying our tent to the ship. One of the other passengers showed me how to do it."

Livia had never felt more useless. "Dear Lord, I think maybe you made a mistake calling me to go with Tatius. I love him, but I can't do anything!" Livia prayed silently. Tatius had told her it was fine to just talk to God, and that was what she was doing.

Finally, somewhat exhausted but proud of his success with the tent, Tatius announced it was ready. He then placed the various bundles, jars, and pots inside the tent.

"Now let's talk for a while, unless you are hungry," said Tatius.

Food was the last thing on Livia's mind. "No, I don't want to eat. I want to know how you got all these things." Livia had watched as Tatius talked to a merchant at the harbor before they boarded the ship. There had been no exchange of money, but soon several slaves began loading a tent with its poles and ropes, along with the items Tatius had just placed in the tent.

"It has to be God's plan, Livia. Everything has happened as if it were directed according to a design," said Tatius with an attitude of awe and wonderment.

"That's all fine, Tatius, but how did you get a tent?" asked Livia with a determination to get practical answers instead of theology.

"Well, you know Paul is a tentmaker, don't you?"

"A tentmaker? Is he not an apostle of Jesus Christ? I'm confused," said Livia with a frown.

Tatius laughed. "He is both. He worked as a tentmaker when he traveled and preached, and he didn't want to have to ask for money from the new Christians. Anyway, he has a friend in Rome who is a tentmaker also. According to Paul, he is very skilled and has an excellent business. I met him twice at Paul's house. Yesterday, as I was leaving the *taberna* where I hired the mule cart, I ran into him. He asked me about my plans. Knowing that he was a Christian, I felt led to tell him I was going to Gaul to serve my Savior. Livia, you won't believe what he told me. He said God had told him to make a tent and then leave it with a merchant friend in Ostia for someone who was going to need it. He then said, 'Tatius, I now know it was made for you. When you get to Ostia, get the tent, use it on the ship, and then take it with you when you land. It's God's tent and His plan.' When we got to the harbor, I found the merchant, and he gave me the tent and then loaded the tent, poles, ropes, plus bedding on the ship for us."

"Oh Tatius, I can hardly believe all of this is real. Did he give you the jars and food also?"

"No, the big water jars and pot are supplied by the captain for all the passengers and crew. I had a little money, and I bought some food. We also have some food from the old Jewish couple. There isn't a large quantity, but I'm afraid we'll just have to make the food last until we get to Gaul."

"I'm so excited about our journey, but I'm also scared. And Tatius, I feel so useless. Do you think I'll ever be of any help to you or the people we'll be meeting?" Livia asked with a trembling voice.

"My dear, you are already a help to me. You have given up everything for me and our mission, and your belief gave me enough courage to begin this new life. I don't think I've told you how much I love you. When I look at you, I feel as if I can do anything if you are with me. I know that sounds boastful, but I believe God has chosen us to be His witnesses to the joy of our salvation," said Tatius.

"I love you too, and I promise to cherish you forever." Livia moved toward Tatius as if to touch him, but Tatius took her hands and said, "I want you to be my wife so very much. I want to hold you in my arms as we sleep in our tent, and I want to join our bodies as one. I say all this, but I know we must wait. On this ship, you must remain my 'sister in Christ.'"

"I know we can't be as husband and wife yet, but what do you mean by '*sister*'? I, I don't want to be your '*sister*'!" said Livia boldly while blushing.

"I'll explain. I pray that I haven't done wrong. While working with our tents, the others passengers began to comment on my wife. The old man said, 'Your wife is lovely. Has she traveled by sea before? She seems quite awed by the experience.'"I then said you were not my wife, but my sister. I added that you had traveled very little and never by water. The old man said that he should have guessed we were of the same family due to our heights. He didn't continue the conversation, and we returned to our work with the tents."

Livia laughed, but she saw that Tatius was troubled by his untruthfulness. "Don't worry," said Livia, "I'll be careful to act as a '*sister*'. He really called **me** lovely. His eyes must have been affected by his age, but he is right about one thing. I am in awe of the beauty of the sea. What did you mean by 'sister in Christ'?"

"In the Church at Corinth, we called all our fellow believers 'sisters' or 'brothers' in Christ. We are all in the family of God. So you are my 'sister in Christ', but it still seems a deception—somewhat like that of Abraham."

"Is Abraham one of your Christian friends at Corinth?"

"No, he isn't," said Tatius, with a laugh. "Livia, Abraham is known as the Father of the Jews. He lived a long, long time ago. The reason I mentioned him is that the Jews say that he claimed his wife Sarah (who really was his half-sister) as his sister rather than his wife on more than one occasion. It's a long story, but I wish I had not had to be deceitful. As for the comment about your being lovely, he is right. To me your beauty exceeds that of this great sea!"

"Your eyes must be bad just like those of the old man. I'm glad you are my '*brother*' or I might have tried to kiss you — you blind giant!" Livia laughed at her own joke. Tatius, being unaware of all the "giant" conversations between Paulus and her, simply smiled. For a moment, after her laughter, Livia felt a deep sense of loss. Paulus and she had such a strong bond of affection for each other, and now they would probably never see each other again. She closed her eyes and prayed in the way that Tatius had taught her, "Oh please Lord, protect Paulus and touch his heart like you have touched mine. Oh, I forgot again, but Amen."

Chapter 7

*A*s Paulus and Silvius were leaving Paul's house that evening, they stopped and talked briefly. Silvius repeated that he had no idea where Tatius had gone, but he now felt Livia and Tatius had probably left together. Silvius told Paulus that he was so sorry for the family division because of their decision. He assured Paulus however, that Tatius would never harm Livia, and that his Christian beliefs would permit nothing improper between them before marriage. Paulus thought, "How can there ever be a marriage without my father's drawing up a contract, and he certainly will never do that?" They bade each other farewell, and Silvius said that he and his wife would pray for Paulus and his family as well as for their son Tatius. His comments were so gentle in tone that Paulus had no stirring of anger over his offer of prayer. He thanked Silvius and walked on home. Arriving home, he found his father in bed, undoubtedly completely exhausted after the visit to Paul's house.

Surprisingly, Paulus slept well, and when he got up, some of his gloom of the previous day had lifted. When he entered the atrium, he found his father already awake, lying on a couch.

"How are you feeling, Father?" asked Paulus.

"Yesterday was very difficult for me, son, and I slept badly. I'm up early because I want to talk to you." Atticus seemed much less angry and agitated than he had been yesterday. Paulus wondered if his father was becoming resigned to the situation.

"We can't find her, Paulus. Tatius told me of the many places he has lived and studied. He could be in Athens, Corinth, Thessalonica, Ephesus or, even here in Italia. Didn't he just return from somewhere to the north?"

"Yes Father," said Paulus.

"I'm not sure what I would do if I did find her. She has brought disgrace on the Livian family. Running away with a man and joining some kind of strange religion are not circumstances that I can forgive. She is no longer my daughter." As he was saying this, Paulus noticed how very pale his father was, and how much the conversation was draining him of energy.

"Father, would you permit me to get a doctor and bring him to see you?"

"No, I have seen several. They know nothing about treating me. They keep giving me cabbage in different forms. It only makes me sicker. I'm not even sure my pain is from the injury I had, but I do know I'm getting worse. I know that I will not live much longer."

"Do you want me to go or send servants to bring my other sisters here to help you?"

"Absolutely not! They have families. Your sister Livia *Prima* talks constantly. I would be miserable with her here. Livia *Secunda* has five very loud children, and I can not bear the noise. Besides, you know she lives near Pompeii. No, Livia *Tertia* was the only one I enjoyed. Not only was she smart and could talk about everything, but she made me laugh. Her actions have disappointed me severely," said Atticus.

"I'm sorry Father." Paulus wanted to say something in Livia's defense, but his father's condition was such that he did not want to disagree with him. Truthfully, he also felt hurt by her leaving, but he understood much more about her decision than his father. He knew that Livia had doubted the existence of their Roman gods long before she met Tatius. He also knew she wanted answers that she had not found in her extensive studies. This new religion seemed to give her answers to many of her questions and also to bring her much joy. However, he could not express these thoughts to his father.

"I need to rest now. I just wanted you to know I'm no longer going to look for Livia. In my will, of course, you inherit everything, but never expecting Livia to marry, I made a request in it that you provide for her. Disregard my request. She has chosen a different life, and her future is no longer our concern. However, there are many business concerns we need to discuss in the next few days."

Getting up slowly, Atticus went to his room. Paulus noticed many of the slaves and servants standing on the other side of the atrium. Seeing Philippa there with them, he walked over to her and asked if she had successfully accomplished her assigned duty of commanding the others. She smiled and said, "Sir, many of these people are my dear friends. I have 'asked' them to do the tasks they usually perform. They have been very cooperative."

"Well, do you think you could 'ask' them to continue in their household duties for a few days, until my father and I decide on how we will manage everything?" Paulus asked with a touch of mockery.

"I shall do my best sir. Do you have any special requests of me?" asked Philippa.

Paulus looked at her carefully. For a moment, he started to make a bawdy comment, but she had such an air of innocence about her that he knew her words were not meant to be suggestive. "I can think of none at the moment," he replied.

"Miss Livia often wanted the tabletops changed or the vases readied for her chosen flowers of the day. I thought, perhaps, there might be some such changes that you would like sir," said Philippa.

He was ashamed to admit he had never paid any attention to either the tables or flowers. "If I think of anything, I'll let you know," said Paulus.

"Very well sir. I will try to please you and your father and do as Miss Livia would wish."

As Philippa hurried back toward the other servants and slaves, Paulus thought again, "She is charming and quite attractive. I wonder why I haven't noticed her before. If she were not a member of our household staff, I might find out just how 'interesting' she could be for a couple of nights!" As he entertained these thoughts, he could almost hear Livia say, "Oh Paulus, don't think of her that way just because she is a servant and you have power over her." He thought, "Maybe that Jew Paul has gotten into my head with his odd ideas about sexual purity!" Turning away, Paulus started into the city on his way to the public baths.

Chapter 8

The winds strengthened as they traveled farther north, and the ocean spray lapped the section of the deck where Tatius and Livia had been assigned. Tatius tried to get Livia to go into the tent where she would have some protection, but even though her *palla*, *stola*, and probably her *tunica* were completely soaked, she refused to leave. Tatius (also soaked) sat beside her, and they talked more about their extraordinary trip and God's plans for their lives.

Suddenly, the ship's captain came near the passengers and ordered them aft and into the small cabin there. Tatius asked, "What is the problem? The ship seems to be fine."

"We've spotted pirates. Everyone must get into the cabin for safety and also to make our work easier. The oarsmen have changed our direction, so we are going nearer to land. It's safer." Tatius could see another ship not too far away.

Tatius and Livia hurried to the cabin, along with the other passengers—two young men (apparently traveling together) and the old man with whom Tatius had talked about his "sister". The cabin was filled with jars, chests (which probably contained food for the captain and crew), tools, tarps, and a few weapons. There was a rough bench and some rather dirty-looking bedding on the floor of the cabin.

"I thought General Pompey stopped all piracy about a hundred years ago," said one of the young men.

While Tatius could have replied to this comment, he remained quiet as the old man gave them a brief history lesson. "As you probably know pirates burned Ostia back in the days of Julius Caesar, and after that time, anti-piracy laws were enacted. It's true that most of the bands of pirates were killed, or at least resettled, but they never completely disappeared. Pompey captured or destroyed hundreds of ships, and killed thousands of pirates, but as time has passed, some are in the waters again. I suppose we are a target because it is very late in the season. Due to our late travels, there are fewer Roman warships on patrol and fewer ships for pirates to seize."

"Do you think we are in great danger?" asked the same young man.

"I don't know. Usually they prefer ships with rich passengers that they can hold for ransom or a cargo ship loaded with expensive materials. This is a grain ship, and we don't look like rich Roman nobles, now do we?" he asked with a laugh. (Livia thought to herself, "If they knew about my family's wealth, they would be surprised. However, my father would probably not even pay a ransom for me now!") The old man continued, "We will probably get much closer to land for a while, and perhaps that will cause them to leave."

Livia was scared. She wanted to hold Tatius, but she didn't want to act in any way that would appear *"unsisterly"*. They could hear shouts from the crew, and what had been a glorious day turned into an evening of fear in a smelly cabin. Livia felt herself getting a little nauseous. The rocking of the ship, which had seemed so soothing, now (along with the bad smells) made her stomach queasy. She was glad she had declined food earlier.

They remained in the cabin for a long time. The men talked about the pirates, the tents, the weather, and Gaul. No one shared any personal information with the exception of the old man. He told them that he had been on a visit to see his son in Rome. Never having met his son's wife or seen his two grandchildren, the old man decided to leave his home in Arelate (Arles) and visit his son and his family before he got too old to travel. He had been in Rome since early spring and was very eager to return home. He obviously loved to talk, and he continued telling about his life in Gaul. He was a widower, with two daughters (both married) in Gaul and another son there as well. His chatter had a calming effect on the other passengers and perhaps that was his intention.

Tatius asked him, "What does your family do in Arelate?"

"Well, my grandfather was one of the veterans that settled there when it became a *colonia*. My family now has a farm on the outskirts of Arelate. We have a vineyard and several large olive groves and export a lot of olive oil to many places, including Rome."

"I thought we grew all our own olives in Italia," said one of the young men.

"Apparently a lot of farmers have left the countryside and gone to live in the city, and there is a big demand for oil for all kinds of things from food to lotions. I've made several trips to Rome for contracts for my olives, but I'm old now and my son in Rome and my other son at home handle most of the business. Even though I haven't seen any pirates on my other trips, I learned a lot about them from the ships' captains. Let me introduce myself. I am called Tullus."

Just when it would have become awkward for Livia and Tatius to have to introduce themselves to the others, they heard shouts. Peeping outside, Tatius said, "The crew seems happy. Something must have happened." One of the seamen then motioned for them to come out. When they were outside on the deck, they could see two Roman warships nearby. They were basically serving as escorts for the ship, and the pirates were no longer in sight.

Livia and Tatius returned to the bench near their tent and Livia began, "Oh Tatius, I wanted to ask questions so badly. How did they know the other ship was a pirate ship? How did the warships know we were in danger? Will the pirates return? How much will this delay our journey? Will I always have to remain a silent '*sister*'? Do you…"

"Livia, Livia," said Tatius with a chuckle, "How can you ask so many questions? I fear I can answer very few of them. I doubt the pirates will return, with the Roman warships nearby, and I would imagine our hugging the coastline caused the Roman warships in port to see we were being targeted. I'm afraid you'll have to wait on the answers to the other questions. Now it's time to eat and drink something and then prepare for the night. As for your remaining silent, I don't think that likely to happen. It's been a long day and I'm very tired, as are you. It is dusk, and we need sleep to prepare us for more adventures tomorrow."

"I'm not sure I can eat," said Livia. "I became sick in the cabin. I do feel somewhat better now, but I'm not really hungry."

"You must eat, even if only a small amount. You will need it for strength. Come, and let's find something you would like. If you eat I promise to let you ask as many questions as you want!" said Tatius teasingly. He pulled back the flap to their tent, and they went inside. Tatius rummaged inside the bundle that the old Jewish couple had given them. He found some cheese, bread, and figs inside. They ate a little and then each drank a large cup of water. "When you need to use that (indicating the pot), I'll go outside." Livia blushed and nodded.

Tatius then began unrolling the bedding. There were two thin woolen blankets. Since it was a warm day, Tatius suggested they spread both blankets on the deck and lie on both of them. Livia said that they could each use their little bundles of clothing under their heads for pillows. As they were trying to get comfortable, Livia felt something hard in her clothing bag. Opening the bag, she took out the pearls that she had almost forgotten she had brought. "Look Tatius, we can use this necklace to buy things in Gaul. It's mine, and I suppose it could be my dowry." Livia said with a smile.

Tatius was so moved by her comment that he forgot for a moment that he was her *"brother"*! He pulled her over to him and kissed her with passion. When the kiss was becoming too passionate, Tatius said they must sleep, and they would have the rest of their lives to become more than *"brother"* and *"sister"*. "Goodnight my love," said Tatius. He went to sleep very quickly, but Livia had to rehearse in her mind all the events of that day and especially the last few minutes.

Chapter 9

Paulus followed his usual routine at the public baths. He thought about going to talk to his Uncle Cornelius, but there seemed little to say. His father was very ill, but he refused to see a doctor. His sister was gone from their lives, and he knew his responsibilities were going to increase. Paulus' father was a man of great wealth, and he had several businesses. Even after his injury, he was able to see clients in his house and continue his business ventures. Paulus knew little about these matters. As he was having a massage at the baths, he suddenly realized his carefree days were probably going to end soon. He thought to himself, "How am I going to run two households (one in Ostia and one in Rome)?" If my father dies, must I continue my guard duty at Paul's house?" For a second he thought, "I sound like Livia with my many questions!" This idea caused him a pang of deep sadness. How he missed her!

When Paulus returned to his house, he learned from the kitchen servants that Atticus had eaten in his room. He went to his father's bedroom and looked inside. He could tell that Atticus was sleeping. Going back into the atrium, he saw Philippa arranging flowers in a vase and placing them on a table.

"For whom are you fixing the flowers? I'm leaving shortly, and my father will certainly not notice," Paulus said harshly.

Philippa paused for a moment and then answered, "Well sir, I suppose I'm doing what Miss Livia would have done. Adding beauty to anything seems a task well worth the effort, and the flowers add joy to my life each time I pass by them." She then gave him a radiant smile and continued working with the flowers.

Paulus walked away and muttered to himself, "By Jupiter, she looks like a tiny goddess in a shabby tunic. I don't understand how she can be so joyful when she is just a servant. But she certainly is attractive. I think I've been without a woman far too long!" Paulus then went into his room in order to prepare for his guard duty.

Chapter 10

Arriving at Paul's house that afternoon, Paulus found Silvius standing quietly at his usual guard post. Paul and Ezra, the scribe, were working on the letter from which Cornelius had read the previous day. Paul nodded a greeting to Paulus and continued dictating his letter.

Speaking to Timothy, who was often present, and Ezra, Paul said, "I want the Jews and Gentiles to understand that the churches of God's family must take lessons from the *Pax Romana*. We must live as a united body of the children of Jesus Christ! Write these words: 'Through the gospel the Gentiles are heirs together with Israel, members together of one body, and sharers together in the promise in Christ Jesus.'"(Ephesians 3:6)

With great emotion, Paul said, "I must make them understand that God loves them all beyond human understanding." He then dictated the following: "I pray that you, being rooted and established in love, may have power, together with all the saints, to grasp how wide and long and high and deep is the love of Christ, and to know this love that surpasses knowledge — that you may be filled to the measure of all the fullness of God."(Ephesians 3:17-19)

Paul then said, "I pray that this letter will be read in the churches after I am gone on to meet my Savior. I've so much I need to say, and I doubt I'll have much more time to teach my beloved brothers and sisters. Ezra, come back in a couple of days. When I have finished fasting and praying over what my Lord wants me to say, we'll complete the letter." Ezra and Timothy then left, and Paul dragged his chains to his couch and lay down.

After a short time, Silvius, breaking his usual silence, asked Paulus, "How is your father today?"

"Not well, I'm afraid. He seems to be getting worse by the day. Since Livia has gone, he has changed so much," said Paulus.

"I suspect he is hurt and probably feels betrayed. Have you told your father that my wife and I are also Christians?" asked Silvius.

"No, I haven't."

"Thank you. I know your father and uncle are powerful men, and if my family's beliefs were known, our lives would be in danger. I fear our Emperor would never accept that one of his soldiers could be a Christian and still be loyal to Rome. It's true that I've served Rome for many years, but now I have a new master — my Savior Jesus Christ," said Silvius.

"Don't you think someone, maybe even your son Flavius, will reveal that you are 'Christ followers'?" asked Paulus.

"Flavius is confused and angry, but he loves us, and I don't think he will tell anyone. Besides, he is leaving for Britannia. I'm only sad that he can't share in the joy of our salvation. But you are correct. I am sure some of my friends are becoming suspicious about us since we no longer attend banquets or festivals where sacrifices to the gods are offered."

"Silvius, how could a veteran soldier such as you risk your life to become involved with this Jesus Christ? He was crucified, **by us!**" said Paulus.

"Yes, Paulus, we crucified Him, but He rose from the dead. I've met some of the people who saw Him after His resurrection. I've heard some of the stories about the Holy Spirit coming forty days later. I've seen lives changed." With a chuckle, Silvius added, "When I came here, I was like you and could not wait to leave. But I've been here for many months, and now I treasure every moment I am in this house. You see, I'm not just involved with this Jesus Christ, but now He is my life."

Paul, who they thought was sleeping, sat up. He apparently had been listening to all of Silvius' comments.

"I have never heard a more eloquent witness for our Lord. When I am gone, you and your family will help shine His light into the world," said Paul.

Paulus was in awe of the devotion of these very different men — one a Jew from Tarsus, the other a veteran Roman soldier. As Paul was making this last statement, several men entered the house. They were there to make plans for another ceremony the next day.

Paulus and Silvius made no further comments as the afternoon passed. Silvius returned to his usual stoic self. Paulus thought about the strange direction his life had taken in the past few weeks. His family would never be the same, and he had doubts that his own future would ever be that of a skilled Roman soldier. He felt he was spending his life in two worlds—both in some ways foreign to him. The world at the Jew's house was one of people working for what they all called the kingdom of God. The other world was his old life of luxury, Roman patriotism, and a lonely house, (full of gloom, silence, and approaching death). He realized all of a sudden that he was no longer comfortable in either of these worlds.

When the replacement guard arrived, Paulus was glad to say farewell to Paul and Silvius. He hoped that sleep would erase some of the turmoil that he was feeling this evening.

Chapter 11

When Livia woke the next morning, she was disoriented for a few minutes. As the light filtered into the tent, she stared around her at their meager supplies and thought this a far cry from her beautifully decorated bedroom in Rome. Tatius was not in the tent, and as she peeped outside, she realized that it was late. Usually up at dawn, Livia's fatigue and the rhythms of the sea had apparently caused her to sleep well into the day. Livia drank a cup of water, and desperately wished for a bath. Taking a little water into her hands, she attempted to wash her face and hands, but aware that this water had to last until they arrived in Gaul, she used very little for her toilette. Brushing her hair back from her face with her damp hands, she went out onto the open deck. Tatius was seated on a bench talking to the other passengers. Seeing her, he walked over and teasingly said, "You must not mind really hard beds! The day is almost gone."

"Oh, it is not! How long have you been up?" asked Livia.

"Truthfully, I slept late as well. We had quite a day yesterday — from a mule cart ride to pirates. We both needed some extra sleep, and when I saw you were sleeping so soundly, I left to give you some privacy. I hope we have another beautiful day."

Livia saw that land was still in view, so they must be following the coastline as predicted. However, the Roman warships were no longer to be seen.

"Do you think the pirates will return today?" asked Livia.

"I doubt they will. We are still close to the coast, and I don't believe they will risk running into Roman warships again."

They both sat down on a bench near their tent. "Tullus said that we are probably about a fourth of the distance to Gaul. I'm not sure how he knows, but I hope he is correct," said Tatius. "You know, Livia, I feel like Abraham setting out from his own country into the unknown."

"There you are, talking about Abraham again. You know I had never heard of him before you mentioned him yesterday. Why is he so important that you keep talking about him?"

"Well, as I said before, he is the father of the Jews. God made a covenant with him that said, 'I will make you into a great nation and I will bless you;...And all peoples on earth will be blessed through you.'" (Genesis 12:2-3)

"How do you know all of that?" asked Livia in amazement.

"The church at Corinth had several Jews who had become Christians. A couple of them were great teachers who told their stories and taught the law found in the *Torah*. Would you like me to teach you more?"

"Yes, I want so much to learn everything about the Jews and their connection to our God," said Livia with enthusiasm.

Tatius then spent the morning telling Livia the stories about Abraham, Isaac, Jacob, and Joseph. He continued with a description of Moses and his leadership, the exodus from Egypt, the giving of the Law, and the arrival of the Israelites into Canaan. Livia listened with great interest.

"So that is why the Jews have always seemed strange. They were told they were to be different. Is that all of their history?" asked Livia.

"No, there is a lot more — from their great fighting men to their kings. David and Solomon were their greatest kings."

"I've actually heard of them. One of my tutors said they had written some good poetry, but I never learned any of it," said Livia.

"I know some of the beautiful psalms, and I will teach you more of their stories and some of their poetry later. What is more important, however, is that Jesus Christ is the Messiah they were promised. The Jewish leaders, however, didn't believe in Him, and they were the ones who had him killed."

"I'm confused. I thought Roman soldiers crucified Him!" said Livia.

"They did, but only because the Jews wanted Him dead. By the time Jesus came, the Jews were looking for a military leader, and they had twisted the laws to their own advantage."

"Oh Tatius, you know so much about our beliefs, and I know so little," said Livia.

"It's not what you know, my dearest. We only have to trust in Him, and in God's grace that gives us our salvation."

About the time Tatius was making this statement, a wave swept over the deck and drenched Livia and Tatius. "Well, that was not the baptism I had hoped you to have, my love," said Tatius. "Let's check on our supplies. They are probably very wet." Going into the goat hair tent, they found that their blankets were a bit damp, but everything else seemed dry. "We must remember to put our blankets on the jars from now on," suggested Tatius. "Now let's eat the rest of the food given us by my old Jewish friends."

"Tatius, what did you mean by hoping I would have a different baptism? What is this baptism?" asked Livia.

As they ate, Tatius told her about Christ's baptism. "Mark, one of Paul's friends, quoted Jesus after His resurrection as saying, 'Go into all the world and preach the good news to all creation. Whoever believes and is baptized will be saved.'...(Mark 16:16-17) We try to follow His command."

"Then I want to be baptized. Can you baptize me? Have you already been baptized? Could I be baptized on the ship? Would it…"

"Stop! Livia, you ask too many questions for me to keep up with the answers," said Tatius with a chuckle. "My dear, we must wait until near a river in Gaul for your baptism. I will explain more about it later."

"Tatius it is so hard for me not to talk when we are around other people. Must I always remain silent?" asked Livia with some frustration.

"Dearest, you speak Latin and Greek with too much polish and sophistication for an ordinary Roman woman. I have traveled so much that I can adapt my speech to the people I'm around. But I fear others would recognize you as a Roman aristocrat immediately."

With tears in her eyes, Livia said, "I am so useless. I can't do anything or even speak. Why would God want me?"

"My love for you is so intense that I thought at the beginning I was confusing my hopes and plans with God's plans. But now, as I see God's presence blossoming in you, I am sure you are part of His holy plan for me and for Gaul. Be patient, my dear one. I'm unsure what will happen, but if He leads us, we can follow with no fears."

When they went back to their familiar bench, Tullus came over to talk with them. The other passengers were drinking wine and laughing loudly, while gambling with several of the members of the crew.

"Ah yes, they spend their youth as if it were water pouring through their fingers. At my age, I've learned to savor my portions of time, because I know I have very little left. Would you mind if I joined you?" asked Tullus.

Tatius said they would be honored and Livia nodded. Tullus remarked on the increasing clouds and the sky which was becoming dark. The day had begun with sunshine and calm waters, but the winds were becoming stronger now.

"Do you not think there will be a storm soon?" asked Tatius.

"I do. Both the wind and waves are much rougher. As you can see, the sea now has become gray. But for now, I think all is well."

"Tell us more about Arelate. Is it much like Rome?" asked Tatius.

Tullus told them that it is indeed a smaller version of Rome in many ways. The city has a forum, an amphitheater, some *insulae*, an aqueduct, and an arena. He said the area is well-known for its fruits and beautiful flowers. (At the comment about flowers, Livia had a hard time not asking questions.) According to Tullus, there is a great river called the Rhone that flows through the city and by his farm as well.

"If you don't mind my asking, what are your plans in Gaul? Do you have family there?" asked Tullus.

Pausing for a moment, Tatius then said, "We are beginning a new life in Gaul, far from the crowded streets of Rome." Tatius knew that he hadn't really answered the question. While they were talking, the ship's captain came over to where they were. He motioned to the other passengers to come nearer. The crew had gotten very busy with the ship due to the increasing winds, so the drinking and gambling had stopped. The captain told all the passengers that the tent poles must be removed from all the tents, and then the tents had to be flattened and tied with more ropes. He told them to get all their supplies, bedding, and water jars and take them to the cabin.

They all began moving supplies, but it was difficult to walk with the high waves. The supplies were finally all placed inside the cabin, and the tents were secured. The captain then told them to get into the cabin. They crowded into the available space, but with all the provisions there was little room. They had to sit on the dirty blankets on the floor.

After a short time, one of the young men called Quintus said they should have made an offering to Neptune before the voyage. He then said," If only we had some incense, we could still burn it in his honor and beg for protection."

Tullus said gently, "I think incense is the last thing we need in such close quarters, especially with the waves throwing us around. I would be happier if someone had the power to say to the waves, 'Peace, be still.'"

With this comment, Tatius turned and looked sharply at Tullus. Livia, noting Tatius' reaction, was dying to ask what was wrong, but she remained dutifully silent. As the ship was being tossed sharply back and forth over the waves, Livia felt herself getting sick, and Tatius was looking rather pale as well. Before long, the two young men who had been drinking so much wine earlier were retching into one of the pots. The smells in the cabin were horrible, and Livia was so afraid she too would become violently sick. They could see the lightning flashes, and the thunder seemed to rattle the ship. When it seemed things could not be any worse, the captain and crew came into the cabin. "We have secured the sails, and we need to be inside until the lightning lessens," said the captain.

Everyone sat quietly and listened to the storm. Livia looked at Tatius, who had his eyes closed. She knew he was praying, and she began praying as well. When she opened her eyes, she saw fear in the faces of everyone except Tullus and the captain. After what seemed a very long time, the thunder and lightning appeared to be decreasing. The captain looked outside and motioned for the crew to follow him onto the open deck. The two young passengers were lying on the floor moaning, but Livia, though nauseous, had maintained her composure.

Tatius suddenly turned to Tullus and said something that Livia found very strange. "If we couldn't have the waters stilled, it would have been nice to walk on the water, would it not?"

Tullus slowly smiled and, seeing that both young men were too sick to notice anything, did something odd with his foot. Tatius then did something quite similar. Livia started to get angry. She knew something significant was happening, but, as usual, she was left out.

"What are you…" she started to ask.

Tatius shook his head and said, "We will be on deck soon, and it will be good to talk again." Livia simmered but took the hint.

Before long, one of the crew told them they could come out on the deck. The storm had passed. Tullus, Tatius, and Livia left the cabin, holding their clothing bags in their hands. Remembering the pearls in her bag, Livia had no intention of leaving the bags with the sick men. When out on deck, the captain asked about the other two men.

Tullus indicated that they were still in the cabin. The captain then said something to one of the crew, and the next thing they knew, the men were being half-carried and deposited on the deck. Tullus went over to the men and began rubbing their faces with a damp cloth. Livia and Tatius sat down on a wet bench, and Livia said, "I'm ready for an explanation. First, you talk about walking on water, and then Tullus and you do some kind of dance in the cabin! Has the storm affected your mind?"

Tatius laughed, "No, my dear. I've just learned an interesting fact. Livia, Tullus is a Christian!"

"How do you know this? He never mentioned God or Jesus Christ," said Livia.

"Do you remember when he said something about being happier if someone would say to the waves, 'Peace, be still?'"

"Yes, I thought the comment odd, but not as strange as your wishing you could walk on water."

"Livia, those were two of the miracles Jesus did. He walked on water, and he calmed the waves. I suspected Tullus was a Christian from his comment, and I then tested him with the walking on water statement."

"What were you doing with your feet?" asked Livia.

"Tullus drew the top part of a fish, and I then drew the bottom part. It is a way that Christians identify themselves to each other. Oh, my dear, I think we have just found another part of God's plan."

Livia was ashamed at her anger and prayed that God would help her be a better Christian. Suddenly she cried out, "Look Tatius, look!" There on the horizon was one of the most beautiful rainbows either of them had ever seen. Tatius smiled to himself and decided it would be wise to wait to tell Livia about Noah, the great flood, and the rainbow. He just silently said, "Thank you Lord."

Chapter 12

For Paulus, the next few days followed a similar pattern. He got up early and met with his father, either in the atrium or in his father's bedroom. Each day, until his father got tired, they would go over business contracts. Atticus helped Paulus understand the deals he had with various importers, tradesmen, and clients. Paulus knew his father had extensive business interests, but he had no idea how widespread they were. Atticus also showed Paulus the amounts that had to be spent for the upkeep of the households in Rome and in Ostia. The expenses for the slaves were astonishing, and the money paid to the overseers of the house and stables in Ostia was much higher than anything he would have imagined. Atticus had several hired servants such as Alexander and Philippa. A generous man, Atticus rewarded those who gave him excellent service. Paulus was ashamed to admit that he didn't even know the names of half of his father's clients, servants, or slaves.

When Atticus went to rest each day, Paulus, with his head spinning from so much information, did something he had seldom done before. He went out into the garden to seek a quiet place to think. In truth, near her beloved flowers, he felt a connection with Livia there. Each day, while in the garden, he followed the routine of talking to Philippa and asking her to manage the household. On the first of these days, he told her he was pleased with her service to him and his father.

Philippa blushed and said, "Thank you sir."

On an impulse, Paulus said, "Since you have done such a good job, would you and Alexander like to have an afternoon off, with no reduction in salary, of course?"

With a big smile, Philippa said, "Sir, we would be most grateful for your kindness. Is there anything else you would like sir?"

Again seeing how delightfully charming she was in her gratitude, he had to resist the desire to make a suggestive offer, but he simply said, "No, that is all." As Philippa walked away, Paulus again wondered why he had never noticed her until recently.

Paulus went each day to the public baths and did a little exercise. There was no time, however, for seeing a race or doing anything else entertaining, and he still had his guard duty.

On the day of the free afternoon for Alexander and Philippa, there was another bread and wine ceremony at Paul's house. As before, there was a lot of food, and the people attending seemed to be of diverse backgrounds and nationalities. As they had the bread and wine service, some of the people openly began weeping when Paul said, "Do this in remembrance of Christ." The crowd was even larger than the other times Paulus had been present at a service.

After the food and the ceremony, Paul again spoke to the crowd. He spoke a few words in Latin, but most of his speech was in flawless Greek. He concluded with, "He is Risen." The crowd then repeated, "He is Risen indeed." Paulus again spotted someone in the back of the crowd that he knew — Philipps's brother Alexander! He looked to see if Philippa were there also, but she was so small, he knew he wouldn't be able to see her in the crowd. He tried once more to find Alexander, but there were too many people. However, Paulus was almost sure it had been him.

"Are these Christians everywhere?" he wondered.

By the time the people finally left, it was time for Silvius and Paulus to leave as well. Paul had already said farewell and retired for the night. Paulus knew the Jew had to be exhausted with the long afternoon and evening.

As Silvius and Paulus walked toward their homes, Paulus asked Silvius, "Do you know a 'Jesus follower' that is a Greek servant called Alexander ?"

Silvius said, "No, I don't think so. But there are so many people who come here. There are many servants and slaves as well as some very important people. Paulus, I plead with you if you know him, do not betray him. I assure you these dear brothers and sisters mean no harm to Rome."

Paulus answered sharply, "I am too busy with my family worries to concern myself with what happens at a prisoner's house."

Silvius said quietly, "Thank you." They then went their separate ways. As Paulus was walking home, he thought, "No wonder Philippa was so happy to have the afternoon off, she wanted to go with Alexander to the ceremony at Paul's house!"

Chapter 13

As the days passed, Paulus watched his father grow weaker. He continued to refuse Paulus' request that his sisters be notified. After a few days, he did ask that Paulus send for Cornelius. Paulus did so, and Cornelius arrived within a short time. Cornelius was shocked at his brother's deterioration.

"Have you sent for a doctor?" asked Cornelius.

"No, they **can not** help me," said Atticus. "I know I have little time left, and I do not want to be bothered by doctors." This last speech completely exhausted Atticus. After a few moments, he was able to say a few words. "Cornelius, will you help Paulus when I am gone. He has a fine mind, but he would do better with your help." With this speech, he groaned and asked for water. One of the two slaves that were always by his bed ran for the water. He took a couple of sips and then seemed to fall asleep. They waited for a few minutes and then went out into the atrium, telling the slaves to notify them if there were changes.

"I do not think he will live long, Paulus," said Cornelius.

"I know."

"Have your sisters been notified?" asked Cornelius.

"He absolutely forbids it and I have honored his wishes. I do so wish Livia were still here. She was always such a comfort to him. I find it hard to believe she would desert us!"

"I'm so sorry Paulus. You know Atticus has always been like a father to me. Since his accident which confined him to Rome, we've grown close. Until the last few weeks, he has always been such a fair-minded man, and I have listened to his counsel about so many things. He was the one who advised me to advocate tolerance to this new Christian cult. Of course, that was before Livia became involved in the group. I think the loss of Livia and the terrible pain he must be suffering have caused him to do and say things he would never have done otherwise," said Cornelius.

"I am trying to be the son he would wish. I've been learning all I can about his businesses. There is just so much to absorb, and I can't stay with him in the afternoon because of my guard duty," said Paulus.

"Don't worry about that for now. I'll handle the matter with your commanding officer. You need to be here. You should probably return to the Jew's house and explain the situation to the other guard, but I'll see to it that you are able to stay here all the time with Atticus."

Cornelius stayed for another hour, but Atticus never woke. He left to attend to the matter of Paulus' orders as well as his other duties at the Senate. The time approached for Paulus to leave to go to Paul's house. He didn't want to leave his father, but he felt he should explain things to Silvius. He had never told Silvius or Paul how very sick his father was.

Atticus remained asleep as Paulus left. When Paulus arrived at Paul's house, Silvius was there, early as usual. For a change there were no visitors. Upon entering the house, he went to Silvius to tell him of his father's condition, but before he could say a word, Paul said, "I'm sorry that your father is so very ill. I have been praying for his soul as well as yours."

Paulus was somewhat shaken. He had no idea how Paul knew of his father's severe illness. At a loss for words, Paulus simply muttered, "Thank you."

Paul then said, "I will leave you and Silvius to talk alone. But I want you to know that if everyone else leaves you Paulus, you are still not alone. Jesus is here, just waiting beside you."

As Paul walked away, Paulus surprisingly took some comfort in these words. He quickly explained the situation to Silvius, who expressed his regrets and said he would pray for him and his family. As Paulus was leaving, he turned and said to both of them, "Thank you for your prayers." Paulus then hurried back to his house.

Arriving home, he found his father still asleep, but very restless. At times, Atticus mumbled things, but the only word Paulus recognized was 'Livia'. Paulus slept the night on a couch just outside his father's room.

Chapter 14

The next morning Paulus rose early and checked on his father. The slaves said he had awakened only once during the night to ask for water. Paulus watched as one of the slaves dipped a cloth into a bowl of water and moistened Atticus' lips. Paulus trembled with emotion as he watched the former strong soldier fade before his eyes. He hurried from the room, not wanting the slaves to see him weep.

As Paulus went into the atrium, Philippa approached him and asked, "Sir, is your father any better today?"

"No, He's failing fast, and I fear his death will be soon," said Paulus. As he said these words, he quickly wiped tears away, hoping Philippa did not see them. However, she did notice and did something completely shocking. She reached out and actually touched his arm for just a moment and said, "Oh sir, I am so sorry. I'll pray for his soul." With tears running down her cheeks, she turned and walked away.

Paulus was taken aback by her sympathy as well as her nerve in daring to touch him. Pulling himself back from his thoughts about Philippa, he quietly said a little prayer to the Jewish God Jehovah to heal his father. (Not that he had any faith in this god, but it certainly could not make things worse!)

As he was eating and drinking a little, one of the slaves came into the room and told him that his father was awake. He went into his father's room and immediately saw that he was much more alert than usual. For a moment, Paulus thought, "Could all these Christian prayers have caused a miracle?"

"Are you feeling better Father?" asked Paulus.

"I have less pain my son, but I think my time with you is very short," said Atticus. He spoke gently, as he always had until the past few weeks.

"You are a good man Paulus. I know you will follow the paths of honor and fairness. I am proud you are mine." As he said these words, Atticus' voice became weaker. He closed his eyes for a moment, and Paulus feared he was gone, but he then heard his faint breaths. The room seemed very quiet and silent.

Suddenly, Atticus opened his eyes and said, "I forgive her, Paulus. I'm sorry I've been so harsh. Son, stay with me." With these words, he closed his eyes again. One of the slaves brought a chair for Paulus to sit in beside Atticus' bed. He seemed to be sleeping, but Paulus heard him mutter several words. One time, Paulus thought Atticus was actually praying, but he wasn't certain.

Time passed, and Atticus struggled for breath as Paulus gently touched his face. In the early afternoon, he gasped for breath one last time and then he was gone. With many of the slaves and servants standing nearby, Paulus closed his father's eyes. All of a sudden, Paulus felt a loneliness unlike anything he had ever felt in his life.

Chapter 15

*T*atius and Livia passed the next few days of their journey to Arelate with no new adventures. Thankfully, the seas were calm, and there were no pirates to be seen. But since they were headed north, the headwinds made travel very slow. Tatius and Livia spent much of the time talking to Tullus, while the other passengers were again content to pass their time drinking and gambling. As they sat watching the gentle rhythm of the waves, Tatius, making sure they were not heard by anyone else, said to Tullus, "Sir, tell us how you became a believer."

Tullus, who loved to talk, recounted his story. Some years ago, he was traveling with his family to Massalia (Marseille). He had gone to arrange some business affairs and decided to take his family to see the bustling seaport. Since they had cousins who lived there, they planned to stay about three weeks with them. One afternoon, early in the visit, his son Marcus, who had been exploring the city, returned, excitedly telling the family a wild tale about what he had just seen. Talking so fast he could barely be understood, he said, "Oh Father, I think I've just seen a great wonder, maybe a miracle!"

"Chuckling at his youthful exuberance, I asked, 'Now what is this great marvel, Marcus?'"

"My son then blurted out, 'There was a group of people singing and praying, and then the boat just appeared out of nowhere.' Making little sense out of my son's statement, I began questioning him. What I found out was that my son had been on the docks watching the fishermen, when he heard a group of people singing. Being very curious, he went to where the sounds were and saw about twenty or thirty people on their knees. Some were crying, some were talking (praying) to a god, and others were singing. Marcus asked a young man standing nearby what was happening. The man explained that a small fishing boat had not returned after a violent storm three days earlier. The storm was so bad that even one of the Roman warships had run aground, so a tiny boat had little chance with such strong winds and rain. According to the young man, the four men in the boat were 'Jesus followers', as were the people singing on the docks. He laughingly said to my son, 'They apparently think they can pray the boat from off the floor of the sea!'"

Tullus then told Tatius and Livia what had so impressed his son. "While my son was talking to the man, they heard shouts and saw people excitedly pointing at the sea. There on the horizon was the boat heading toward shore. All four men were singing and praising God as they rowed to the dock."

"But how did **you** meet these Christians?" asked Tatius.

Tullus laughed as he recounted the story. "By a remarkable 'coincidence', one of the men in that boat was a trader with whom I had business matters to arrange a few days later. When I met him, he told me how they had survived. They had managed to get the boat to a tiny islet which had almost no protection. As the winds raged around them, they were praying for God's grace as they prepared to die. The rain beat upon them, and yet, neither they nor the boat were harmed. However, the waters were so turbulent that they had to wait until the seas calmed to return home. They gave all the credit for their lives being spared to this Jehovah. My trading partner invited me to his house for a worship service. I thanked him, but of course, I declined," said Tullus.

"I still don't understand how you became a believer," said Tatius.

"I didn't go to the service, but my son did. He had witnessed the boat's returning and was much impressed by these people. I'll tell you more of the details later, but I will just tell you now that before we left Massalia, we were followers of Jesus. I knew nothing about a Jewish God named Jehovah. Most of the believers in Massalia were Roman or Greek, but a few were Jews who said this Jesus was their Messiah. I wanted to know so much more, and then I found out that there were a couple of Jewish families living in Arelate who followed Jesus. I have spent the last years learning so much from them. My home is now a house church just outside Arelate, and all my family have become believers, including my son and his wife in Rome," said Tullus.

Tatius and Livia listened to his story with amazement. It was obvious that Tullus was completely at peace and very sure of his faith. Tullus then looked at Livia, who was crying softly, and said to Tatius, "Now tell me your story and that of your uh *'sister'*."

Tatius was surprised. They had been so careful to act as brother and sister. "Why do you think she is not my sister?" asked Tatius.

Tullus smiled and said, "I'm an old man now, but I still recognize the kind of love shared only by lovers."

Livia blushed and unable to remain silent any longer asked, "Do you think the others have noticed?"

Tullus replied, "I doubt it. The crew seems too busy, and the two young men are so involved in their drink and games that they pay little attention to anyone else. Now, I'm ready to hear about you."

Tatius looked at Livia inquiringly, and she nodded her head. He then told Tullus the story of his becoming a Christian, his meeting of Livia, and their developing love. He hesitated for just a moment, and Livia began telling him about her family and how she had chosen to flee with Tatius after becoming a believer. They told him that no one knew where they were going, including God's servant Paul.

"Did you say Paul? Are you talking about the Apostle Paul who is being held in Rome? Do you know him?" asked Tullus excitedly.

Tatius joked, "Livia, he can ask questions almost as fast as you." Then turning to Tullus, he said, "I have known him for some months now. He has been my teacher and mentor, and my father is actually one of his guards."

"I have been to a couple of the bread and wine services at his house. I had so wanted to talk to him about my situation and ask for his guidance. But there were always so many people present. For the sake of my son and his family in Rome, I've tried to be discreet, so I didn't insist on seeing him. Please tell me all about what you have learned from him," begged Tullus.

"That would take weeks," said Tatius. "If I might ask, what is the situation where you need his guidance?"

"We need a leader. My sons and sons-in-law are very busy with our growing businesses and have little time to help our church. I have tried to guide our little group of believers, but my knowledge is so limited. We have an old rabbi living nearby who is a believer who has taught us much, but he is very feeble and is going blind. We have been praying for God to send us someone who can help us convince all of *Gallia Narbonensis* that Jesus is God's son and that He is risen from the dead!" said Tullus with great emotion. Then taking Tatius' and Livia's hands, he said, "I think perhaps the two of you are the answer to my prayers."

"I am not sure of that sir, but I do know God has paved the way for us to come to Arelate," said Tatius.

"Oh how I have been praying that God would send us someone with the gift of teaching and preaching the good news! I'm willing to lend my home for a church and visit our sick and needy, but I can not teach or preach!" said Tullus.

"Well, I do feel God has called me to witness to the power of his salvation. As for having the gift to teach your little flock, I'm going to let the Holy Spirit direct me where I need to go. As I told you, I became a believer in Corinth. While I was there, they read and reread a letter Paul wrote to the church about gifts. There had been some conflict in the church about which 'gifts of the Spirit' were most important. I memorized parts of the letter. He wrote, 'There are different kinds of gifts, but the same Spirit.'(I Corinthians 12:4)

He continued in the letter saying that believers are like the human body, with each part serving a function. He said, 'Now you are the body of Christ, and each of you is a part of it. And in the Church God has appointed first of all apostles, second prophets, third teachers, then workers of miracles, also those having gifts of healing, those able to help others, those with the gifts of administration, and those speaking in different kinds of tongues.'(I Corinthians 12: 27-28) I have no doubt that you, Tullus, have many of these gifts."

Livia then spoke through her tears, "I do not see any possible use God has for me. I don't know how to do anything!"

"My dear, someday I'll tell you more about what he said, but one thing I do want you to know. He talked a lot about a gift greater than all those mentioned, and he said it was the most important of all gifts," said Tatius.

"Oh Tatius, don't tease us. I want to know what the greatest gift is now!" (Livia had never been known for her patience.)

"Please tell us," insisted Tullus.

"Well, Paul wrote, 'If I speak in the tongues of men and of angels, but have not love, I am only a resounding gong or a clanging cymbal. If I have the gift of prophecy and can fathom all mysteries and all knowledge, and if I have a faith that can move mountains, but have not love, I am nothing. If I give all I possess to the poor and surrender my body to the flames, but have not love, I gain nothing… Now these three remain: faith, hope, and love. But the greatest of these is love.'"(I Corinthians 13:1-3, 13)

"Oh, I must hear more Tatius," said Livia, and Tullus nodded in agreement.

For the next couple of days, the three met in one corner of the ship, and Tatius taught them much of what Paul had told him personally and also what he remembered about the letters he had heard read in Corinth.

While they were talking about the Corinthian letters, Tullus suddenly asked, "Where are you staying in Arelate?"

Stammering a bit, Tatius replied, "I am not sure."

The Light Will Come

Just as I thought," said Tullus. "You have no place to stay. Well, it is settled. You are coming to my house!"

"But that is too generous of you sir," said Tatius. "You hardly know us."

"Nonsense! God has planned this, and I'm certain he has placed us on this ship together. Now, I think the matter of your being *'sister'* and *'brother'* must be settled very quickly. After we get to my house, your marriage should be planned immediately!"

Fearing Tullus thought they had been living as man and wife, Livia said, "We have been as *'brother'* and *'sister'* like Abraham!" said Livia with fervor.

A bit confused about the Abraham reference, Tullus smiled and said, "I believe you, dear children." While they were having this discussion, one of the other passengers yelled, "I see land." Tatius and Livia trembled as they saw the port of Arelate and a new life just coming into view.

Chapter 16

Paulus sat in the garden enjoying the quiet of the early morning. It was a cold winter day, but Paulus felt the temperature outside no more chilly than his heart. "Oh I miss Livia so much," thought Paulus. The last two weeks had passed with Paulus performing his expected duties ably (with the help of his Uncle Cornelius), and Paulus had even remained in control when dealing with his difficult older sisters. But it had not been easy.

"Father was certainly right not to want them here during his illness," thought Paulus. "Their constant bickering and hysterical behavior would have caused his death much earlier."

Paulus could not forget the arrival of Livia *Prima* with her husband and children shortly after his father's death. They had entered the house with their entourage of slaves carrying several trunks. One of the children immediately started screaming, "I don't like it here. I want to go home, now!"

Ignoring her daughter, his sister had demanded to know why she had not been notified that her father was so sick. Pointing her finger at Paulus, she said, "If I had been here, I would have taken care of him, and he might still be alive. Oh, I **can not** believe Livia *Tertia* would desert him like this!"

Paulus had clenched his hands behind his back, fighting his anger. He wanted to yell that his father had not wanted to see her, but he knew that would be so hurtful that he held his tongue. "Perhaps time with the Jew Paul has calmed my temper," thought Paulus. He had stayed away from much of the planning of the house for mourning. He should probably have been grateful for his sisters' help. They had given Philippa extensive orders, constantly changing their minds as to the food to be served for the guests who came to pay their respects to the family and the arrangement of the furniture. His sisters had decorated the house for mourning and argued at length about which tunic their father should wear. Paulus had finally intervened and ordered him dressed in what he had worn when returning from one of his military campaigns. Atticus' body had been cleaned by the slaves, dressed, and then placed in the atrium with his feet toward the door, so that he could walk away in an afterlife. Of course the family had followed the tradition of not changing clothes or bathing until after the funeral.

Paulus had tried very hard to do honor to his father by carefully following the usual funeral customs for a prominent man. As he was recalling the funeral, he thought how very grateful he was to Cornelius. Two of his father's other brothers had returned from their foreign posts to attend the funeral, but even though older, they had wanted Cornelius to deliver the eulogy. "What a wonderful tribute he had given." thought Paulus. The body had been taken to the Forum and Cornelius had spoken to the crowd about his brother with much eloquence and emotion. The next part of the ceremony, Paulus wished he could forget. The large procession taking the body from the Forum to outside the city had seemed offensive to him. The musicians, mourners singing dirges, and the paid actors wearing the wax masks of their ancestors all seemed to be just a big spectacle. But the worst part had been when he had had to light the funeral pyre with its foods, oils, and, of course, his father's body. Paulus shivered as he thought of seeing his father's face just as he was putting the torch to the pyre. He had staggered, and one of his uncles had steadied him. He felt as if his own life was being burned as well.

After the fire had burned, his father's bones were taken and placed in a large urn. That urn was then placed in the Livy family crypt with many of his ancestors, and yesterday, Paulus had "swept" death from the house according to Roman tradition. He had also thankfully said farewell to his sisters and their families as they left for their homes.

"It is so good to have quiet in the house again," thought Paulus. As he was enjoying the solitude, he looked around the garden and noticed that Alexander was not there. The garden had been repaired and tended after the onslaught of his nieces and nephews, but it was unusual that Philippa's brother was not working. He got up and went into the atrium where the slaves and servants were still cleaning after the departure of his family. Seeing Philippa talking to one of the maids, he walked toward her and inquired about Alexander.

"Oh sir, I was going to explain a little later, but I've been so busy. Alexander is very sick. He has a terrible cough and is so sick that he can eat nothing. I came alone today," said Philippa.

"You walked here alone before daylight?" asked Paulus.

"Yes sir. I knew there was still a lot of work to be done in returning the house to order, and I did not want to let you down sir," said Philippa.

"You know it isn't safe for a woman to walk alone in the dark. I'll send a couple of the servants with you this evening as you go home. Oh, and I'll send some juices and broths that might help Alexander recover more quickly," said Paulus.

"Thank you, sir. You are a kind man," said Philippa with a blush as she returned to her duties.

"Well, that's a compliment I've never had before," thought Paulus. "Me, a kind man? I doubt she would say that if she knew some of the thoughts I've had about her recently."

Paulus spent the rest of the morning working on his father's business affairs. After eating a few bites, he decided to reward himself with an afternoon at the baths. But before he left, he instructed two of the slaves to take some supplies to Philippa's home and to accompany her when she left.

Chapter 17

Livia watched the crew and passengers as they gathered the tents and remaining supplies and unloaded them from the ship. She could do little to help. Tullus had told them that there were shops along the docks where they could sell their tent. He assured them they would not need it any longer, and they would have everything they would need at his home. As the others worked, Livia began to worry about their future.

"How will Tullus' family react to two strangers in their home?

"How can we be married without my father making a contract?"

"Will there be Roman soldiers sent by my father in Arelate?" (She doubted that, since no one knew where they were.)

"Will I be able to talk to people without their guessing I am Roman nobility?"

"How can I be of help as a witness for Jesus if I can't speak?"

"Will Tatius be disappointed in me as a wife?" Her father had seen to it that she had an excellent education. She loved to read and learn, but she had always had slaves or servants. She couldn't cook or clean. She had only given orders to others, but she could do little (except in a garden).

"I know that Tatius loves me and I love him, but will I know how to love him as a wife?"

Livia was getting a headache and also becoming very fearful, when

Tatius walked toward her and smiled broadly at her. He whispered, "You make my world shine with happiness. Don't you worry, my dear one. God has chosen this road for us, and we will not fail." He walked away to continue his work, but his words had helped her.

After the tents, jars, and other supplies were placed on the dock, Tatius and Livia gathered their little bags of personal supplies (including her necklace) and got off the ship. For a few moments, they continued to sway on land as they had on the ship. When they saw each other going from side to side as they walked, they broke into laughter. Tullus began talking with a group of men near one of the shops. It was obvious that he knew several of the men. Not quite knowing what to do, they stood and waited for Tullus. He soon returned and said he had sold their tent and supplies for them. All they had to do was agree to the deal. Tatius walked over to the men and accepted the arranged transaction. Then one of the men gave Tatius money, and he returned to Livia.

"I just hired a mule cart to take us to my house," said Tullus. "It will be a bit crowded, but we'll be fine. We'll pass through the city of Arelate, and you'll get to see a bit of our 'Little Rome'. I wish it were just a little earlier in the season, so you could see more of our beautiful flowers, but you will see some things in bloom. Our weather here is very mild and quite temperate." While he was talking, a mule cart arrived. How all this could have been arranged so quickly was impressive. He was quite an organizer. It was obvious why Tullus was such a successful businessman. Livia remembered Tatius' telling them about the different gifts that people have and Tullus' wishing he could be better at teaching. "Perhaps he is a poor teacher, but he certainly has many other talents," thought Livia.

The weather was indeed lovely. There was a light breeze from the sea, and the sunlight made the water look bright blue in the distance. As Livia was helped into the mule cart, she took one last look at the ship and thought, "Another step into the unknown!" Praying silently, she asked, "Oh Lord of the Jews and now of me, please make me into the wife and 'Jesus follower' you want me to be. Oh, and Amen."

As they traveled through the city, it was as Tullus had described. There were *insulae*, public baths, a Forum, an amphitheater, shops, statues to various gods, and a couple of Roman temples. As they passed neatly dressed people in the streets, Livia became acutely aware of her own condition. Her clothes were soiled and neither she nor Tatius had been able to use enough of their precious water to get clean. As they passed a public bath, she saw Tatius looking at it longingly. Seeming to guess their thoughts, Tullus said, "At my home there is a bath, and I will ask my servants to bring us a lot of water from a nearby stream for bathing. I am tired and eager to get home, but there will be time for a visit to town later. My land is not far north of town."

Traveling a bit farther, they passed a huge aqueduct, and then they saw a large river. "That's the Rhone. It's a forceful river with many tributaries. I have one tributary on my land that is quite lovely. It's perfect for baptisms!" said Tullus with a smile. A couple of days earlier, they had talked about Livia's desire to be baptized.

As they began passing groves of olive trees, Tullus informed them that they were now on his property.

"Oh, one thing I forgot to mention," said Tullus. "I have no slaves. I freed all those I had a few years ago. It seemed wrong to me somehow to worship with some of my slaves who were believers, call them 'brothers' and 'sisters' at a service, and then return with them to my household and consider them my property. I prayed about it a long time. Finally, I had the papers prepared and gave all of them their freedom. If they wanted to remain with me, I would pay them wages, provide lodging for them, and treat them as servants or employees. Most stayed, but some left."

Tatius and Livia were astounded. "But do you not lose money having to pay workers rather than owning slaves to work in your household and business?" asked Tatius.

Tullus chuckled, "I was worried at the beginning, but I just felt it was what I should do. However, my fields, olives groves, and vineyards produce far better than any of my neighbors' lands. My free servants work with a sense of pride and loyalty, and they have chosen to be where they are. They are part of my family."

Tatius and Livia were silent. Livia had lived with slaves doing almost everything, and while not wealthy, Tatius' family had a couple of slaves as well. It was evident that Tullus had chosen to follow what he felt Jesus would have him do, no matter the cost. They were quiet as their journey to this remarkable man's home continued.

After a very short ride through the olive groves and vineyards, they arrived at Tullus' home. Livia was shocked at its size. It was as large as her house in Ostia. As they climbed out of the mule cart, several people appeared from the house and buildings near the house. They approached Tullus with a smile, and a couple of the older men gave him a warm embrace. Tullus made the introductions of Tatius and Livia to his workers. He said that Tatius and Livia were two dear friends who would be staying with him for a time, and they would need separate rooms and bathing supplies as soon as possible. The servants left immediately to make preparations. Tullus introduced his house staff, his stable manager, and his farm managers. He then sent one of the young men to his younger daughter's house to tell her and her husband that he had returned. Thankfully, he also told the young man to inform them of his guests, but he said that they were all so very tired from the trip to please wait until tomorrow morning to come see him and his visitors. "He's giving us time to rest and more importantly to bathe!" thought Livia. Both Tatius and Livia were at a loss for words when watching and listening to Tullus. He gave orders kindly, but with assurance. Everyone responded as if they were eager to please him, and he seemed capable of handling all situations.

"Welcome to my home," said Tullus to Livia and Tatius, as he indicated with his hand that they were to enter. Livia was very impressed with the house. The atrium was almost as large as that of her house in Rome, and the *impluvium* was splendid, with an inlaid pool. What surprised Livia most was the condition of the house. It was spotlessly clean and even had beautiful flowering vines on the tables. When her family went to her home in Ostia, it was days before everything was clean and well-arranged. Tullus had been gone for months, but the house and grounds had obviously been well-tended. A lovely young woman showed them to their bedrooms. Livia's room was charming and very feminine. According to the young servant named Flora, her room had been Tullus' older daughter's room. Tatius was to stay in his older son's room. Livia was overcome with so many feelings. She was so grateful, so overwhelmed with the amazing circumstances that God had obviously planned, and so very aware that she looked absolutely dreadful! The young woman said that Tullus had ordered a bath prepared for her immediately, and clothes that had belonged to his wife were to be made ready for her use. Livia felt the tears begin to fall as she thanked Flora. After Flora left, Livia prayed quietly, "Oh dear Jesus, I am so unworthy of your trust and love. My family and my home are gone, but I don't feel alone because you are my Savior. Please guide me as I learn how to be your child. Amen."

Chapter 18

Paulus sat in the *tablinum* working on his family's business accounts. He had seen clients for the past two days and was now verifying some information from those transactions. He found that he could do the work with few problems, but it was tedious and rather dull.

"Well, this is certainly not the way I intended my life to be. I should be off with my friends in the service of the Great Roman Empire, not checking for errors in accounting! It isn't fair!" thought Paulus.

As he was pitying himself for his loss of "fun", he saw Philippa pass in the atrium. He had forgotten to inquire about Alexander. "Truthfully, if I were a 'kind' man as Philippa had said, I would have insisted she stay home to help care for Alexander. But I'm so dependent on her running the household, I don't want to offer her a chance to not come to work," thought Paulus. He had remembered to have a couple of his slaves go to her home in order to accompany her to work early in the morning. She had insisted that she would be fine in the evening if she left before dark. Getting up from the table with his papers, he went into the atrium and called for Philippa in order to ask about her brother.

Coming slowly to where he stood, she asked, "Sir, do you need me?"

Paulus was shocked at her appearance. Usually so neat, she looked somewhat disheveled. She was very pale with bright red cheeks, and it was obvious she was sick. He noticed she was holding on to a table as they spoke.

"Philippa, you must go home. You are sick," said Paulus.

"There is so much still to do here. I'll..." As she was saying these last words, she swayed, and Paulus grabbed her just before she hit the floor. When he shouted for help, one of the maids and a couple of the male slaves came running. Philippa was unconscious. Paulus gently carried her to a couch. The maid ran and got a wet cloth and began rubbing her face, as Philippa's *palla* fell to the floor. He was very alarmed, and it suddenly dawned on him that he actually cared about her condition, besides needing her to run the household! She slowly began to revive and tried to get up from the couch, but Paulus pushed her back and told her to remain still.

Obviously embarrassed, Philippa said, "Oh sir, I'm sorry. I've just not been able to eat, and I'm very tired. Alexander is so very sick, and I don't know what to do." Tears had started to run down her cheeks as she talked.

"Well, you are going home. I'll have a *lectica* brought here for you," said Paulus.

"No, No, I couldn't bear that sir. I hate *lecticas*! Besides, I must get some food and oil for my family this evening. I'll be fine in just a few minutes. I don't live far from here, and I walk it every day."

On a sudden impulse, Paulus said, "I'll go with you, and a couple of the slaves can take some supplies with us."

"Oh, you can't do that!" said Philippa.

Paulus was taken aback. A servant could not tell him what to do! Now he was all the more determined to accompany her home. Besides it was a good excuse to leave the boring business matters behind.

"Just as soon as you can sit up and drink some broth, I am taking you home!" said Paulus. He began giving orders to a couple of slaves about food and oil for her family.

Tears still flowing, Philippa slowly sat up. She drank some of the broth but refused to eat anything. Paulus walked over and picked up her fallen *palla*. He noticed how very thin and shabby it was. There were holes that had been sewn many times and the material was threadbare. Turning to one of the maids, he said, "Get a cloak from Livia's room for Philippa." He knew it would be much too large for her, but she needed to be warm.

With the cloak around her and the food ready, he, Philippa, and the slaves left the house. He had to support her several times as they walked down the hill. She was such a tiny little thing and looked almost like a child in Livia's huge cloak.

"This isn't the way I have imagined holding her!" he thought to himself.

After a slow walk, due to Philippa's condition, they arrived at the *insula* where she lived.

"I can go on alone now," said Philippa.

"Nonsense! You are too unsteady. We'll go with you to your apartment." He was being thoughtful, but he also was enjoying touching her even if only as a support.

After climbing what seemed like endless stairs, Paulus, Philippa, and the slaves arrived at her family's apartment. The halls leading to the apartment were very dirty, and the smells were oppressive. However, Paulus recalled the halls leading to Silvius' apartment had been very bad as well, but when you entered his home, it was lovely. At her door, Philippa thanked him, turned to open the door, and again started to fall. Paulus grabbed her and opened the door while announcing their presence. As Paulus entered with Philippa, he saw the apartment. It was almost bare. There was a well-used couch, an oil brazier, some rough shelves containing a few things, and a table. Alexander was lying on a cot in one corner of the room, and a woman who looked like an older version of Philippa sat on the floor beside him with a wet cloth in her hand. Startled at the intruders, the older woman rose from the floor and with eyes wide with fear said, "Oh, what has happened now?"

Philippa replied, "Mother, don't worry. I'm just a little tired. This is my kind master, Paulus. He has brought us supplies and also assisted me as I was somewhat unsteady." Paulus thought her explanation of her condition very simplified. Philippa's mother then came toward them slowly. Paulus saw that she dragged her leg and walked with much difficulty. As if guessing that Paulus was wondering about her lameness, Philippa explained, "Not long after my father's death, my mother was knocked down in the street by slaves carrying a *lectica*, and she was gravely injured. We were young, but Alexander and I saw it happen." As Philippa was speaking, Paulus had to support her to keep her upright. Paulus saw she was near falling, so he guided her to the couch. Her mother followed and thanked him for aiding Philippa. Turning to Paulus as she sat down on the couch next to Philippa, her mother said, "Sir, I am called Helena. I owe my life to your uncle and father."

"What do you mean?" asked Paulus with surprise.

"Your father and uncle saw the accident when I was injured. They had me taken to a nearby inn, sent for a doctor, and ordered one of their slaves to stay with Alexander and Philippa. There were many other witnesses, but they turned away. I'm sure you already know the rest of the story," said Helena. Paulus didn't agree or disagree. He was simply stunned that he had never heard any of this from his father or Philippa. Recovering for a moment, he asked about Alexander. Philippa's mother said he was a little better. Paulus could see that he had slept throughout the conversation.

"Philippa has helped care for Alexander at night for several days, and she has slept very little. With her work at your house and her work here, she is exhausted," said Helena. With tears running down her cheeks, she continued, "Sir, please forgive my rudeness in talking so much. Thank you again for the supplies and for helping Philippa."

Paulus prepared to leave but said he would check on her again tomorrow. He was hesitant about leaving the three of them, but he knew he must. "Farewell," said Paulus. "I will return tomorrow to see about your welfare."

Philippa regaining her strength for a moment said, "Sir, I'll try to be at work tomorrow if…"

Paulus cut off her words. "I forbid it! You and Alexander will rest until recovered. As I said, I will see how you are tomorrow." With these words, he hurried from the room, and his slaves followed.

As he walked home, Paulus was troubled by thoughts of the terrible poverty of Philippa and her family. He knew there were beggars in the streets and other people who seemed poorly clad near the shops and market stalls. However, he didn't know them, and he gave them little thought. But he knew Philippa. He mumbled to himself, "How can she be so cheerful and so concerned about making my home beautiful when she has nothing?" Her family obviously survived on what Philippa and Alexander earned in his household, and Paulus knew from studying his father's accounts that they were receiving the same amount they had been paid for years. He also knew that food and oil prices had greatly increased during the time of Emperor Nero. "No wonder Philippa's *palla* was threadbare," thought Paulus. He was greatly disturbed by what he had seen.

As he entered the atrium of his house, he saw the beautifully arranged plants on the tables and the ornate couches throughout the room and shivered with a new awareness. He was sure that with Alexander sick and Philippa the only one working, there was little money for food. Philippa had probably been sitting at night with her brother to give her mother some rest. "Lack of sleep and little food! It was no wonder she was sick," thought Paulus.

"All I was concerned about was her skill in running my household, and she said that I was a kind man. Ha! That's a joke. What would she think if she knew my only thoughts of her were having her in my bed!"

Paulus spent the rest of the evening finishing the work he had been doing on the business accounts, but he had trouble concentrating. His mind kept returning to that sad little apartment where Philippa and her family were trying to survive.

Finally Paulus decided to retire for the night, but his sleep was fretful and disturbed.

Chapter 19

Livia was very nervous as she sat on the steps at Tullus' house. Today she was to marry Tatius. She was happy, but facing old fears as well. It wasn't that she did not love him or that she doubted his love and commitment to her, but she was still unsure about her role in this new life. She desperately wanted to not only be a good wife to Tatius but also a useful child of Jesus.

The past couple of weeks had been wonderful, but in many ways overwhelming. After arriving at Tullus' house, Tatius and Livia had been surrounded by loving attention, comfortable rooms, and delicious food. She had learned the routine of the house and had tried to be helpful in any way possible. But that was part of the problem. Tullus' household was very organized and self-sufficient. Neither Tatius nor Livia could really contribute anything very useful. Livia had never felt unneeded before. For the last few years, she had supervised the running of her father's house and had had her garden to enjoy. Now, she mostly remained quiet and listened as Tatius talked with Tullus about the "church" at Arelate. Of course, there had been some times when she felt happy and at peace, especially when she was with Tullus' younger daughter Julia. Livia and Julia had liked each other immediately. Only recently married and with no children, Julia had a carefree spirit that always made Livia laugh. Sometimes, Livia, Julia, and the servant Flora would laugh and giggle like young children when they were together. It felt so good to be able to talk freely with people again. Julia never questioned her about her family and simply accepted her as a friend of her father.

The highlight of the last week had been Livia's baptism. Tullus had invited several people for the ceremony: Tullus' son Servius from Arelate, his older daughter Claudia and her husband and children, Tullus' servants who were believers, a few other "Jesus followers," and the old rabbi who was to perform the ritual. Livia could hardly think about it now without crying. Many different people spoke briefly, including Tullus' two daughters! The group had sung psalms of praise and then prayed for her. The old rabbi told of Jesus' baptism by John the Baptist at the beginning of his ministry. Finally the moment arrived, and Tullus baptized her in the river, while the rabbi prayed for her salvation. Before the baptism, he had asked her if she believed that Jesus was the Son of God, who was crucified, and then rose from the grave. She had said "yes". Livia was overcome with a profound peace, and as the tears fell down her cheeks, she saw tears in Tatius' eyes as well.

After the baptism, Tullus had announced that there was to be a wedding in one week at his house. Tatius and Livia were to be married, and all were welcome to this joyful celebration.

Preparations began almost immediately, with Julia (who obviously had some of her father's organizing skills) taking charge. Since she had married recently, she knew exactly how to plan a wedding. Julia had told Livia that the "Jesus followers" or Christians, as some were now calling them, adopted parts of the Roman, Gallic, and Jewish customs in their wedding ceremonies.

"It will give me so much enjoyment to plan for your wedding," said Julia. "Don't worry about anything."

The day had finally arrived. Even though she knew it impossible, Livia wished her father and Paulus could be there. There was still a strong longing for her family. Julia suddenly appeared on the steps and said, "I'm almost as excited as I was on my wedding day. Come, we must get you ready." And Julia led Livia away.

The house was filled with the smells of late blooming flowers, many unknown to Livia. On the way to the spacious atrium where the ceremony was to take place, the perfume of the flowers began to have competition from the aromas in the kitchen. In the bedroom, Julia began helping Livia with her clothes for the wedding. The old rabbi was already there talking to Tatius. Livia didn't know if their conversation was about God or what Tatius must do to be a good husband!

With Flora's help, Julia divided Livia's long black hair into the traditional six tresses and then wound them around her head into an elaborate coiffure. Julia then helped Livia into a white tunic and then a saffron veil, *stola*, and *palla*. The yellow color made Livia's raven black hair look like glistening coils. While her clothes were according to the Roman tradition, the food and floral decorations were the beautiful products of Arelate. The only customary food served was the *spelt* cake (actually a kind of wafer) that was always part of a Roman wedding.

When they heard the singing of a psalm in the atrium, Julia told her, "It's time my dear, and you look beautiful." Livia doubted that, but she prayed that Tatius would find her so. She walked out with Julia as her matron of honor by her side.

Tatius and Livia joined hands and then sat on the couch. The contract was read, and the witnesses put their seal on it. Livia then said the traditional phrase, "*Ubi tu Gaius, ego Gaia*" (where you are Gaius, I am Gaia). This concluded the Roman part of the ceremony. The old rabbi then sat across from them and told them, "God created male and female, but with this marriage, you are now to become one in the eyes of God." Reading from an ancient scroll, he recited psalms of joy and praise to God. Taking their hands, he then prayed, "Oh dear Lord, watch over these dear children. Help them as trials and testing come, and lead them to be witnesses to your salvation. In the name of the Father, Son, and the Holy Ghost, I hereby proclaim you married in the eyes of God and man." Tullus then offered a moving prayer for them, and to Livia's surprise, Tatius looked at her and said,

"You gave up everything for me and our Savior Jesus Christ. I pray that I can always be worthy of such trust, but even if I falter, my Lord Jesus will always be your perfect redeemer and companion." He then kissed her hand. Livia smiled at him and thought to herself, "No one has ever been as happy as I am at this moment."

Several of the women and children began singing a traditional wedding song. After the singing finished, Tullus said all were welcome to eat and celebrate the marriage of Tatius and Livia. It was a great time of feasting and joy. However, on the official contract, Livia and Tatius had listed their true names, and there was a possibility of danger if Livia's family were to see the records kept in Arelate. Livia thought about her *bulla* left in Rome, which seemed so long ago. In many ways the action of leaving it behind symbolized her ending of her old life. Now, she thought, "I am truly a new person — Livia the wife of Tatius and the child of Jesus Christ the Son of the God Jehovah!"

Chapter 20

Paulus got up feeling as if he had not gone to bed. The visit to Philippa's apartment had greatly bothered him, and he found himself again this morning thinking about her family's condition. He had promised to return there today, and he intended to keep his word. In truth, he both dreaded it and looked forward to it. He was slowly realizing that he was very attracted to Philippa. Of course, there could never be a serious relationship between them. After all, she was a Greek servant! He also knew that if she were a "Jesus follower" as he was convinced, she would never agree to become his mistress, and he had too great a sense of honor and fairness to force himself on her. So it was foolish of him to even think about her.

After eating a small amount, he summoned a couple of slaves and told them to gather more food and oil for a visit to Philippa's house. He knew that both Philippa and Alexander were greatly respected and liked by the slaves and other servants, and he could see that they were pleased by his show of kindness. Although the household was running much less smoothly during Philippa's absence, his concern for her family was genuine and not selfish in nature. As he (with his slaves following) walked to her *insula*, he thought about his life and its tedious quality. Shockingly, he found he not only missed his father and Livia, but he also missed hearing the many plans and discussions at the Jew's house. The fervor and joy that Paul and his friends displayed in their talks about their "Risen God" were almost contagious. Of course, he knew they were deluded, but their enthusiasm was a far cry from the tedium he felt working with his father's accounts.

As they climbed the stairs to Philippa's apartment, Paulus was struck again by the decaying smells and the deplorable appearance of the building. Arriving at the door of her home, Paulus hesitated a moment and then knocked. To his surprise, Philippa opened the door. While still somewhat pale, she looked much improved from the previous day.

"Sir, please come in," said Philippa. "We were just eating some of the food you so generously brought us yesterday."

Paulus saw Philippa's mother again seated on the floor beside Alexander. However, today Alexander seemed much better. "Thank you for the food, sir," said Alexander weakly. "I'm sorry I haven't been able to work." With this statement, he seemed to tire, and he closed his eyes.

Helena, Philippa's mother, also thanked Paulus again for the supplies brought yesterday, and then seeing the slaves with their arms full of more food and oil, she began to cry. Paulus became even more uncomfortable.

"Mother is very tired," explained Philippa, "as am I. But I believe our prayers are being answered, and Alexander is going to recover."

Helena suddenly exclaimed, "You know we have not always been like this. We were once proud Athenians with possessions and family. At one time, my husband…"

"Oh, Mother, my master is much too busy to listen to our story. Besides, you told him last time about your accident. Don't you remember?" asked Philippa.

Not liking the decision of his hearing their story or not being made by Philippa, Paulus said, that he would indeed like her to continue.

Helena began again, "At one time, my husband was a brilliant scholar, with special achievement in philosophy. His father was a lawyer and wanted him to be one as well, but my husband had dreams of opening his own school in Athens. I was a disappointment to my husband's family as well. My parents had died, and I was raised by my elderly grandparents, and there was no dowry. When we married, he was a successful tutor for several young men who were studying in Athens. While reluctant to accept me, my husband's large family gradually began to soften to both the marriage and my husband's work. When Alexander and Philippa were born, everyone was charmed by them. You did know that they were twins, did you not?"

"No. I did not," answered Paulus with some embarrassment. They had worked for his family for years, and he knew little about them. "But they look nothing alike," said Paulus. Actually that was not completely true. It was simply that Philippa was so tiny, and Alexander was as tall as Paulus. But their coloring and features were similar.

"Yes, they were the darlings of our friends and family," said Helena. (Paulus stole a glance at Philippa and saw her obvious embarrassment). "We were doing quite well with our little family. We had a large apartment with a room where my husband gave lessons to his students. However, my husband's dream was still to have his own school. With a family to support and no help from his family, this dream seemed unattainable. One day, by chance, he met a wealthy Roman businessman who was most impressed with my husband. He visited the classes at our apartment and then made my husband an offer. 'Come to Rome and tutor my two sons and my two nephews. I will pay for you and your family's transport to Rome. I will also set you up in an apartment and pay you double what you earn in Athens.'"

"My husband was tempted but declined by saying that he wanted to work for his dream of running a school. A couple of days later the same man approached him and offered to help him establish a school in Rome under his sponsorship, after he had worked as a tutor for his family for a year. My husband Stolos was very confident in his teaching, and after some serious consideration, he agreed. His family was furious. Not only was he to be a tutor to 'Romans', but he would be taking their adorable grandchildren away as well. Of course, the children, at six years old, were delighted to be going on an adventure."

"Mother," interrupted Philippa, "my master is a busy man. You must shorten the story."

"I'm sorry," said Helena. "It's just that I relive it so often in my mind that I tend to tell too much. Anyway, after we came to Rome, the gentleman did as he promised. We had a nice apartment, and Stolos was a success at his teaching with new clients asking for his services. Unfortunately, instead of saving money, my husband furnished our place with many unneeded luxuries. Oh, we were so happy. He worked for his clients, he taught our children, and I ran the house. The Roman gentleman began making plans to help him establish a school. They were together examining an older building for a possible school site, when the roof caved in, killing both the Roman gentleman and my husband instantly. I had two small children, a lavishly furnished apartment, and no income. I wrote to Stolos' family, and they sent us a little money, but since they disapproved of me and the move to Rome, they didn't help for long. I began selling our furnishings to support us. I was at the market selling some of our possessions on the day the *lectica* hit me. Of course, you know the rest of the story."

Paulus thought to himself, "I don't know half the story. I can't imagine what it must have been like — a foreigner, crippled, no income, and with two small children. What recourse could she have other than putting the children into domestic service? At least my father had treated them kindly."

"Oh sir, we have been very blessed. We are happy, we have a kind employer, and my brother is getting well. My mother has just been through a very difficult time with Alexander' sickness," Philippa said by way of apology for her mother's long speech.

"I understand," said Paulus. "I am sending someone with more supplies tomorrow. I forbid your returning to work for two more days. I must leave now, and I hope your family is well soon."

The Light Will Come

"I'm sure I'll be well by then sir, and thank you again," said Philippa.

Alexander stirred and said weakly, "Thank you."

Helena, somewhat subdued by shame at her long tale about their life said, "I'm sorry for talking so much sir. Please forgive my rudeness." At this she stood clumsily from the floor and bowed to him slightly.

Again overcome by the sadness of their plight and the contrast to Philippa's cheerful outlook, Paulus said his farewells and hurried, with his slaves following him, back to his house.

Chapter 21

The following morning as Paulus was finishing his breakfast, he was surprised by a visit from his Uncle Cornelius. They greeted each other fondly. Cornelius sat on a couch in the atrium and drank a small glass of wine, while Paulus finished eating.

"I wanted to check with you before I met with your commander. Since you have so many of your father's business affairs to handle, I assume you want to be discharged from the military. I can use my influence to expedite the discharge."

Paulus was upset. He had wanted to be a soldier all his life, following in his father's footsteps.

"I, I hadn't really thought about leaving," stammered Paulus.

"But son, I don't think you have much choice. Your father ran many businesses, and now there is no one to run them. How would you manage your households? I'm too busy with my duties as a Senator to be of much help. There can be no foreign campaigns for you. Too many people would suffer. You must remain in Rome."

"Could I not remain a soldier and stay in Rome?" asked Paulus.

"And do what? Would you want to keep guarding the Jew? I thought you were unhappy with that assignment. Perhaps there could be other prisoners you could guard, but is that not demeaning to you as a member of the Livian family?" asked Cornelius.

"I wouldn't mind returning as a guard for Paul. The other guard

The Light Will Come

Silvius is quite congenial, and the conversations at the Jew's house are often interesting," said Paulus, being careful to not appear too interested in the 'Jesus followers'.

To Paulus' surprise, Cornelius seemed to guess Paulus' feelings and said, "I understand. I find this sect fascinating as well. But I'm afraid the Emperor does not share my interest. He sees them as a threat, and I suspect he will not tolerate them much longer."

"I'm certainly not a 'Jesus follower', but I do want to continue in my guard duties for now. I'm not ready to leave the military yet. Would you please arrange for my return to my guard duty?"

"If you are sure, I'll tell your commander today, and you can report at any time," said Cornelius.

"I may go there this afternoon. It will relieve the boredom of all these business accounts. Farewell Uncle, and thank you again."

As Cornelius was leaving, Paulus realized he was looking forward to returning to Paul's house. "What a difference in today compared to that first day as his guard!" thought Paulus with a smile.

Chapter 22

*L*ivia sat on the grass and listened as Tatius talked to the small group of believers. He was telling them about Paul's conversion on the road to Damascus. As Livia had already heard this story from Tatius, her mind drifted to the last few weeks.

It was hard not to smile as she thought about her wedding. With Julia directing everything, all went as planned. Tatius told her later that she was the most beautiful bride in the world. While she knew that to be untrue, she was still very flattered. With the ceremony and the feast which followed it finished, the guests finally left. After their departure, Tullus said that he had a little surprise for them. Livia could not imagine what it could be. Tullus then told them that he and some of the servants had been working for the last couple of days cleaning and repairing a small house where his son, who now lived in Rome, had once lived. Tullus said that he had prayed about it, and tomorrow he wanted Livia and Tatius to have the house and the surrounding land. The grounds were in disarray and the house had not been used after his farm manager, who had lived there for a while, moved to his own home. According to Tullus, all his children were established in their own places, and he wanted this to be a home given to Jesus and his messengers — Tatius and Livia.

Tatius and Livia were stunned. Livia cried until Tullus finally said, "I refuse to have you shed tears on your wedding day. Rejoice!

The Light Will Come

God has joined you in marriage, and he has now planned a home for you. Dear children, I know that you are going to be a blessing to me and my family, and I thank God for you. Go now to the room prepared by my servants as your wedding chamber. We've not followed the Roman tradition of anointing the door with oil or hanging wool on the doorposts, but Flora and her friends have made the room comfortable and welcoming. I pray that your lives together will be long and happy. God's peace and joy be with you."

With this, he directed the servants to show them to the room. When Tatius and Livia entered, they were delighted. There were flowers on the table and over the door. Candles were burning in the corners of the room, giving a soft glow to the interior, and silk curtains were hung over a dressing area. No one could have asked for a lovelier place for a wedding night!

In the days that followed, Tatius and Livia were overcome with so many emotions. Their love continued to grow, and the feelings of gratitude toward Tullus were without measure. Livia smiled to herself as she thought about the fact that now they were no longer "brother" and "sister". Most of their days were spent working at their new home. Livia learned quickly how to clear weeds and clean floors. Although the house had been hurriedly cleaned, there was still much to do. The furnishings were sparse; however, compared to the tent on the boat, everything seemed luxurious! The house was on a hill with a lovely view of Tullus' vineyards in the distance. To Livia's delight, there was a small stream at the foot of the hill and land at the back of the house where she could plant flowers and vegetables. Tullus' servant Flora had promised that she could easily teach Livia how to cook, and Livia was eager to learn.

Livia stirred from her musings as she heard Tatius say that they would now partake in the ceremony of bread and wine as instructed by Jesus. Livia knew of this ritual, but this was her first experience being part of it. The old rabbi stood with Tatius, as Tatius quoted the words of Jesus that were so familiar to all believers, "Jesus took bread, gave thanks and broke it, and gave it to his disciples saying,

'Take, and eat; this is my body.'"(Matthew 26:26) The rabbi then took a loaf of bread and broke a piece from it and ate it. He then passed it to Tatius who did the same. The loaf was then passed to the rest of the group. There was complete silence. When it was Livia's turn, her hands shook as she placed the bread in her mouth. Tatius then said, "Then He took the cup, gave thanks and offered it to them, saying, 'Drink from it, all of you. This is my blood of the covenant, which is poured out for many for the forgiveness of sins.'"(Matthew 26:28) When the cup of wine was passed for all to drink, Livia felt tears running down her face. As she drank, that peaceful joy that she had sought for so long filled her whole being. She looked at Tatius, whose face was shining with a kind of joyful determination.

New thoughts then began swirling in Livia's mind.

"I can learn to be a useful wife."

"I can learn from Flora the language of the native people here in *Gallia Narbonensis*, and then I can tell other women about Jesus Christ!"

"Tatius already has a job as a tutor for several boys. Why can't I tutor some of their sisters?"

"I can go with Julia to town and buy furniture with the sale of my pearl necklace."

"I can grow lots of vegetables and give them to the poor."

"I can…" Livia stopped herself suddenly and prayed, "Oh Jesus, forgive me. I can do nothing. Please use me as your humble servant. Oh, and Amen."

Tatius closed his remarks with the words that Jesus said to his disciples after his resurrection, "Therefore go and make disciples of all nations, baptizing them in the name of the Father and of the Son and of the Holy Spirit, and teaching them to obey everything I have commanded you."(Matthew 28:19-20) Livia's heart soared with optimism and joy. She thought to herself, "God surely has led us to this place, and I know many people will become believers here. If only my family in Rome could just hear Tatius' words, maybe they would believe as well." It then occurred to her that Paulus had spent endless hours at the great Apostle Paul's house, and it had had no effect on him. She then looked up and saw Tatius walking toward her with his hands outstretched, reaching for her. With the sun on her back, the smell of springtime blossoms in the air, the sounds of a psalm being sung, and Tatius beside her, Livia felt that calming peace fill her once more.

Chapter 23

As Paulus walked toward Paul's house, he remembered how angry and frustrated he had been the first day he made this journey. In just a few months, his whole life had completely changed. In those days, his chief worry had been whether he would get his favorite exercise instructor at the baths or how to get time to see a race during his training regimen. Now, his days were filled with decision-making about his father's businesses as well as the responsibility of running the house in Rome and sending instructions to his overseer in Ostia. He had little time for races, games, or any amusements. He was very lonely, but with his time so occupied, he had not even thought about seeking pleasure with the temple prostitutes. At times, he felt that Philippa had somehow bewitched him, but in truth, he knew her to be an innocent in a rough world. Strangely enough, after the visit to her apartment, he found himself feeling protective of her and her family.

"Well," he thought, "Certainly I can forget my personal struggles when I begin my guard duty."

When Paulus arrived at Paul's house, he saw that there were several other men there already. While visitors were not unusual, such a large group so early in the afternoon seemed a bit odd. Entering the atrium, Paulus spoke to Silvius in greeting. In response, Silvius said, "Good afternoon Paulus. I am very sorry about the death of your father. He must have been a great man. I was at the Forum for his funeral and found the tribute given by your Uncle Cornelius very impressive."

"Thank you Silvius," replied Paulus as he took his familiar position opposite Silvius. "I miss him more than I can express. I don't suppose you've heard anything from Tatius?"

"Not a word. None of my contacts have heard anything about his whereabouts or that of Livia. I'm sorry Paulus." Looking at Silvius, Paulus saw the pain in Silvius' face. "He must be suffering deeply for the loss of Tatius," thought Paulus.

Paulus didn't see Paul for a moment. There was a group surrounding him. "Is there something happening today? There seems to be a lot of enthusiastic conversation taking place."

"I think I'll let Paul explain it to you, if you don't mind. He will notice that you are here in a little while," said Silvius.

A few minutes passed, and then suddenly Paul saw Paulus. Dragging his chains, Paul came forward and spoke to Paulus.

"You have my sympathy, Young Paulus, for the death of your father. By all accounts, he was a fair and honorable man."

"Thank you," replied Paulus.

As if a sudden revelation had come to him, Paul then said, "But I believe you will surpass your father in greatness one day." He then turned and walked back to the other men.

Paulus was stunned. His father had been a fearless soldier and then a wealthy businessman. He was respected and admired by everyone. He, Paulus, would probably never be able to fight for Rome or have half the power and influence of his father. "The Jew is certainly wrong about me!" thought Paulus.

Paulus quickly became interested in the conversation of Paul and the other men. There was apparently some differences in opinion about a course of action for the people in Philippi. Some felt Paul should write a letter immediately to help settle some matters, but others thought that the letter could wait considering the news they had just had.

Paulus was very curious as to this news. Whatever it was, the whole group was very excited and in good spirits.

Paul calmed the men for a moment and said, I'll write a letter to the Philippians later. Perhaps I will even be able to see them in person if I am set free. But I must go to Spain first if that happens.

Unable to bear not knowing what was happening, Paulus walked over to Silvius and asked, "Is Paul being released?"

"There have been rumors that he is to be freed without a trial. Talk in the palace is that Emperor Nero has become less worried about a rebellion, but I know nothing for sure," said Silvius.

Their conversation was cut short as the group began singing a psalm of praise. After the song, Paul began to address the group. "I am so happy that I don't know how to thank God enough."

There were many false rumors floating from the palace daily, and Paulus was surprised that a rumor would cause such excitement. Then he heard Paul say, "Even if I'm never free, it doesn't matter. What is important is that Peter is coming to Rome." As tears ran down Paul's face, he said, "My courage is restored and my faith is made stronger in the surety that God has a plan for us all. It's true that Peter and I had our differences in Jerusalem, but he is the Apostle who was with Jesus throughout his ministry and death. He saw the empty tomb, he saw the Risen Lord, and he will be here in Rome. May God's name be praised!"

"Who is this Peter?" asked Paulus of Silvius.

"He is one of the original twelve disciples, called by Jesus himself. He traveled with Jesus, he heard him teach and preach, he saw him die, and he saw him after he rose from the grave. He is one of the greatest apostles if not the greatest. Any day now, he is coming to Rome!"

Paulus could hear the excitement in Silvius' voice. Paul continued, "We Jews were one of the most exclusive peoples on earth. We were the Chosen Ones. Now, we "Christians" know that God has his arms open to everyone!"

As the hours passed, the conversation flowed. There was

continuing talk about the problems at Philippi and whether a letter was needed, but most of the discussion was about Peter's coming to Rome. No one knew exactly when this would happen, but it would be soon.

As the time of Paulus' guard duty was drawing to a close, Paulus heard the prayers of Paul and his friends. When he started to leave, He heard Paul say, "With Peter here, I have hope that all of Rome will become believers." Paul continued, I **know** that someday "at the name of Jesus every knee should bow, in heaven and on earth and under the earth, and every tongue confess that Jesus Christ is Lord…"(Philippians 2:10-11)

As Paulus and Silvius left, Paul and his friends were so involved in conversation that they didn't appear to notice their departure. After walking a short distance in silence, Paulus and Silvius said their farewells, and Paulus continued his walk toward home. Every time his boots hit the pavement, he heard these words echoing in his mind, "At the name of Jesus every knee should bow, at the name of Jesus every knee should bow, at the name of Jesus every knee should bow." He stopped and then started walking again. With each clanking of his boots on the pavement, he began hearing again and again the refrain, "And every tongue confess that Jesus Christ is Lord." (Philippians 2:11)

"What is wrong with me?" wondered Paulus. "I must sleep and give my mind some rest!" Still he kept hearing the words, "Jesus Christ is Lord!"

Part Three

Chapter 1

*P*aulus leaned against the railing on the dock at Ostia and watched the sea. It had rained earlier, but the skies were now clear with a pleasant mist blowing from the water. He looked out at the azure water with its gentle waves and thought how the waves with their constant folding had a soothing effect on him. Sometimes, Paulus felt as if his life prior to the past two years had been similar to those waves. It had flowed with an orderly movement, and his future seemed settled. Oh, but that was definitely not the case. The calm waters of that time had been too soon roiled with storms which he could never have imagined. At times, he wished he could turn back time to those carefree days when he had few worries and little responsibility. But that time had forever changed. Like the lovely blue waters rolling toward the distant horizon, his life was plunging into the unknown.

As Paulus was thinking about his past, a small boy wandered over to him and asked, "Are you a sailor?"

Somewhat taken aback by the boldness of the boy, he answered a bit sharply, "No, of course not!"

"Well, I've seen you here before, and I just thought you might be waiting for your ship or something. I think I'm going to be a sailor someday. I want to see what is on the other side of all that water! It might be better over there," said the boy.

Paulus finally turned and looked carefully at the little boy. He appeared to be no more than six or seven years old. "Are you here all alone?" asked Paulus.

"Yes sir," replied the boy respectfully. Apparently the child had recognized by Paulus' speech that he was an educated man and "sir" seemed appropriate.

"You shouldn't be here alone. Won't your parents be worried?" asked Paulus.

"Oh, I don't have any parents anymore. They died in the fire. My two sisters died too. I was outside of our *insula* playing, and the fire almost got me. See my leg." At this he pulled up his tunic and showed Paulus his scars. Pausing for a moment, he then said, "You know, sir, sometimes I wish the fire had gotten me too."

Paulus was so intrigued by the little boy that he left his own reveries and took more notice of the child. He was dirty and disheveled, but there was remarkable alertness in his black eyes. There was no doubt about his intelligence as well as his charm.

Paulus asked, "Where do you live? Do you have family here?"

Suddenly becoming shy, he lowered his head and said, "I guess I do, sir."

Intrigued by his response, Paulus asked, "Do you live with family in Ostia?"

"Well, I stay with a man who says he is my cousin, but I'd never seen him before the fire. He found me in a camp at the Campus Martius and brought me here."

Looking around to make sure no one else was around, the little boy said, "I don't think my cousin and his wife like me very much. When they don't think I'm listening, they talk about how they hate having another mouth to feed." Speaking very softly, he said, "I think the Emperor gave them money to take me."

"Why do you say that?" asked Paulus.

"Oh, I must go. If I'm late, I won't have anything to eat. They say it is bad enough that they have to feed me, and I don't want them angry at me again. They hit really hard! Farewell sir."

As he was leaving, Paulus shouted, "Son, what is your name?"

"I'm called Antonius sir. Maybe I'll see you again," said the little boy as he began running up the hill toward the city of Ostia.

"What a clever and charming little boy!" thought Paulus. "It's a shame he had to leave. I wish I knew more of his story."

Paulus sat down on one of the benches near a stall selling tents. As he watched the tentmaker busy at his sewing, his mind was suddenly pulled back to the only tentmaker he had ever known, the Jewish prisoner Paul. He found himself thinking about him more and more.

When Paulus returned to his assigned duty after his father's death, he began listening to the words of Paul and his friends with a lot more curiosity. As foolish as they sounded, their words were so filled with fervor that their enthusiasm was almost contagious. Many of those days were filled with excitement for the Jews at the impending arrival in Rome of Peter, one of the original followers of the man named Jesus Christ. Paul and his scribe were very busy trying to finish a letter to believers at Philippi. While Paulus had casually listened to the other letters that Paul had written to the Colossians and Ephesians, he found himself much more interested in this letter. Philippi was a city Paulus had heard about from his childhood. It was at Philippi that Marc Antony had defeated Cassius and Brutus in one of Rome's greatest battles. Also, his father Atticus had spent several months there as a young soldier and had told Paulus that it was a place he hoped Paulus could see one day. According to Atticus, Philippi was a wonderful city combining the eastern and western worlds and retaining the best of both cultures. Paul apparently had also loved his stay at Philippi, and the bond between the Philippians and Paul had remained strong.

As he sat watching the tentmaker, Paulus still recalled parts of that letter. Paul had started the letter by telling the Philippians, "I thank God every time I remember you."(Philippians 1:3) Then he had continued, "Now I want you to know, brothers, that what has happened to me has really served to advance the gospel. As a result, it has become clear throughout the whole palace guard and to everyone else that I am in chains for Christ."(Philippians 1:12-13) Paulus remembered how shocked he had been to hear the palace guard discussed in a letter to the followers of this new sect of Jews.

Looking at the waves on the water, Paulus couldn't keep from wishing he could return and listen to the Jew more carefully. Those days now seemed so far away. The horrible things that had happened in Rome between that time and now made Paulus remember those days with nostalgia. As Paulus' mind returned to some of the events of the terrible months that had just passed, he recalled a phrase in the letter that Paul had pored over and reworded several times before he finally had his scribe write them on the papyrus. He said "Forgetting what is behind and straining toward what is ahead, I press on toward the goal to win the prize for which God has called me heavenward in Christ Jesus."(Philippians 3:13-14) Paulus wondered, "Did he have any idea how awful the future was to be?" While he was pondering this, the tentmaker approached Paulus and said, "I've seen you here for several days now sir. If you are planning to make a journey on one of these ships soon, I could make you a good deal on one of my fine tents."

"No, I'm staying here in Ostia. I just like to watch the fishing boats and the bigger ships as they come and go," replied Paulus. "Sometimes, I wish I were on one of those ships."

"Well, there is a merchant ship going to Arelate in a few days. It's a fine sailing vessel. I know the captain, and a good man he is."

"I'm afraid my responsibilities must keep me firmly in *Italia*, but if I ever need a tent, I'll remember you."

"Thank you sir," replied the tentmaker as he returned to his work. As Paulus got up to leave, he thought, "For some reason I feel drawn to Arelate. It is said to be a nice part of Gaul, but I know no one there."

Chapter 2

The next day Paulus spent the morning handling the paperwork of the businesses he still had. Many of his father's vast holdings had been obliterated by the fire, but there were contracts which still had to be signed. He also felt the responsibility of feeding and housing a large household of servants and slaves. After having a bite to eat, Paulus decided he would go to the baths, but on his way there he changed his mind. He felt the draw of the docks and water once again. Seating himself not far from where he had been yesterday, he again settled into watching the rolling tides. He was just beginning to feel some peace in his emotions when he heard,

"Sir, I see that you've come back again too."

Looking up, Paulus saw the little boy from the previous day. In truth, he was delighted to have him for a companion.

"Yes. I can relax on the docks. Nobody wants anything from me here," said Paulus.

"Me neither. And nobody yells at me and hits me here," said Antonius.

Paulus was again struck by the sad situation of the child. "Do they hit you a lot?" asked Paulus.

"Oh, just when I'm in their way. Did you lose your family in the fire too?"

"No son. None of my family died in the fire, but my home burned, and I lost some dear friends," replied Paulus.

"Was your home in one of the *insulae* that burned like mine was?"

"No, I lived in a house a short distance up the Esquiline Hills."

As he said these words, Paulus rehearsed in his mind the events leading up to that horrific day. He could still remember leaving Paul's house on that summer evening. Silvius and he were walking down the street, when they saw a fire in the distance.

"It looks as if our *vigili* have work to do tonight," said Silvius.

"I would hate to be fighting a fire on a hot night like this," said Paulus. "But they are very well-trained, and it will probably be extinguished quickly."

They then said farewell and went to their homes.

When Paulus arrived at his house, he could see the fire and smoke from the hill where his house was located, but he went to bed with no more thoughts of the fire.

The next morning when he woke, he found some of the servants talking about the fire. They said that it was serious enough to have destroyed parts of the business areas around the Forum as well as many of the shops at the Circus Maximus.

When Philippa and Alexander arrived at the house, Philippa approached Paulus and asked, "Sir, have you heard about the fire?"

"Yes. I am going to go now and check to see if my warehouses have had any damage. But the fire is far from here and neither your *insula* nor my house will be in danger."

"Farewell and be careful sir. I don't want you to get hurt," said Philippa as she walked away.

Paulus had then eaten a little breakfast and hurried on his way. As he walked, he replayed in his mind Philippa's comment about not wanting him to get hurt. In the past few weeks, he had developed a genuine affection for Philippa, her mother, and brother. What had started out as an act of merely paying an obligatory visit to Alexander had become a pleasurable diversion for Paulus. He had visited the family three or four times during Alexander's illness. In truth, he envied the closeness of their little family. As for Philippa, his attraction to her had become a serious distraction. Paulus smiled to himself as he thought about her concerned eyes when she had said farewell to him.

Arriving at the center of the business district, Paulus was shocked to see the ruins of what had once been much of the commercial area of Rome. People were wandering around looking for salvageable items. Many of the ruins were still smoldering and were much too hot to search, and the firemen were still on alert throughout the area. Paulus quickly saw that some of his warehouses were gone, but others were untouched by the fire. The wind had apparently carried the flames to certain buildings and left others intact. Knowing there was little he could do to assess the damage until everything had cooled, Paulus had sought out his Uncle Cornelius at the Forum. He found him at the portico talking with a couple of other senators. Paulus was surprised at how close the fire had gotten to the Forum. Seeing Paulus, Cornelius immediately stood and invited Paulus to join them. Paulus asked about the damage. Cornelius told him that the fire had been mostly in the poorer districts, but several people had died. "Fortunately," according to Cornelius, "the *vigili* have succeeded once again in saving the city!" While Paulus was remembering that first day, he felt a tug on his tunic. Turning, he saw the little boy who had been silent while Paulus thought about the beginning of the fires.

"Do you see the fire in your mind when you try to sleep sir?" asked Antonius.

"Sometimes. But mostly, I hear the screams," replied Paulus.

"Me too. Some nights I smell it too. If I hadn't disobeyed my mother, I might have saved her. Do you think she died because I disobeyed?" asked the boy in a quivering voice.

Suddenly touched by the sadness in the little boy, Paulus said, "Oh, I am sure that wasn't the cause of your family's death. Do you want to tell me what happened?" asked Paulus.

The child nodded and began his sad tale. "It was three or four days after the fires first began. I know because I heard my father and a neighbor talking." Interrupting his story, he said to Paulus, "I like to know what is happening. My cousin says that I am nosy. Anyway, I wanted to go play with two of my friends who lived in my *insula*. Even though she was worried about the fires, my mother said that I could go if I would stay just outside in the street. But it was such a nice day, and we wanted to have room for a big sword fight, so we ran to a little park nearby. We were having a great time when we heard yelling. Before we knew what was happening, people started running past us screaming, 'The fire is coming! The fire is coming!'"

Tears ran down Antonius' little face, and he stopped talking.

"I'm sure it was awful," said Paulus as he put his arm gently around the boy. "Would it make you feel better to tell me the rest of your story?"

"I don't know. I wasn't very brave, you know. I tried to run back to get to my family. I wanted to be a noble Roman and save them, but the crowd pushed me forward. I fell once and the fire overtook me, but a man picked me up, put out the fire on my tunic, and pulled me into the mass of people. They ran and I ran with them until we were near the river. If I had gone back, maybe I could have saved them."

"Do you know for sure that your family died in the fire?" asked Paulus.

Antonius nodded slowly. "My two friends were saved too. They took us, along with a lot of others, to a really big place called the Campus Martius. Have you ever been there?" asked the boy.

"Yes, I know it well. Go on with your story," said Paulus quietly.

"Well, one night, my friends and I slipped past the guards and returned to our *insula*. No one would answer our questions, so we decided to find things out for ourselves. There were so many people with no homes. I was hoping my family was somewhere looking for me. But when we got to our street, there was nothing but ashes. On the corner, near the park where we were playing, there were a few shops that were not burned. We went into one and asked if maybe some people had survived in our *insula*. The two men inside told us that no one had gotten out besides those living on the first floor."

Suddenly looking up at Paulus, Antonius said, "My father didn't make much money. He worked in a warehouse near the Circus Maximus. We lived on the eighth floor."

Paulus was afraid to ask which warehouse. He owned several in that area, and he didn't want to know if he had been the employer of this poor child's father.

It was remarkable that a child so young could have such an adult conversation. Paulus couldn't keep from wanting to know more.

"What did you do then?"

"Oh, we walked back to the Campus Martius. All three of us were too sad to even talk. There isn't any more to my story. We slept on the ground there, and they fed us. It would have been fun if my father and mother and sisters had been there too. One of my friend's aunts found him, and he went to live with her. He knew her well and really liked her. After a long time, my cousin brought me here. I'm not sure he is my cousin. How did he find me? He lives in Ostia."

"Well, maybe he went to Rome and searched for survivors in his family?"

"But I don't know him. I know they gave him money to take me. I found out at the camp that the Emperor gave money to people to take children home with them. I heard my cousin say to his wife that maybe they needed to go find another 'cousin' and then they laughed. They aren't very nice, you know. They don't live by the rules my parents followed."

"I'm sorry," said Paulus, again struck by the intelligence of the boy, as well as his sad plight.

"Oh, it's not too bad. I like watching the sea here at Ostia. I'd never seen it before I came here. If I watch the water, I feel much better."

"So do I," replied Paulus.

"I've told you everything. Do you have a fire story too?" asked Antonius.

"I do son. If you want to hear it, I'll be here tomorrow, and I'll tell you about it then. I must go for now. Stay safe Antonius." Paulus got up and walked toward the business district to check on some of his clients. As he walked, Paulus thought to himself, "What utter foolishness! I'm going to make a little boy my confidant! But what a remarkable child he is."

Chapter 3

While Paulus was at the docks, Philippa walked about the house at Ostia, checking to see if there was any more cleaning that needed to be done. The first few days after their arrival in Ostia, Philippa had been so stricken with grief that she had done little except sit quietly in the garden and pray. At times, she wanted to die, and at other times, she questioned God, "Why, Lord? Why am I left?" Often, her grief was so overpowering that she felt she could hardly breathe. At night, she had nightmares and would awaken in a terrible panic. But as time passed, Philippa became more aware of her surroundings. Seeing how poorly the house and grounds had been maintained, she asked Paulus if he would like her to organize the servants and slaves to begin a complete cleaning of the house. He had been too preoccupied with work and trying to house the members of his staff from Rome at Ostia to notice the neglect. The house was smaller than the Roman house, and there was a small household staff already living there. Now both households had to be combined. Philippa remembered what she said the day she had approached Paulus. He was working with some papyrus in the atrium. Philippa had asked, "Sir, would you like me to help with the household staff? I would be willing to do as I did in Rome, if it would please you."

"Are you well enough?"

"Oh, I still limp a little, but my foot is healing fine. I need something to do, sir. I think it would help to be busy. If you would permit it, we could do a thorough cleaning of the house and grounds. I would like to be of some use sir."

Paulus had replied that he would be delighted to have her oversee the staff. As he looked at her, he realized that part of her sparkling vitality seemed gone, and always tiny, she was now much too thin.

Giving him a faint smile, she had left. Since that day Philippa had thrown herself into the work. The house was now spotless. The gardens were tended, and even the grounds around the stables were well-kept. Due to the extra staff, Paulus had had rooms built onto the stables to accommodate the new people. He had given her permission to furnish them as she wished. Using furniture that had been stored in a shed nearby, she was able to make the rooms rather comfortable. In fact she had asked to move there, but Paulus adamantly refused. He said she didn't need to walk the extra distance with her bad foot.

As Philippa sat for a moment, thinking about the past few weeks, she looked at her foot, and thought to herself, "I don't know if this foot is a blessing or a curse, but it has certainly altered the course of events of my life forever."

Philippa closed her eyes for a few minutes and rehearsed yet again the horrible, strange night that had so changed her life.

Fires had been raging in different parts of the city for five or six days but had not touched the *insula* where she and her family lived. The wind had carried the flames in the opposite direction. Of course, Paulus' beautiful home where she and Alexander worked was unaffected. As the fires burned in the distance, Philippa had approached Paulus and asked permission to leave immediately if there appeared to be any danger of the fire spreading to the *insula* where they lived. (After all, with her mother's leg so damaged, she would have great difficulty leaving their apartment in case of fire.) Paulus readily agreed and said that both she and Alexander could leave if there was any sign of fire coming their way.

All had continued as normal for a couple of days more. Paulus had even gone to his guard duty with no problems. Then, there was a sudden shift of the wind. From the upper floor of Paulus' house, Philippa and one of the other servants saw smoke coming closer. Philippa started down the steps shouting that she could see the fire. Not watching her step in her haste, she had tumbled down the stairs. Paulus, Alexander, and many of the other servants came running. Though not seriously hurt, her foot was badly sprained. It began to swell almost immediately, and she could barely stand. Wincing with pain, she had said, "Alexander, we must go at once. The fires are coming this way!" Since the *insula* was just at the foot of the hill, their mother could be in great peril.

Alexander looked at Paulus for permission. Paulus said, "Hurry and go!"

Philippa had tried to follow him, but she could barely walk. "No, Philippa," said Alexander. "You will slow me down. Stay here. I'll get to Mother."

Alexander ran out the door. Philippa tried to hobble after him, but Paulus restrained her. "He is right. He can go much more quickly without you. I'm sure he'll get there in time. Come, sit down and rest your foot," said Paulus. She had obeyed, but she wept quietly as she sat on one of the benches.

After that, things had only grown worse. One of the slaves in the upstairs shouted that he could see the flames jumping from building to building at the foot of the hill. They watched in horror as it seemed as if all of Rome were burning. The smoke rising from below began to burn their eyes and make them cough. Paulus had his slaves fill huge pots with water from the *impluvium* to use if the fires got close. Reluctant to believe that his house with its marble walls and columns could be in danger, Paulus, as a precaution however, gathered the pages of his business accounts and money and put them with Livia's and his mother's jewelry in a small portable chest, which he kept nearby.

Some time passed, and the air began to be unbearable. The *vigili* could be seen fighting the fires on the streets below, and they could hear screams of terror. Finally sensing they were truly in peril, Paulus ordered all his slaves and servants to gather food and water supplies and follow him further up the Esquiline Hill. He had two of the strongest servants help Philippa. She didn't want to leave, knowing that the fires were in the direction of her *insula*, but Paulus finally told his servants to carry her. She was such a tiny thing that she was not a heavy load. They had formed a mournful procession and walked up the hill. Continuing until they were at the very top of the hill, the entire group then stopped in an area where there were no houses and few trees. The land had been cleared for houses, but none had yet been built. They sat on the ground and waited for the flames to follow them, but the wind changed again, and the air finally began to clear. After a few hours, Paulus decided he must return to his house. Taking four of his slaves with him, they began the trek back down the hill. Philippa had pleaded to go with them, but Paulus refused. Even she knew she could scarcely stand much less walk. Paulus left his portable chest with his valuables in her care and started toward the house. Philippa began openly praying to Jehovah for the safety of her family and the men. Most of the servants and slaves were startled at this strange praying, but a few bowed their heads with her.

As she waited, Philippa would not let herself think about what might have happened to her mother and Alexander. She just continued praying. After a time, a kind of peace settled over her, and surprisingly, she fell asleep. When she woke, she was shocked to realize it was nearing nightfall. Paulus had returned and was seated on the ground not far from her, talking to a group of the servants. Forgetting her ankle, Philippa had jumped up and then quickly tumbled to the ground. Her foot was even more painful than earlier.

From her prone position, she cried, "Oh sir, what do you know about the fire? Are my mother and brother safe? Has your house burned? Could I not go see if my *insula* burned? Do you..?" Paulus walked over to her, thinking she sounded like Livia with her many questions.

"Philippa, I don't think there is any good news. My house is in ruins. Of course, the columns, pools, and marble floors are still there, but all the furniture, tapestries, clothing, etc. are gone. It's just a black hull. I couldn't get down the street to where your apartment is located, but one of the *vigili* said the whole complex had burned. When the fires have cooled a bit, I'll go see if I can learn what happened to them. But for tonight, we must rest and wait."

Philippa had cried and prayed most of the night. She had had heaviness in her heart that seemed to tear out her insides. When she finally drifted off to sleep, Paulus was watching her. (What Philippa did not know was that Paulus ached to go to her and hold her and comfort her. He too feared the worse, especially with her mother's lameness, and he found himself grieving for the tiny family he had enjoyed so much.)

Philippa remembered the rest of that time as if she were in a dream. Paulus found out that everyone on the top floors of Philippa's *insula* had perished.

After a couple of days, they trekked to the ruins of Paulus' house, and members of Paulus' household collected what few things were salvageable from the house. They didn't delay long at the ruins but continued their long walk to the estate of Paulus' Uncle Cornelius. It had been spared by the fire, and he had opened his house and gardens to Paulus and his huge staff. Philippa's foot was a problem, and they had slowed their procession for her. It had been a horrible march. The stench of burned flesh was overpowering. There were still smoldering fires everywhere, and bodies were piled along the streets. Philippa begged to go by her old *insula*, and Paulus wouldn't argue with her. So the entire group walked by the pile of rubble that had once been her home. When she saw it, she somehow sensed that her family had left her and were now with God.

After a short stay with Cornelius, they had come to Ostia. Paulus went back to Rome a few times to check on his business affairs, and, unknown to Philippa or anyone else, he had also checked on the Jew Paul. The house where Paul was kept was spared by the fire, and Silvius' family and apartment had escaped the fire as well. Silvius told Paulus that he had informed their superiors that he could do the guard duty without Paulus, and with such a disaster before them, no one cared very much about the Jew.

Philippa had been miserable those first few weeks. She longed for her mother and Alexander. With her foot and ankle so bad, she had been unable to work, so she just sat and grieved. Paulus had been very considerate, but she felt completely alone. If not for the comfort of Jesus as she prayed, Philippa was sure she would have gone mad. "How do people bear losing their family and friends if they have no hope of seeing them again in heaven?" she wondered.

Now as she sat on a bench in the garden, Philippa realized that time had softened the grief to some extent. She could enjoy the sunshine and flowers as she had with Livia so long ago. She liked the countryside, where the house was located, and she found a new love — horses. She found her way to the stables quite often. She knew it was silly, but she talked to them as she petted them, and they responded with complete devotion to her. She even dreamed of riding one of them someday. As she sat watching the butterflies flitting form one flower to another, Philippa thanked God for his grace and comfort and asked Him for guidance and strength in the days ahead.

Chapter 4

*A*s Paulus returned to his house that evening, he thought about the little boy he had talked to that morning. He had talked with several traders and merchants trying to revise some of the business deals he had made before the fire, but after each discussion his mind returned to little Antonius. He could sympathize with the boy and his loneliness. With his father and mother dead and Livia lost to him, he felt as if he too had no family. Sure, he had other sisters, but he had never been close to them.

Walking up the steps to the house, he saw Philippa arranging flowers on a table in the atrium. He stopped and watched her for a moment. He still remembered her response of long ago about wanting to add beauty to the world. She, like little Antonius, had lost all her family, yet she was smiling and singing as she placed the different flowers in a pattern she liked.

"I see you are walking much better. It's good to see you enjoying yourself, Philippa," said Paulus.

Blushing at his hearing her sing, she hurriedly said, "I'm better. I see such beauty in these flowers that for a moment I felt at peace. Sir, I've wanted to ask you some questions for days now. Would you mind if I asked them today?"

Paulus, though tired from a very busy day, could not refuse Philippa. "Of course. You may ask me questions at any time. What are they?"

"Well, the servants have heard rumors that our Emperor has been having 'Christ followers' killed. Is this true?"

Even though they had never talked about it, Paulus knew Philippa was a Christian. He had heard her prayers, and also he had seen Alexander at Paul's house.

"Yes, there have been some executions. But I don't think they will send anyone to find 'Christ followers' in my house. They would be safe here," said Paulus.

"Oh, but I'm worrying about my friends in Rome who are Christians. If you wouldn't mind, sir, tell me what has been happening in Rome."

"Come, sit down, and we'll talk," said Paulus. It was so nice to have someone with whom he could share things. Except for his Uncle Cornelius, he had really not talked much with anyone since Livia's leaving and his father's death. So he began telling her about the news from Rome.

"Philippa, our Emperor blames the fires on 'Christ followers,'" said Paulus.

"Why would he think that? You don't believe that, do you?" asked Philippa with surprise.

"No. I've been around many of these Christians while on duty guarding the Jew Paul. They seem to be a very peaceful group, but many bad rumors are spreading rapidly about them."

"What kind of rumors?" asked Philippa with great emotion.

"Well, some believe that they eat children!"

Horrified, Philippa exclaimed, "That is ridiculous! Why would they think something as disgusting as that?"

"I suppose it's because of the 'bread and wine ceremony'. I've seen the ritual several times, and at first, I was shocked by the words. But I finally realized that it was a remembrance ceremony and not a cannibalistic rite. Still, there are people who blame the Christians for the fire and also for any missing children. They fear the children could have been sacrificed for the ceremony."

Philippa was in shock. Never had she realized the serious consequences for her friends who were openly "Christ followers".

"But surely they will be protected in Rome just as the Jews are."

"But Philippa, they are not just Jews. Are you a Jew?"

"No sir," said Philippa meekly. "I'm Greek."

"Yet, you are a 'Christ follower' as are many others. I think our Emperor is concerned about any group who will not bow down to him as a god, and perhaps, he feels that their rejection of our gods will cause others to turn away from our Roman ways. Anyway, I hear there have been executions."

"Sir, do you know anything about your prisoner Paul? Is he safe?" asked Philippa.

"On my last visit to Rome, I went by his house for a brief visit to see about Silvius and his family. Everyone was well, including Paul. However, Paul was in deep sorrow, and there were people constantly coming and going. I didn't speak to him. He had received some news about a man named Peter being executed and …"

"What? Peter is dead! It can't be true, sir. He was the great disciple." At this news, Philippa was so overcome with grief that she began sobbing. "Please tell me what happened," begged Philippa.

Surprised at her emotional outburst, Paulus at first refused but then said, "I know very little, but I don't think you need to become so upset. I'm sure this Peter could not be that important."

"Oh sir, he walked and talked with Him! He…" Suddenly overcome by emotion, Philippa stopped.

"Walked with whom?" asked Paulus.

"With my Lord sir. When He lived here, Peter ate with Him. He touched Him. He heard him speak and teach. He saw Him on the cross. He saw Him after He rose from the dead. Peter was to begin everything. What will become of us now sir?"

Paulus heard her say "us" and it stabbed him in the heart to realize the complete devotion she had for these people. It also made him know that she, too, could be taken and executed at any time. Paulus reached out and patted her gently. "Dear Philippa, I'm sure your God has plans for your safety. As for Paul, he is a Roman citizen and he is very much alive. All will be fine."

Philippa got up and began to walk away. "What on earth am I saying?" thought Paulus. "I doubt that everything will be fine." As for Paul, Silvius had told Paulus that things were getting worse, and that Paul was to be put on trial soon. "Oh well, it was an innocent lie. Maybe it will ease her pain."

Chapter 5

The next day, Paulus came to a spur of the moment decision. He had been cooped up in Ostia for days, so he decided to ride one of his many horses into Rome and perhaps spend the night with friends at the Campus Martius. He thought to himself, "It will be good to get away from my business responsibilities and my household at Ostia." Somewhat disquieted over his conversation with Philippa the previous day, he knew a brisk ride would be good for him. So on impulse, he made his way to the stables. Just outside one of the stalls, he heard a woman speaking. Since there were no women who worked in the stables, he hurried to see who was there so early in the morning. As he approached the stall, he realized it was Philippa.

"What could she be doing here?" thought Paulus. He quietly entered the stall and listened. She was talking to a horse and stroking its mane! Out of sight, he strained to hear what she was saying.

"You are so beautiful," said Philippa. "I wish I could ride you some day. We could see fields of flowers, feel the wind on our faces, and smell the ocean. I bet all our worries would disappear on such a ride," said Philippa.

Revealing himself, Paulus asked, "What are you doing here, Philippa?"

Startled to have been caught talking to a horse, Philippa

stammered for a moment and then finally said, "I think the horses understand me. We dream together of rides never to be taken."

"Why not?" said Paulus. "It's a bit unusual for a woman to ride, but I see no reason why you can't live your dream."

"Oh, I've never even been on a horse, sir. I know nothing about riding."

"It's decided then. When I return from Rome in a couple of days, I am teaching you to ride."

"Oh, but sir, you have too much to do to bother with me, and I'm not sure how proper it would be."

"I care nothing about being 'proper'. It would give me great enjoyment to see someone with such a love for horses learn to ride. I'll look forward to it. Farewell Philippa, and continue your conversation with this fine fellow," said Paulus with a smile as he patted the horse.

"Thank you sir," answered Philippa with a blush.

Chapter 6

*A*s Paulus rode toward Rome, he thought about his conversation with Philippa. He knew that he had already crossed the barrier between master and servant several times. However, with the deaths of her mother and brother, Paulus felt he should be her protector. In truth, his feelings were so conflicted. His strong attraction to her had made him often forget that she was not a Roman, but only a Greek servant. True, she was intelligent and very capable of running his household, but not only was she Greek (which would not have been a serious disadvantage), but she was without family and completely penniless. There would be no dowry for her to find a suitable husband, and to make matters worse, she was a "Christ follower".

"Why does she have such power to attract me?" thought Paulus. "She does nothing to make herself seductive, yet at night, my thoughts are filled with erotic dreams about her. But when I actually see her, I find myself wanting to shield her from lecherous rakes such as me!"

Continuing his ride, Paulus forced his mind to change from thoughts about Philippa to his visit to Rome. He had thought about going to see his Uncle Cornelius, but he decided that his old comrades would have more information on the aftermath of the fire as well as news about the executions of "Christ followers". Also, he was a little wary that his uncle might think he had an undue interest in these Christians if he asked him too many questions.

When he arrived at the Campus Martius, he was surprised to find civilians still camped on some of the familiar training fields. Seeing Claudius, an old friend, walking near one of these fields, Paulus got down from his horse and walked over to where he was.

"Greetings, Claudius," said Paulus. "How are you this fine day?"

With a jovial smile, Claudius answered, "Well, it's good to see you again, Paulus. I've not seen you since your father's funeral. You do know I served under him in my very first campaign outside of *Italia*. A fine soldier, he was, Paulus, a fine soldier."

"Thank you for your kind words. My father always spoke highly of you as well. Since the fire, Claudius, I have moved to Ostia and I know very little of Roman news, but I am surprised to see that there are still people in tents here."

Looking about him to make sure no one else was nearby, Claudius said, "It has been very difficult. There is so much unrest throughout the city. Many of these people are angry that they are homeless, and they blame everyone. There are even rumors about our Emperor setting the fires himself. Of course, we soldiers here know that he was at Anzio when the fires began. Some even place the blame on the *vigili* for not being more aggressive when the fires first started. Now, others are saying that some sect of Jews called 'Christ followers' started the fires, and I'll admit they are a strange group. I, myself, recently heard one of them making some crazy claims."

Paulus tried to be casual in his questioning, but he was actually quite interested in Claudius' story. "You've piqued my curiosity about this sect. I once guarded one of them, a Roman citizen named Paul. Was he involved in the group making the strange claims?"

"I know nothing of this Paul. The incident I witnessed involved a Jew named Simon Peter. He was standing near one of the Jewish meeting places, and he began quoting some man who had apparently died. He kept saying 'Repent and be baptized, every one of you, in the name of Jesus Christ for the forgiveness of your sins.'(Acts 2:38) A large crowd began to gather, and some of his followers tried to get him to leave, but he continued talking. I was with some other soldiers near the crowd's edge waiting to see if there was going to be a disturbance. The man spoke with such fire and enthusiasm that I felt compelled to listen. Though he spoke the Greek of an uneducated man, his words were really odd but powerful. He talked about a Jew named Jesus, who he said rose from the dead. Then he said that a great church would begin here in Rome. He looked to the sky and prayed loudly asking that the kingdom of God be established today. That's when a group of soldiers from the Praetorian guard arrived and arrested him and several others with him."

"What happened then?" asked Paulus.

"I wasn't a witness to anything else, but apparently the Emperor had heard about Peter and these Christians and had given orders to arrest Peter and his friends if they made any public comments. They were taken away, tried, and executed very quickly. It was a strange event. According to some of my friends, Peter asked to be crucified upside down, because he was a follower of this Jew Jesus who had been crucified. Peter said he wasn't worthy to die in the same manner as his savior. My friends said that Peter and his friends died singing and praising their god. Some kept saying, 'He is coming again soon', while others just prayed to Jehovah, the apparent name of their god. One of the other men, according to my friends, kept saying as Peter was crucified, 'This is the rock on which the church will be built.' What that means, I do not know, but those who witnessed the executions were affected by these men. By Jupiter, I'm rather glad I wasn't there. Of course, I'm sure now that this Simon Peter is dead, the strange group will disappear."

"Was a Roman named Paul ever mentioned?"

"No, I don't think so."

"Our world has certainly become more complicated with the fire and all these odd groups. Thank you, Claudius, for telling me the news. Take care. I think I'll ride on into Rome and perhaps check on what is left of my old house in the Esquiline Hills."

Even though he was very tired, Paulus mounted his horse and began to ride, knowing that he was not going to his old home but to Paul's house.

Chapter 7

When Paulus arrived at Paul's, everything there seemed much as it had been on that day long ago when he had first arrived for guard duty. All was quiet, and there were no crowds outside. Silvius was at his usual place.

"Greetings, Paulus," said Silvius warmly. "I am surprised to see you again so soon, but I'm glad you are here. Are things still calm in Ostia?"

This was a rather long speech for the usually taciturn Silvius. "It seems so," replied Paulus. Coming into the house further, Paulus saw Paul in the corner of the room with his head bowed and his eyes closed. With a bit of hesitation, Paulus ask Silvius, "Is he ill or is he sleeping?"

"I don't think he is sleeping. He has slept little for the past several days. He just prays and talks to his many visitors. Things are bad for him, Paulus. He is to be tried in two days, and I think there is little chance he will escape execution. He seems resigned to this being God's will."

"You've been with him so long Silvius. I know you are a believer in his strange doctrine and care for him. Would it not be easier for you to let another soldier take your place if Paul is sentenced to death?"

"I won't leave him. I intend to stay with him until he takes his last breath on earth!"

"And then what?" asked Paulus.

"Well, I have my years with the military completed. Paul has counseled me to take my family and leave Rome. I'll probably do so. All I know is that I must stay until he dies. Perhaps I can give him some comfort. I just pray that I can keep my composure and not betray my true feelings to my fellow soldiers."

"Silvius, do we have a guest?" asked Paul as he stood and rubbed his eyes.

"Oh, it is you Paulus. I was too preoccupied to see who had entered. I am so glad to see you one last time. Are you adjusting well to your new life in Ostia?"

Paulus couldn't believe that Paul would bother to chat about Paulus' life when his own was probably going to end soon. "I am well, as is my household," replied Paulus.

"I'm glad that the great Livian family has been spared. Silvius tells me your house here was destroyed and that you are living in Ostia. I came through Puteoli on my way to Rome. They say it is much like Ostia. I like port cities, and I also like the sea, despite some very nasty voyages. The sea's orderly flow has always calmed my soul," said Paul.

"How strange!" thought Paulus. "He has just described my feelings exactly."

Paul continued, "Things are going to end for me shortly, young Paulus. I have been saying my farewells, and I want to talk to you for a little while." As he was speaking, Paul walked as far as his chains would allow him to go toward Paulus.

"Son, I know the last couple of years have been very hard for you. With the death of your father, Livia's leaving, the loss of your home, and your new responsibilities, you must feel so alone now. I pray that God will give you peaceful joy in the near future."

"How could he know about my feelings of loneliness, and how could he know about Livia's search for 'peaceful joy'?" thought Paulus. Replying a bit gruffly, "Well, it has been a bit difficult, but I have it all under control now." As he said these words, Paulus thought to himself, "What a liar I am!"

With a smile, Paul replied, "I have very little under my control, but I am at peace. 'For to me, to live is Christ, and to die is gain.'"(Philippians 1:21)

As Paul was speaking, Paulus took note of his appearance. Looking so much older than when they first met, his shoulders were now stooped, his eyes looked tired and weary, and his hands trembled. There seemed little of the intensity he had first witnessed in the Jew's words and actions.

As if he knew Paulus' thoughts, Paul said, "Please excuse my weariness. I fear I have slept little these past nights, but I do not want to neglect any last minute details. I have been praying for guidance. I'm not afraid to die, but I do fear leaving undone something that my Lord expects of me before leaving this earth. Others have taken the message to the far corners of the earth, but there are so many people who still do not know that the promised Messiah has come for everyone." Stopping to look at Paulus for a moment, Paul suddenly closed his eyes. Paulus somehow knew that Paul was praying for him. Uncomfortable in the circumstances, Paulus looked at Silvius, hoping that he would say something to end this encounter. Instead, he saw that Silvius also had his eyes closed. "Our Emperor would be delighted to have a 'blind' guard!" thought Paulus sarcastically. Paul interrupted the uneasy situation by opening his eyes and saying, "I know you still find little truth in my words, but I also have been assured that you will change your opinion. That gives me great peace."

"Who assured you of such nonsense?" asked Paulus angrily.

"My Lord and Savior, Jesus Christ. But don't become angry. I don't want our last time together to be filled with rancor. Paulus, have you heard from Livia since the fire?"

"No, and I don't ever expect to do so", replied Paulus curtly.

"Well, I don't agree. I believe that sometime in the future, you will see her and Tatius again. I don't know where they are, but I have calmness when I pray for them. I think they are well and happy in the Lord." Paulus turned to look at Silvius, who still stood with his eyes closed, and Paulus could see tears running down his cheeks.

Suddenly changing the subject, Paul said, "You do know I'm to go to trial in two days. I intend to present my defense as I did to Governor Antonius Felix, Governor Porcius Festus, and then King Agrippa. I will try to humbly tell the truth." With a little smile, Paul straightened his shoulders and with renewed vigor began to tell again the story of his conversion.

"I was on my way to Damascus, when a light brighter than the sun blazed onto me and my fellow travelers. I fell to the ground and then I heard a voice saying, 'Saul, Saul, why do you persecute me?' (Acts 26:14) "Then I asked, 'Who are you, Lord?' And I heard 'I am Jesus, whom you are persecuting.' The Lord replied, 'Now get up and stand on your feet. I have appeared to you to anoint you as a servant and as a witness of what you have seen of me and what I will show you. I will rescue you from your own people and from the Gentiles. I am sending you to them to open their eyes and turn them from darkness to light, and from the powers of Satan to God, so that they may receive forgiveness of sins, and a place among those who are sanctified by faith in me.'"(Acts 26:15-18)

As Paul was speaking, the power of his words that had so impressed Paulus earlier returned. Even though Paulus had heard this story before, this time it seemed as if Paul were reliving the experience. Paul suddenly stopped and looking directly at Paulus said, "It took a light from heaven to change me. My heart and mind were too hardened to see and believe. But your heart is softer, and you will understand and see when the time is right."

While he was finishing this statement, two men came into the room, each in great distress. They began, "What should we do. They are throwing our friends to the lions!" said one of the men. The other man, with tears running down his face said, "My brother and his family were set afire and burned to death. Will our Lord return soon and save us?"

Paul turned from Paulus and said in a gentle voice to the men, "I don't know when He will return, but we are already saved. Our bodies may be burned, crucified, or torn by lions, but we have the ultimate salvation in Jesus Christ. Let me pray with you for a while."

Turning for a last look at Paulus, Paul said, "Be ready when the light comes down on you. I am convinced after that time, Paulus, you will be the most important Livian of them all. Farewell dear Paulus."

Paulus was greatly disturbed by this strange conversation with Paul. He found himself unable to say anything. Unsure whether to be angry or shocked, he found himself thinking of many questions.

"Why does it disturb me so much to hear of the deaths of these 'Christ followers'?"

"Why am I reluctant to leave this place that I have loathed so much in the past?"

"What did he mean that I am to be the most important Livian of them all?"

Recovering from his ponderings, Paulus turned to leave, and as he passed the ever quiet Silvius, he wished him well and walked out of the house. Passing through the front door, he couldn't seem to refrain from one last glance at the three kneeling figures on the floor. They didn't notice his leaving, and Paulus found himself regretting being unable to say a 'farewell' to Paul. But he mounted his horse and headed back to the Campus Martius with a heavy heart.

Chapter 8

Paulus remained in Rome at the Campus Martius for another day. During that time, he relaxed at the excellent public baths there and also enjoyed watching various types of drills and exercises of the young soldiers. Many of the older soldiers were eager to gossip about the arrests and executions occurring on a daily basis. One old veteran, who had been one of Paulus' own drill instructors, was particularly talkative.

"These rebels are getting exactly what they deserve," said the old man. "You know they started the fires, and they aren't loyal to the Empire. I hope they are all killed!"

"Do they have a leader here in Rome?" asked Paulus casually, even though he wanted to know much more.

"Not that I know about. They had one in Jerusalem, but he's dead. We crucified him," said the old man. "But we are getting rid of these Christian vermin quickly. Our Emperor has made an example of the lunatics. Some have been covered with animal skins and thrown to hungry dogs, others were thrown in pits of bears or lions, and some have been set afire and used as human torches. This little group will be crushed in no time!"

Paulus walked away thinking about the old soldier's comments with a shudder. Of course, beheadings and crucifixions were fairly common, but these methods of death seemed particularly brutal. The trials and executions were also being discussed in other parts of the camp that night. After listening to one of these conversations, Paulus said, "You know I used to guard one of these 'Christ followers'—a Jew named Paul. He's a Roman citizen. Have you heard anything about him?" One soldier spoke and said, "He's to go to trial tomorrow, I think. His family was supposed to have saved some Roman soldiers years ago, and they have retained high status as full citizens through the years. But unless he is willing to renounce this Christ as a god and worship our gods, he will die."

Paulus moved on to another field. Here he remained quiet and thought about what the man had just said. He remembered the story Paul had told him earlier about the rescue and care of his ancestors and others near Tarsus. Nighttime approached, and he found himself filled with regret about Paul's coming death. He even considered returning to the Jew's house. For what reason, he was unsure, but he finally decided he could do nothing, and his obligations were to those who depended on him in Ostia. So he slept fitfully in one of the barracks and planned his return home in the morning.

Chapter 9

Paulus left Rome early the next day. As he rode, he enjoyed the cool, fresh morning air. Riding along one of the lanes, he passed a large group of flowers in an open field. Usually completely disinterested in plants or flowers, today he was suddenly struck by the beauty of their many different colors. He slowed his horse and stopped to look at a particularly stunning bunch of red and yellow blossoms. Getting down from the horse, he walked over to them, bent down to smell them, and felt a moment of peaceful calm. On impulse, he picked a large group of the prettiest flowers to take to Philippa. Perhaps, the flowers, he thought, would ease her pain when he told her the news he had learned in Rome. Climbing back on his horse with the flowers in his hand, he started back on his journey to Ostia. After a short distance, he looked at the flowers and suddenly thought, "I am becoming a complete idiot! I'm sniffing flowers and then gathering them like a girl. What kind of man am I?" He then threw the flowers away and rode the rest of the way with new determination to forget Philippa, Paul, flowers, and executions, and instead concentrate on his businesses in Ostia and Rome. As he continued the journey, he thought, "Perhaps I will rebuild my house in Rome. Anyway, there are lots of important things I need to attend to and none of them involve flowers, 'Christ followers', or Paul!"

It was late when Paulus arrived at his house in Ostia. He led his horse to the stables, and one of the slaves took the horse to feed him and rub him down. Paulus was exhausted physically and emotionally after the long trip. Thankfully, Philippa had gone to bed for the night, and he didn't have to recount the information he had learned in Rome. Paulus went quickly to bed and determined to be gone very early the next morning. He wanted to postpone the conversation with Philippa as long as possible.

Chapter 10

The next day, Paulus woke before dawn, quickly dressed, and headed to the atrium for a quick exit from the house. However, when he walked in, there sat Philippa on one of the benches near the door.

"Have you been here all night?" asked Paulus.

"No. I've just been very restless and couldn't sleep the past couple of days. I feel that things are bad in Rome. I just know it in my soul," said Philippa.

"Well, I don't know anything about your soul, but you are right about Rome. There are many trials and executions there. Paul is to go on trial today. There is a lot of violence in Rome now. Philippa, you must be cautious about your prayers, even here in Ostia."

"Oh sir, I'm not important, and I doubt anyone would even miss me if I were to be executed," said Philippa.

With a sudden burst of emotion, Paulus exclaimed, "You are wrong. You are important to me, and I would, I would. . . Just be careful, Philippa."

Paulus hurried out the door. He had to get away before he said too much. He knew where he had to go—the docks. He needed the calming of the ocean.

When he arrived at his favorite spot near the water, he immediately looked for his young friend Antonius, but he was nowhere to be seen. Paulus was disappointed. When he talked with the little boy, his own troubles seemed fewer. He walked around the pier for a while, watching the seas and the bustling commerce on the docks. Finally, he was able to focus his attention on matters of business. He walked to one of his warehouses, arriving just in time to meet with a trader with whom he had dealt before. With the massive rebuilding in Rome, materials such as lumber were in great demand, and Paulus was able to arrange some excellent deals that would be very profitable to him for some time. He spent the entire day talking to different traders and merchants and arranging for storage of the merchandise. Thanks to his father's excellent reputation in matters of business, he found that he was able to make deals with little difficulty. At the end of the long day, Paulus was pleased with himself for being able to successfully carry on his father's affairs so well. He stayed in town until late and then walked to the docks once more. The sun was just beginning to set, and the colors reflecting on the water were absolutely beautiful. He found himself wishing he had someone with whom he could share the stunning scene. As he leaned on the rail, peering into the multicolored waves in the water, he thought to himself, "What is wrong with me? Yesterday, I was picking flowers, and today I'm watching a sunset and thinking like a poet! What has happened to the soldier whose *gladius* was feared by all?" Angry with himself for such silly sentimentality, he roughly kicked a couple of rocks into the water and headed for home. However, he did search one last time for little Antonius, who was nowhere around.

Chapter 11

Paulus spent the next few days at his house in Ostia. He had some calculations to do for his business, but he spent most of the time riding around his property inspecting the vineyards and orchards that he had had cleaned up after his move to Ostia. Mostly, he just wanted to be out of the house so as not to see Philippa. He had no news from Rome about Paul, but he couldn't stop wondering what had happened at his trial. He even considered giving a riding lesson to Philippa in order to distract himself, but he was too glum to be interested in teaching her to ride. Also, he couldn't bear any questions about Paul, and of course, if he were honest, he feared his own responses to being alone with her. When he met her in the house, he was formal and courteous but didn't pursue a conversation. She, too, seemed subdued and not eager to talk.

On the third day after Paulus' return from Rome, he decided to go into Ostia to the baths. It was a dreary day. It had rained during the night, and Paulus thought he would probably have few companions there. Before going to the baths, he decided to go to the docks to watch the sea for a while. Upon arrival, he saw the back of a familiar figure. Peering at the sea was little Antonius.

"Well, I thought you had deserted me, Antonius," said Paulus cheerfully as he approached the boy.

The Light Will Come

Hearing Paulus, Antonius turned toward him and said, "I'm still here sir."

Coming closer, Paulus was horrified at what he saw. Antonius' face was battered. One eye was swollen shut, and Paulus saw that he had huge red marks on his shoulder at the neck of his tunic. Touching him gently on the head, Paulus asked, "Son, what happened to you?"

"Oh, I'm getting better. I was hurt bad for a few days, but I can walk now. I'll be well in just a little while," said Antonius.

"But what happened to you?"

Paulus had seen beatings before, and he knew that was what he was seeing. But he still wanted to hear it from the child.

"Well," he then hesitated and stopped.

"Go on. Tell me," said Paulus with authority.

"I don't think my mother and father would be proud of me, but this is what happened. A few days ago, I was playing and didn't know it was so late. When I got to my cousin's house, he and his wife had already eaten. They told me that they had warned me not to play so late, so they said, 'Go to bed. There'll be no food for you tonight!' I went to bed like they said, but I couldn't go to sleep. I hadn't eaten anything all day. So I slipped into the kitchen and got a piece of bread and a fig, and then I started back to bed. I guess I made some noise because my cousin grabbed me and yelled, 'Thief! I don't know why we ever took you! You're not worth the money. I'll teach you never to steal from me again'. He then started to hit me. I ran and that made him angrier. He caught me and just hit me again and again. Then he got a piece of leather and beat my leg where I was burned." Antonius pulled up his tunic, and Paulus could see the open wounds on the skin still tender from his burns.

Paulus wanted to hold him and give him comfort, but he was so battered and bruised that he was unsure where to touch him.

Antonius interrupted his thoughts by asking, "Do you think my father would be very mad at me for stealing? I didn't mean to steal. I was just so hungry. They are giving me less and less food, and I just wanted some bread." Paulus could see tears running down his dirty, swollen face. Here was this remarkable child in obvious pain, crying not from his wounds but because he had done something wrong. The little boy had so touched his heart that all other matters seemed unimportant to Paulus.

"Son, I know your parents would not be angry with you. It wasn't stealing. You were just getting your own supper. Come sit and let's talk for a while."

"I'll mostly listen sir, if you don't mind. It hurts to talk very much," said Antonius.

"I want you to tell me the name of your cousin and where you live. I want to talk to him," said Paulus.

"No! No! He'll be angry I told you what happened, and he'll beat me again. It'll hurt really bad on these bruises. Please don't talk to him!" pleaded Antonius.

It was at that moment that Paulus made a decision that he knew would change both their lives.

"I promise he will not hurt you. I will see to that. Now take me to his house."

"But sir, he might hurt you too!" cried Antonius.

"Son, I am not afraid. I am a trained soldier. Let's go."

"Wait, I…" Paulus then saw that the boy could barely walk. No wonder he hadn't been to the pier two days ago.

"I can carry you if it is too hard for you," said Paulus.

"Oh no! I am a Roman. I am tough," said the boy.

They then started the slow (due to Antonius' condition) trek to his cousin's house. It was farther from town than Paulus had expected, and Antonius was obviously in pain, but he walked bravely onward.

"I was hoping to see you today. That's why I came to the pier. I could probably have walked there yesterday, but I was so ashamed for you to see me. I… I know it's wrong to steal. My parents are…" Antonius then stopped talking and said no more until they arrived at the house. It was small but neat, with a nice garden beside it. Paulus strode to the front, and as he walked up the steps, a large, middle-aged man came out the door.

"Well, here you are," he said to Antonius. "You're back early today. I guess you'll not be late again," he said with a little chuckle. Looking at Paulus, he then said, "Who are you and why are you with my boy?"

"Is he your son?" asked Paulus innocently.

"No, but I take care of him. I don't have children, just my cousin here." With that, he grabbed Antonius harshly by the arm and the boy yelped in pain.

"He seems to be hurt," said Paulus. "I was wondering if I might be able to offer some money for a doctor for him." In truth, Paulus doubted he needed a doctor, but if he judged the situation correctly, he thought the mention of money might change things.

"Well, he did have a bad fall," said the cousin, who by then had noticed the expensive tunic and the gold-braided belt Paulus was wearing.

"Now who might you be?" asked the man.

"I am called Paulus of the Livian family from Rome."

The cousin immediately heard the aristocratic speech and the authoritative manner of speaking of a patrician Roman family.

"We are humble, working people, just doing our duty by helping care for this poor orphan," said the cousin.

"If you could spare the time," said Paulus graciously, even though he was seething with fury, "would you mind having a private conversation with me for a moment." As he was saying this, he was thinking, "Be calm! Be calm!"

"But of course sir," said the man with a smile.

Leaving the boy and a woman, who was obviously the wife of the cousin, on the steps, they walked to the edge of the garden.

Paulus began carefully. "This may seem strange to you, but I've been looking for a boy to train for work in my stables. I talked to this boy at the docks, and he seems very energetic and intelligent. I would be willing to pay quite generously to get the appropriate child. May

I ask if you are a close relative? I wouldn't want to interfere with the courts if you are adopting him."

"No, we are not near relatives, just distant cousins. We have no plans to adopt him, but of course, he is very dear to us both."

"Of course," said Paulus. "But I would be willing to give a handsome sum to relatives of a child who would serve me well. Would you be interested?"

Paulus was amused at the man's attempt to be pondering the offer.

"How much are you offering?"

Paulus stated a sum he knew would seal the deal with the obviously greedy cousin. Paulus also saw the gleam in the man's eyes as he winked at Paulus, and Paulus realized that the man thought Paulus wanted the boy for his own "pleasures".

With a knowing smile, he said, "Well, when he is clean, he is a handsome lad, and I would not want to prevent his learning to be a fine stable hand." He then laughed.

"Do you have documents from the authorities concerning him?" asked Paulus politely, even though he could barely contain his anger.

"No, just their agreement to pay a very small sum for his care for a year. The year is almost up."

Paulus reached into his belt and took out a gold coin and gave it to the man. "Nine more of these will be delivered at your house tomorrow. I will send a scribe with papyrus for you to sign before you have the coins. I hope we have an agreement."

"Oh, we do sir. We do," said the man as he stared at the coin.

"I would like to take the child with me now. Perhaps, he needs a doctor due to his 'fall'."

"That is very quick. I think it best that he remain with us until the deal is complete."

Paulus glared at him with a stony expression and said, "The boy will come with me or you can return the coin now."

"No, no. That will be fine. Antonius," he yelled, "come here quickly."

The boy hobbled over to them with a look of dread in his eyes. "Here I am sir," he said to his "cousin", while looking with questions toward Paulus.

"Young man, you are to go with this fine man. He seems to think he can use you." At this remark he chuckled. "Be sure and tell him what good care we have taken of you. Farewell." With this comment, he walked back toward the house without another look at Antonius.

"My emissary will be here tomorrow with the papyrus," shouted Paulus at the man. Saying nothing more to the "cousin", he turned to Antonius and said, "We must go now. Tell your "cousins" farewell as you get your things."

Antonius went into the house and returned with his meager possessions. They then walked away very slowly with no conversation between. When they were out of sight of the house, Paulus said, "Let me carry you son. I know you are in pain."

"Oh no sir. It would hurt just as much for you to touch me. What is happening? Where are we going sir? Will they be angry that I'm going with you?"

"I thought it hurt you to talk," said Paulus, with a grin. I'll explain later. Now we need to find a mule cart to take us to my house where you'll now be living."

"But, but I don't understand. I…" said Antonius tearfully.

"I don't understand either, son. Now hush and let's find an easy way to get you home."

Chapter 12

Paulus hired a mule cart to transport them to his house. Antonius brought with him all his possessions which consisted of a change of clothes (really only rags) and a shabby little chest. Clutching the little chest, Antonius told Paulus, "My special treasures are in here. They are just a few things I've found and aren't really valuable to anyone but me. I'll show them all to you someday."

As they were riding to the house, Paulus watched as Antonius peered into his little chest. Antonius then took something out and said, "Here's one of my treasures." At this, he handed Paulus a small white stone. "I found this near the water several days ago. It was all alone. No other rocks were around it. I was sorry for it, so I picked it up. It's very pretty."

Hearing Antonius' words, Paulus found himself strangely moved by this story. He was almost sure that Antonius felt he was like that stone.

"Well, it's a very nice rock," said Paulus as he turned it over in his hand. "I'm glad you rescued it." He then gave the stone back to Antonius.

"I have some other things I'll show you later, but they won't make me worth anything to you sir. Maybe the Emperor will give you money for me, but I don't know."

"Son, I don't want any money to take care of you. I just want you to be part of my household now. By the way, I thought it hurt you to talk."

Antonius then laughed for the first time in Paulus' presence. "My cousin says I talk too much and ask too many questions. But I'll try not to bother you sir."

Paulus replied, "Don't worry about that. You just have to get well so that we can walk to the pier together."

They didn't talk much more for most of the rest of the trip.

Paulus and Antonius arrived at Paulus' house just before sunset. There had been a steady drizzle most of the day, but the sun had returned by the late afternoon. The house and gardens looked lovely bathed in the diminishing sunlight.

"You really live here?" exclaimed Antonius.

"Yes. This is my home and land," said Paulus, gesturing with his hand to show that he owned the fields and woods around the house as well.

"I see a horse! Oh, there are several horses. Do you think I could touch one?" asked Antonius.

"Later," said Paulus with a chuckle. "Now, you need a good bath and some clean clothes. Get your things, and you'll meet my household."

Antonius hobbled up the steps and then hesitated before going into the atrium. "Go on," said Paulus, "I'll pay the mule cart driver and then I'll be with you." Antonius waited. He wasn't going into that big house alone with all those people he could see through the doorway. When the driver was paid, Paulus joined Antonius and actually took the boy's hand. "Come, there is nothing or no one to fear here," said Paulus.

When Antonius saw the interior of the house, he stared in wide-eyed wonder. "This must be the biggest and most beautiful house in the world!" exclaimed the child.

"It's hardly that, but it certainly needs a little boy to make it complete," replied Paulus.

Philippa, along with several of the other servants and slaves appeared. Paulus announced, "Antonius will be living with us. Make him welcome. He needs a bath, food, and some treatment for his wounds." Paulus directed a couple of the servants to draw water for a bath. Then to two of the kitchen maids, he said, "Bring some soup and warm bread into the atrium for us to eat." Then to Philippa he said, "Antonius lost all of his family in the fire as did you. I want you to tend to his wounds. He will have lots of questions, when his mouth heals," said Paulus cheerfully.

The house staff seemed to bustle with activity. Usually, they were preparing for bed, but tonight, they were to prepare for a small and mysterious new member of the household.

With his hand gently touching Antonius' shoulder, Paulus said to Philippa, "Antonius has a serious request which I want us to honor tomorrow. He wants to touch a horse. I think we can arrange that, don't you Philippa?" Paulus said with a twinkle in his eyes.

"I'm sure we can sir," replied Philippa.

"Now let's get you settled in for the night young man. First there will be food, then a long bath, and bed."

"But, but what, uh why…" began Antonius, but Paulus interrupted the child.

"There will be plenty of time for explanations later. What you need is treatment for your wounds and rest. I know you like to know what is happening, but tonight you must simply trust me. No one will harm you here, and when you wake tomorrow, you will be properly introduced to some horses."

By this time, a servant had appeared with water and clean towels for washing their hands. Shortly thereafter, steaming bowls of soup and warm bread were brought in by servants. Antonius' face lit up when he also saw butter and honey. Paulus smiled to himself. "Nothing heals wounds any better for a child than honey and bread."

Strangely, Paulus found himself more at peace and even happier than he had been for weeks. There had been so much turmoil, change, and sorrow in his life for the past few months, and he knew that he had just made what was perhaps a rash decision, but this little boy had captured his heart.

Chapter 13

The next three days were filled with delight and wonder for Antonius. Paulus, too, found himself looking at the world with a new sense of awe. When Paulus, Philippa, and Antonius went to the stables the first morning after his arrival, the excitement in Antonius' little face was contagious. Paulus found himself completely relaxed and free from his worries and responsibilities.

"Philippa talks to the horses when she's lonely. They like her," said Paulus. At this, Philippa began rubbing the mane of an older mare.

"Go ahead. Touch her. She's gentle," said Philippa.

Antonius tentatively rubbed her lightly. Paulus saw that one of his eyes was wide with excitement, but the other eye was still badly swollen and almost shut. "He needs cold water on his eye," he said to Philippa. Then to Antonius, he said, "When you are better, I'll teach you to ride. I've made a promise to give riding lessons to someone else as well." At this comment he gave Philippa a knowing look.

"Do you really mean it?" cried Antonius.

"Yes son," said Paulus.

"I think this is the best day of my life!" said Antonius. "It's the nicest day since my family died. I know that for sure," said Antonius as he continued petting the grey mare with more confidence.

The next couple of days passed with new things for Antonius to discover every day, and Paulus found himself enjoying tasks that he had usually thought boring. As he inspected areas of the gardens and the house itself, his constant "shadow" with his squeals of surprise and interest made Paulus appreciate the good fortune he had in life.

Philippa and Antonius became friends very quickly. When Antonius was not with Paulus, he was with Philippa asking question after question.

"Sir," said Philippa on the second day, "I think we have someone who can ask more questions than Miss Livia."

"You may be right. Just wait until his mouth heals. I suspect the questions will increase," said Paulus with a smile.

Paulus had told Philippa about the little boy's situation, even about the exchange of money. Paulus sent his emissary on the second day after Antonius' arrival to the "cousin's" house and the exchange of coins and documents was completed. No one, besides Philippa, was aware of the arrangements.

On the fourth day after Antonius' arrival, Paulus left Antonius in Philippa's care and went to Rome. He told Philippa, Antonius, and the other staff that he had to make a business trip there but would return very shortly.

While Paulus was confident that Antonius' "cousin" was satisfied with the deal, he intended to make certain there were no legal problems with his keeping the child. He had become more and more sure every day that he wanted to adopt Antonius as his son. Adoptions in Rome were commonplace, but they usually involved family members being adopted. He was unsure exactly how one should proceed when a child was not a relative, but he knew his Uncle Cornelius could help him with the legal process. So he decided not to delay, but get the matter settled immediately.

As Paulus traveled on the familiar road to Rome, he thought about Paul as well as Antonius. Before leaving, Philippa had begged him to find out Paul's fate. Paulus had been so preoccupied with the little boy that he had not thought very much about the Jew and his trial. He knew the trial had already taken place, but he had pushed the possibilities of its outcome from his mind. It was obvious that Philippa hadn't done the same.

She pleaded, "Please sir, I have prayed and prayed, but I have no peace about him. I must know if he is still alive."

Wanting to know the answer himself, he agreed to find out the outcome. Of course, he had already intended to ask Cornelius the trial results even before Philippa's plea.

Riding alone with no distractions, Paulus wondered if Cornelius had been present at the trial, and if so, if he had voted for execution. In the past, Cornelius had been moderate in his views about this new sect. In fact, on the visit to Paul's house with his father Atticus, his Uncle Cornelius had seemed quite impressed by the Jew. Paulus' own feelings had certainly softened since his first day on guard duty. There were many reasons for his change in views: Livia's becoming a convert, finding out that Philippa and her family were "Christ followers", Silvius' faith in the sect, and Paul's story about his ancestor. But Paulus knew, if he were honest, that Paul's words and actions also had had a strong impact on him. "Of course, I don't believe in this Jesus' being raised from the dead, but these Christians (as some were now calling them) are a remarkable group of people. They have strange ideas such as love being more important than a sword and their god listening to them when they talk to him. In no way can I see them being a threat to the great Roman Empire, but I will be very interested in what Uncle Cornelius has to say," thought Paulus to himself.

Chapter 14

When Paulus arrived in Rome, he decided to go straight to the Forum, where his uncle spent most of his time. As he rode through the center of Rome, he was amazed at the amount of construction that was taking place. On his last visit, he had heard that Emperor Nero was building a new palace where so many buildings had been destroyed by the fire, but he was surprised by the size of the palace and grounds. Huge gardens and even a lake were being made in the middle of the complex. With so many Romans homeless due to the fire, he knew his uncle would have some negative opinions about this extravagant project. Upon his arrival at the Forum, he tethered his horse, and then searched for his uncle. He found him quite easily, just outside the *Curia*. He was talking with a group of other Senators, all quite regal in their senatorial togas. On seeing Paulus, Cornelius left his comrades and walked over to him.

"It is so good to see you, Nephew. I've intended to travel to Ostia to see you, but I have been rather occupied here. With the Senate and our business affairs, I find I have little time. Are you here for very long? I know Mucia and my girls will want to see you. They so enjoyed your stay with us after the fire, even if it was a bit crowded."

"I was hoping to spend the night at your house. I'd like some time to ask you for some important advice," said Paulus solemnly.

"Is there something wrong?" asked Cornelius.

"No, no. I think it is something very right. However, I do need direction on the proper legal steps to take."

"Well, it so happens that my work here is finished for today. Let me say farewell to my friends, and then we can walk to my house."

"I have my horse and need to take him to a stable. Is there still one on the west side of the Forum?"

"Yes, it is still there. It will take very little time for you to stable your horse, and then we can have a nice stroll."

After completing their duties, they began their journey. On the way, Paulus remarked on the clearing of the ruins from the fire and on the construction of the new palace.

"Yes, it's going to be quite spectacular. There is to be a huge lake, multiple gardens, and a grand palace with massive columns." Looking around to make sure no one was within earshot, Cornelius said, "Unfortunately, there are new rumors circulating that our Emperor set the fires in order to have this land in the center of Rome for his *Domus Aurea*. Of course, he insists that the 'Christ followers' are to blame, and I don't really know what to think. A lot of our temples were destroyed in the fire, and many think this sect wanted to get rid of all of our gods and traditions by burning our temples. But I've been at the trials of several of these fanatics, and they mostly seem to be simple people with dreams of some kind of a spiritual kingdom after death. I've been on the jury of some who seemed to welcome death, but I somehow doubt either our Emperor or this sect had anything to do with the fires. But I may be wrong."

"Do you know anything about the Jew Paul?"

"Yes, he was executed three days ago. I was not part of the trial, but I've heard the scene at his trial and execution was quite dramatic. The *Praetor* let him speak in his own defense before passing judgment on him. I was told by one of my friends that the entire hall became quiet as he spoke about his life and mission. Let's face it Paulus, the Jew was no ordinary man. He had Roman citizenship; therefore, he was sentenced to be beheaded."

"He was under our guard and could not be responsible for any fires. What were the charges against him?" asked Paulus.

"Since he refused to bow to a statue of our Emperor and continued to talk about the kingdom of God, there was no choice but to charge him with treason and anarchy."

"It might surprise you, but his speech at the trial so impressed some of the jurors and spectators that they are still talking about it. I wish I had been present. I'll have to admit that I was amazed at his eloquence and passion when we visited him."

"He was a very unusual man," said Paulus.

"Yes, it's a pity he had to die. They knew he set no fires, and it was apparently true that his ancestors were highly honored for their service to our Roman soldiers many years ago. But he wouldn't deny that Jesus Christ was the son of God. If he had just done that and pledged his loyalties to our gods, he would have been freed."

As they continued their walk to Cornelius' house, they talked about Roman politics, the massive rebuilding program in Rome, Paulus' business affairs, and his house in Ostia. Finally, Cornelius asked, "As we've talked, I find nothing amiss in your life, my son. What is this advice you are needing?"

Hesitating for just a moment, Paulus then said, "I need to know the legal procedures necessary to adopt a child."

"Adopt a child! This seems quite sudden. Whose child do you wish to adopt, Paulus?" asked Cornelius with some alarm.

"His name is Antonius," began Paulus. He then proceeded to tell Cornelius the entire story of the little boy. After he finished, he said, "He is a special child, who will add much to the Livian family."

"Are you sure you want to do this?"

"I'm completely certain."

"Well, since the fire the rules of adoption have been greatly relaxed due to the large number of orphans who lost parents in the fire. The adoption procedure is called *adrogatio*. In the past, there was a meeting of officials of the *Comitia Curiata* to approve an adoption, but since there are so many children who have no parents, the Emperor has given authority to the magistrates to legalize adoptions."

"Is it difficult to petition for an adoption with one of these magistrates?" asked Paulus.

"Son," chuckled Cornelius, "if you have the money to accompany the request, it can be finalized in one day. I can take care of the matter for you tomorrow. I assume you know he will become your legal heir when the seal is put on the papyrus?"

"Yes, I know that."

"And I presume, you have gold with you to speed up the transaction?"

"Yes. I have come prepared, Uncle Cornelius. This child has become very important to me and has given me much joy. I want him for my son."

"Well, I am looking forward to meeting your Antonius. Leave everything to me. I'll take care of it tomorrow."

"Do I need to be present?"

"Ordinarily the answer would be yes, but we Livians are not without influence. My word and your petition will be enough, and it would probably be easier for me without you. I can more easily call in personal favors alone."

"I appreciate your help so much. I have some things I need to do tomorrow. For one, I want to check on my old house."

"That's a smart idea. You need to make sure there are no squatters living in the ruins. Are you going to rebuild?"

"I haven't decided. I like living in Ostia. Somehow, I feel drawn to the sea, and I am so near it there."

"You have plenty of time to make a decision."

They continued their conversation until they reached Cornelius' house. When they arrived, Cornelius' wife Mucia and their daughters greeted Paulus with great enthusiasm. They all wanted to know about Ostia. The evening passed agreeably with a good meal and congenial talk about many matters. Before retiring for the night, Cornelius said, "Paulus, you know there are many fine Roman families with daughters who would be very interested in you for a husband. I'm sure there are girls with fine dowries who would be a good match for you. I would be happy to help with the contract. Now that you are to have a son, isn't it time for you to have a wife?"

"Thank you Uncle Cornelius, but at the moment, I'm trying to adjust to many changes. I don't want to marry until I'm more settled."

"I suppose that makes sense, but certainly this adoption is a big change."

"Yes, but the child's situation forced me to act. But I am still sure that I'm making a wise decision."

After he was in bed, Paulus thought about Cornelius' marital counsel. He admitted that he would like to have a wife, but for some reason, every time he thought of a woman, he saw Philippa's face.

Chapter 15

Perhaps due to the long ride from Ostia and the festive evening with Cornelius and his family, Paulus slept rather late the next morning. Going into the atrium, he encountered Mucia who was arranging flowers in one of the urns. "Good morning to you Mucia," said Paulus.

"Good morning Paulus," said Mucia cheerfully. "I hope you slept well. Cornelius left early, but he left a message for you. He said that he must get an early start to make sure the gold is properly delivered and the matter sealed. I don't understand what that means, but I've repeated his words."

"I know its meaning and thank you. I have a little business to which I need to attend. I'll be gone most of the day, but I'll be back tonight. I hope I haven't caused too much hardship for you and your staff."

"Of course not," said Mucia. "I hope you have a successful day. The weather certainly looks very nice." With this, Mucia returned to her flowers. Paulus grabbed some bread and grapes and hurried from the room.

Paulus began his walk through the streets leading to his old house. Just before he started up the hill, he looked at the bare area where Philippa's family had once lived. There was no rebuilding of those *insulae* as of yet. A couple of small shops had opened, but the rest of the area was still a ruin. He felt a moment of strong regret as he made his way up the Esquiline Hill to what was left of his house.

When he arrived, he saw that it was just as he had left it. The marble walls and columns were still in place, and it gave him a desolate feeling. As he walked into the garden, he saw that weeds and wild vegetation had overrun the grounds that Livia and Alexander had kept so beautifully. It seemed to Paulus that it was a house of gloom. He made a decision at that moment. He was not going to rebuild here. It brought back too many happy memories that could never be repeated. No, he knew that Ostia was now going to be his home.

After looking at the house, Paulus stopped by one of his warehouses to talk to his manager. There were no problems to solve there. As he left, he stopped for a moment and thought, "Do I really want to go there?" But he then convinced himself that it was the polite thing to do. So Paulus started walking to Silvius' *insula*. "It's not that I'm so interested in Paul," he thought to himself, "but I do want to make sure that Silvius and his family are safe."

At Silvius' apartment building, he paused for a moment, dreading the visit and wondering what he was going to say. Finally he entered and began the familiar walk down the dingy hall. He knocked on Silvius' door and Silvius opened it. "Greetings Paulus," said Silvius. "Please come in."

When Paulus entered he saw that the beautiful apartment was now reduced to chaos, with chests piled with utensils and decorations, tapestries in a stack, and furnishings gathered on wooden pallets. It was obvious that they were moving. In one corner, he saw Herminia, Silvius' wife, sitting on the floor putting jars and urns in a chest. By the look on her face, Paulus could see she had been crying.

"I don't want to disturb you. I can see you are preparing to move," said Paulus.

"Yes Paulus. It is now time for us to leave Rome. Herminia and I are going to Greece, along with Titus and his family. Herminia has family who live in Thessalonica. Many of our friends have already been executed, and we know it's only a matter of time before we will be arrested if we remain here."

"I'm sorry Silvius. I truly do not believe 'Christ followers' set the fires, but it would be so easy to stop the trials. All any 'Christ follower' must do is bow to our Emperor and reject the notion of this Jesus Christ's being a god."

"Oh, it isn't quite that simple. For us there is only one god, Jehovah, who sent his son Jesus Christ to earth to save us."

"From what I see, it doesn't look as if he is saving you," said Paulus sharply.

"It isn't a salvation of the body, Paulus, but a salvation of the soul."

"This talk is too philosophical for me. I've just come to see if you and your family are well, and if you have heard anything from Tatius and Livia."

"I have heard nothing from them, and I have no idea where they even are. I pray daily for their safety."

Silvius continued, "Paul advised me to take my family away from Rome. He has friends in Thessalonica who are Christians, and he believed it would be a place where we could raise our grandchildren in our beliefs. Perhaps I will die for my faith one day, but Paul assured me that I can still serve my Savior now here on earth for a while. Paulus, I want to thank you for not revealing that I have become a convert to this new faith. It would have meant a quick death for me and probably my family."

Abruptly, Paulus changed the subject and said, "Silvius, tell me about Paul's trial and death."

"It is something I will remember in detail for the rest of my life. The trial began with the *Praetor* asking if he were guilty of treason. He replied, 'No, your honor.' The *Praetor* then asked for evidence to be presented against him. There were two rolls of papyrus on which several Jewish leaders in the provinces had written that Paul claimed that the kingdom of God was at hand, and there were a couple of Roman witnesses who said that crowds gathered at his house for a feast that included eating flesh and drinking blood."

"Did they not call you as a witness?"

"No. Lucien, one of the other guards, was called to give a full account of the meetings at Paul's house, including the bread and wine ceremony. While somewhat biased, he said that the people attending were strange and emotional, but the ceremony had no blood or flesh in it."

The *Praetor* then asked, "Are you now a believer?"

The crowd became quiet while Lucien said, "Most certainly not! I only believe in our gods, including our latest god, Emperor Nero!"

"I was sure I would be called, and I was prepared to tell the truth which I knew would lead to death. However, the *Praetor* simply turned to Paul and asked, "Do you as an honorable Roman citizen renounce your belief that this Jesus Christ is God, and then will you bow to our god Nero?"

"No, I can never do that."

"Do you have anything to say in your defense?" asked the *Praetor*.

"Paul then began to speak. Paulus, I have rehearsed his words and have memorized them. I must do so to tell the world what he said. He began by telling the story, that you've heard, of his conversion on the road to Damascus. The room then became very strange."

"What do you mean 'the room was strange'?"

"Well, there had been a lot of noise with jeers and laughter during the trial. But when Paul began speaking, the room became very quiet and still. It was as if Paul were alone with God. He knew he was going to be sentenced to death, but he looked around the room and after telling his life story, he said these words, 'In all these things we are more than conquerors through him who loved us. For I am convinced that neither death nor life, neither angels nor demons, neither the present nor the future, nor any powers, neither height nor depth, nor anything else in all creation, will be able to separate us from the love of God that is in Christ Jesus our Lord.'(Romans 8:37-39) Grace to all who love our Lord Jesus Christ."

"With these words, he bowed his head. The *Praetor* hesitated for a moment and then sentenced him to be beheaded. The crowd finally came to life, and some jeers returned but not as many as before. Tears ran down my face, and I longed to go to him. But it felt as if invisible hands were staying me. I just waited. Two members of the Praetorian guard then took him away."

"Was, was he tortured?"

"No. I followed as they led him to the grounds where he was to be executed. I was permitted to stay with them even though my official duties were finished. No one touched him except the guards who were leading him."

"Did he say anything else?"

"Yes. As they were placing the blindfold on him, he said, 'The time has come for my departure. I have fought the good fight, I have finished the race, I have kept the faith. Now there is in store for me the crown of righteousness, which the Lord, the righteous Judge will award to me on that day — and not only to me, but also to all who have longed for his appearing.'"(II Timothy 4:7-8)

"They then placed him with his head over a block of wood, and as the executioner was raising the axe, Paul said, 'The Lord be with you all.'" As Silvius was relating these last words, Herminia began to sob quietly, and tears ran down Silvius' face as well.

Paulus didn't know what to say. He was moved by the words of Silvius and in truth deeply saddened by the death of Paul. To lighten the conversation a little, Paulus said, "Silvius, I have heard you say more in the last few minutes than in all those months we were guards together."

"Yes. I seem to have become much more able to talk about everything, especially about my belief in the resurrected Christ. Paul said that I should pray for a gift to use for God, but I never expected it to be speaking. I listened to Paul all those many hours, and now I want to tell what I learned from him. I want to tell the good news."

"The good news! It seems to me there is no good news but only bad news for you 'Christ followers'!"

"Oh, but there is good news Paulus. Paul often quoted the good news of these words of Jesus, told to him by one of Jesus' first disciples.

'For God so loved the world that he gave his only Son, that whoever believes in him shall not perish but have eternal life.'"(John 3:16) Silvius said this with great passion.

"This Jesus, whom you call the son of God, was crucified by us! He died, Silvius! What makes him different for our Emperors who died that we now worship as gods?"

"I know you don't believe it, but I'll say it anyway. He rose from the dead. He talked and walked with his followers after his crucifixion. Now this is the good news. I believe, and I feel his presence in my life. Furthermore, even if I perish today, I'll have eternal life with him."

Paulus was becoming more uncomfortable by the minute. Changing the subject, he said, "I'm somewhat curious. What became of Paul's body or do you think his head returned to his body and he is walking and talking again also?" His tone was extremely sarcastic, but Silvius answered calmly.

"No, his body was treated with respect due to his status as a Roman citizen. It was given to a small group of Jews who buried him in a private garden. Strangely, no one interfered with the removal of his remains, nor did they arrest any of the people who took the body."

Herminia approached them and whispered something to Silvius. He then said, "Oh Paulus, I would so like to talk longer, but my wife has reminded me that we must hurry. Titus is to be here soon."

"I'm sorry for have taken so much of your time. Thank you for seeing me, and I wish the best to you and your family. Farewell."

"Farewell Paulus, and I pray that what Paul believed about your life will happen very soon," said Silvius.

Paulus turned and walked out the door. Silvius and Herminia stood and watched him go down the hall of the *insula*. Paulus paid little attention to his surrounding as he walked back to Cornelius' house. He couldn't stop thinking about all the things that Silvius had said. Not only did he find the last words of Paul very moving, but the last statement of Silvius had made him recall the words Paul had said to him. "Be ready when the light comes down on you." It was all so confusing and disturbing. As he walked, he decided not to tell Cornelius about his visit to Silvius.

Passing by one of his favorite public baths, Paulus stopped to spend some time there. It had been a long time since he had treated himself to a rigorous workout and baths. He was a bit disappointed that none of his old friends were there, but he still enjoyed the exercise and relaxation of the waters. However, even in the baths, he rehearsed the conversation with Silvius.

When Paulus arrived at Cornelius' house, it was late in the afternoon, and his uncle was already home. On seeing his arrival, Cornelius said, "Greetings, Paulus. Have you had a good day?"

"Yes. I have taken care of some small duties and enjoyed an afternoon at the baths," said Paulus.

"Well, I have good news for you." With this statement, Cornelius walked to a small table and picked up a sealed scroll. "Here, Paulus. This document completes the adoption procedures. You are now Antonius' father."

"I am surprised that it happened so easily. Thank you so much Dear Uncle."

"I had to use a little persuasion, but with help from my friends and a little gold, it is finalized and legal."

"My gratitude is beyond words," said Paulus.

"It is my pleasure, and I'm looking forward to meeting this child who so quickly stole your heart. Now I am famished. Let's eat and enjoy the evening together," said Cornelius.

Paulus spent an enjoyable evening with Cornelius and his family. At the end of the evening, Paulus told them that he needed to leave very early the next morning. He had to get his horse from the stables, and he then had a long ride to Ostia. So he thanked Cornelius again and retired for the night.

Chapter 16

*P*aulus began his ride to Ostia shortly after dawn. It was another beautiful day, but Paulus was too occupied with his thoughts to even enjoy the scenery that he had so admired a few days ago. He had made decisions that were going to change his life, and there were other things to ponder as well. He now had a son for whom he would be responsible. His uncle was right. He was definitely at the age when he should marry, and he knew several girls from patrician Roman families that would be suitable. But he just wasn't interested. He was only attracted to one woman, a tiny Greek servant named Philippa. His thoughts also kept returning to the death of Paul and the strange conversation with Silvius. "Oh yes," Paulus thought, "my thoughts have become those of a serious man!"

He arrived at Ostia in the late afternoon and immediately took his horse to his stables for one of the servants to feed. When he entered the stables, he heard Philippa speaking.

"Yes, I think Hector would be a good choice when you have a lesson. You like people, don't you Hector?" said Philippa.

Paulus then made an entrance and startled Philippa, Antonius, and even the horse, Hector.

"Shhh. It's fine, Hector. Don't be alarmed," said Philippa to the horse as she calmed him. Then turning to Paulus she said cheerfully,

"I'm afraid you've found me in a conversation with another horse. What is worse, I have introduced Antonius to my horse conversations."

"Oh sir, we have had so much fun," said Antonius. "I think the horses like me. When can I sit on Hector, sir? I'm ready. He knows me and…"

"Stop," said Paulus with a smile. "Now let's begin again. Greetings to you, Antonius and Philippa."

"Greetings sir," replied both Philippa and Antonius.

"I see that you are much better. Your eye looks less swollen, and I can tell your mouth has recovered," said Paulus jokingly. "And your leg, is it healing?"

"Oh yes sir. You can see," replied Antonius. "It won't hurt at all when I am on a horse." It did look much better, but it was evident that Antonius had only one thing on his mind—sitting on a horse and then riding it!

Laughing at the exuberant child, Paulus said, "I think we should see if Hector likes a talkative child on his back tomorrow. Then we can begin your riding lessons!"

"Thank you, sir." He started toward Paulus as if to hug him, but then he stopped and said, "I don't know why you have been so kind to me, but I'll try not to pester you with my talking so much. Oh my, I'm talking again!" said Antonius.

Paulus then went to the boy and put his arm around the boy's shoulders, "Son, I have many things to discuss with you in the morning. Now I need to talk to Philippa. Go to the house and tell the servants I have returned and would like dinner." Looking at Antonius' dirty hands, Paulus said, "Also, you need to wash those hands for a very long time."

"Yes sir," replied Antonius. He then ran (his legs obviously a lot better) toward the house.

Paulus asked Philippa to sit on one of the benches just outside the stables and wait while he gave instructions to the stable attendants. After leaving his horse with them, he returned to where Philippa was sitting. He immediately sat down beside her, and she stood, knowing that it was improper for a servant to sit with her master.

"No, no, sit Philippa. I have many things I want to tell you," said Paulus.

"Oh, is it about Paul?" asked Philippa fearfully.

"Yes, and there are other things I need to tell you as well," said Paulus.

"First of all, I'm sorry to tell you, but Paul was beheaded a few days ago. If you like, I can tell you about his trial and his words of defense in court. I have information from a soldier who was there."

"Yes sir, please do," said Philippa as she began to cry quietly. "I want to know everything about him."

Paulus then told her the information he had learned from his Uncle Cornelius and Silvius. Philippa listened without interruption. Paulus finished by quoting Paul's last words, "The Lord be with you all." Philippa began to sob softly.

Paulus couldn't prevent himself from putting an arm around her shoulders and pulling her toward him. For a moment, she cried on his chest as his other arm gently encircled her. She remained against him for just a moment, and then, realizing the situation, she pulled away.

"I'm sorry sir. I didn't mean to lose control," said Philippa as she rose from the bench.

"Was there something else you wanted to tell me?" asked Philippa.

"Oh, if she only knew what I want to say," thought Paulus as he remembered her tiny body in his arms. He had felt her heart beating against his chest, and it was almost more than he could stand not to tighten his arms around her and kiss her.

"Sir, is there something else?" asked Philippa again, bringing Paulus out of his momentary daze.

"Uh, yes Philippa. There is something quite important I want to share with you. I have adopted Antonius. It was finalized yesterday."

"I'm so glad!" said Philippa as she reached out and touched his hand lightly. "He is an absolutely delightful child. I have spent quite a bit of time with him while you were away, and I do so enjoy being with him. He makes me see everything with a renewed joy. He will be a wonderful son to you sir," said Philippa. She had now stopped crying and was smiling.

"I must go. I have duties to perform. Good evening sir," said Philippa as she walked away.

Paulus remained by the stable door. He couldn't stop remembering the way his heart raced as he had held Philippa, and he could still feel the touch of her hand on his as she shared the joy of his adopting Antonius. "If only she would consent to being my mistress," thought Paulus. But he knew that as a "Christ follower", she would reject any such suggestion, and he feared any such approach of this kind by him would drive her away.

Walking toward the house, his thoughts drifted back and forth from Antonius and his adoption to Philippa, the tiny servant, who unknowingly had completely addled his mind.

Chapter 17

Paulus was up at daybreak the next morning. Usually after a long day of riding, he was so tired that he slept quite soundly, but the previous night, he couldn't seem to get the many new developments of the past few days out of his thoughts. He had been in the atrium for only a few minutes when little Antonius dashed into the room. Seeing Paulus, he said hopefully, "I suppose it's too early to have a riding lesson on Hector, isn't it sir?"

"It is a bit early. But before we get involved with any horses, there is something I need to tell you."

"Do you want to send me back to my cousin? I promise not to talk so much," said Antonius fearfully.

"No, my boy. I'm not ever going to send you back to him. Let's go outside for a few minutes while I tell you some new information."

As they were walking outside Paulus asked, "By the way, why are you up so early?"

"Oh, I couldn't sleep. I was too excited about sitting on a horse. I could just see myself on Hector, riding over the fields. I had to get up so the day would hurry and begin!" said Antonius with obvious excitement.

Ignoring the little boy's comments, Paulus began with his serious news. "Antonius, when I went to Rome yesterday, I adopted you as my son. Now, you will be able to stay here with Philippa and me and all the horses forever."

"I don't know the word 'adoption'? What does it mean?"

Paulus considered how to explain it to a child. "Well, your parents died in the fire, and you had nowhere to live except with your 'cousin'." Paulus continued, carefully choosing his words. "My parents died as well, and I was all alone just as you were. I didn't have a son, and I decided **you** would be a fine son for me. If we became father and son, then we wouldn't be alone but would always have each other. So I asked a magistrate to let me adopt you—meaning I can be called your father. They gave me a scroll with a seal on it. The scroll says that you are now a member of the Livian family, and I must take care of you as a son."

Paulus wasn't sure what reaction he had expected, but he certainly hadn't expected silence. Finally Paulus asked, "What's the matter? I thought you liked it here. Don't you want to live with me?"

"I'm just thinking about it all. Being adopted doesn't mean I have to forget my own father, does it?"

"Certainly not," replied Paulus. "I would never want that."

"You do know I ask a lot of questions, and I might get in your way. My cousin says…"

"I don't care about your cousin's opinions. I like you Antonius just the way you are, and I want you to be my son."

"I think I can do that," said Antonius as if he were negotiating the deal himself.

Paulus smiled as he thought again, "What a remarkable little boy!"

"Sir, there's a secret about me I should probably tell you if you want me as your son," said Antonius.

"You can tell me now," said Paulus.

"Uh, well maybe it can wait until after I get to sit on Hector and go for a ride," said Antonius while flashing a big smile.

"Whatever you decide will be fine," said Paulus, even though he was very curious as to what big secret Antonius could have.

Changing the subject, Antonius said, "I really like Miss Philippa.

We've become friends, but she's not very good at pretend sword fighting. I guess it's because she's a girl."

"Probably so," agreed Paulus with a chuckle. "Come let's eat something, and then we'll see what Hector thinks about letting you ride him."

Chapter 18

*T*he next few days passed with Antonius living his dream. He learned how to sit on a horse, how to mount and dismount (with the help of a stable hand due to his size), and finally how to ride around a field with someone leading the horse.

Both Paulus and Philippa were so occupied with the energetic child that they had very little time to discuss Paul's death or the events in Rome. It seemed there were few places Antonius did not investigate. He roamed the gardens, hills, and fields near the house where he found bugs, frogs, and various other interesting creatures that he brought back to the house to share!! Having lived most of this life in Rome and then in the restricted environment at his *"cousin's"* house, this newfound freedom was wonderful for the boy. The melancholy child that had first spoken to Paulus on the docks was no more.

One morning, Paulus decided to go for a ride to check on one of his vineyards that was located on the other side of the woods from his house. As he approached the stables, he heard Philippa and Antonius in a serious conversation. He was curious as to what they were saying, so he kept very quiet and listened.

"You do think it's good that I'm 'dopted, don't you?" asked Antonius.

"It's adopted, and I think it is wonderful. Master Paulus is a fine man, and he really cares about you. It's sad when you lose all your family, and you don't matter to anyone. I know. I lost my family in the fire as well."

"Yes, I know. Father Paulus (his new title for Paulus) told me. But you do matter to someone — me!" At this, Paulus could see that he wrapped his little arms around her. "You do know that Father Paulus cares a lot about you too."

"Oh, my dear, I'm just a servant to him. He trusts me to manage his household. That's all."

"I don't think so. I see how he looks at you. It's like my father used to look at my mother. I believe he **really** likes you. Maybe you'll even get married. That's what I think! Now let me show you what I found on the other side of the hill, a nest of birds." At this he took her hand and they started for the door. Paulus ducked behind some stacks of hay so they wouldn't see him.

After hearing this discussion, Paulus decided to postpone his ride and walk instead to the docks alone. He and Antonius had gone to the pier a couple of times together, and they had watched the tides and enjoyed the sounds and smells of the docks. But today Paulus wanted to be alone, and he knew of no better place to be than by the sea.

Chapter 19

*L*eaning on the same railing where he had watched the azure waters weeks ago, he thought about Antonius' comments to Philippa. He was stunned by the child's words and by his amazing perception. He considered for a moment his feelings for Philippa. He trusted her, he admired her, and he was greatly attracted to her. If he were honest, he knew he loved her. But she was a servant. She had no dowry, and she was a foreigner. To marry her (since she was Greek), he would have to get special permission from the courts. Of course, that would be granted, but his status as a noble Roman would be greatly diminished. There would be no patrician family alliances through a contract of marriage. But he was being absurd to even think about it. He had to remember something even worse about Philippa—she was a "Christ follower". Their two worlds were too different to ever be joined!

He watched the rippling water of the tides rolling into shore and renewed his resolve to forget Philippa. He had businesses to run and a new son who gave him great joy. Despite Paul's prediction of his being a great Livian, he was going to be an ordinary man, content with his new life in Ostia.

A few more days passed with life settling into a normal (or as normal as it could be with Antonius around) routine. Paulus and Philippa talked about the household needs, and Antonius continued his riding lessons. Philippa also began to ride. She had such a natural affinity for horses that she needed few instructions. There were comments from some of the other servants to her about a woman riding a horse, but she just said it was her master's suggestion.

One day Philippa and Paulus were standing just outside the stables watching Antonius ride. (He was now permitted to ride with no one leading him.) He was on Hector, his favorite, and all seemed well, when they heard a yell and saw Antonius fall from the horse. He didn't get up immediately, and both Paulus and Philippa started running toward the child. Philippa began praying, "Oh God, please don't let Antonius be hurt. Dear Jesus, we need him so much. Please help him."

Paulus quickly outran Philippa, and as he left her behind, he almost unconsciously began repeating the same prayer, "Please God, help him. Please help him."

When he got to the child, he saw blood running down his cheek from a cut on his forehead. Paulus gathered him up in his arms to take him to the house. Antonius suddenly opened his eyes and looked at Paulus and said, "Ouch! I think I fell off the horse, but it wasn't Hector's fault. You see, I saw a baby rabbit, and I turned loose of the reins. I know I should have held on to them. Why are you crying, Miss Philippa?"

Paulus turned to see Philippa standing behind him. Tears were running down her face, and she was saying, "Thank you Jesus."

"I bet Philippa prayed for me and that's why I'm not hurt. She prays a lot," said Antonius to Paulus. Seeing the boy had a mere flesh wound, Paulus put him down. Antonius then reached for Philippa and hugged her. She was so happy with relief that she then turned to Paulus and hugged him. Paulus held her for a few moments longer than necessary, and he looked over her head at Antonius. The child had a gleam in his eye and was smiling. Turning her loose, he then said, "You are going to make my hair become silver overnight if you have any more accidents like that!"

"Oh, I'll be more careful, I promise," said Antonius, who was now skipping merrily beside them as if nothing had happened.

Chapter 20

The next day Paulus found Philippa in the atrium alone. He gathered all his courage and asked her if she would mind answering a few questions.

Somewhat alarmed, she said, "I'm sure I would be glad to reply to any questions you might ask sir."

"It's about your beliefs. I'm just somewhat curious. How did you become a 'Christ follower'?"

Pausing for a moment to hide her surprise, she replied, "Several years ago, there was a Jewish couple who lived in our *insula* who were 'Christ followers'. They befriended my family. We had recently come from Greece and felt very alone, and my father and mother talked many long hours with them. The couple had a few people who would meet in their apartment for prayer and worship. My parents, Alexander, and I started going to the services. One day we all prayed together, and we believed. It wasn't like a dramatic light from heaven such as I've heard people say happened to Paul. But we all **knew** that Jesus Christ was the Son of God, and he had brought salvation to us."

"But there was no salvation for your father. He died. His new religion didn't help him!"

"No sir, it didn't prevent his death, but he was at peace when he died. In fact, he told us that we would only be separated from him for a short time."

"What do you mean by that?"

"Well sir, we believe that Jesus Christ conquered death and rose from the dead. Because of Him, we too shall conquer death and have eternal life," said Philippa.

"This is too complicated for me. To believe all this I would have to be struck blind by a light like Paul, and I doubt that is going to happen!" said Paulus.

"I'll pray that there will be a sign for you sir."

"Oh, I'm not sure I want that. I'm just curious about this new religion. That's all. Perhaps we can talk another day. I have some business matters which need my attention," said Paulus. Truthfully Paulus was becoming uncomfortable with the fervor of Philippa's words, much in the same way as Paul's last speech had disturbed him.

As Paulus walked toward town, he thought again of Paul's assertion that he too would have an awakening light. He had listened to Paul, Silvius, and now Philippa, but there was no light or sudden peaceful joy as described by Livia. No, all he had was a headache and a remembrance of the way Philippa's eyes shone when she talked, as well as how her lips simply begged to be kissed.

Chapter 21

The following day, Antonius and Paulus went for a walk together. When they came to a big oak tree, they stopped and sat in the shade for a while. Antonius said to Paulus, "I like to look at clouds. They change shapes all the time, you know. I like to imagine what they look like."

"Yes, they do. What do you see in those big white ones above us today?"

"Oh those are easy. I see a lot of sheep talking to each other," Antonius said.

Paulus laughed. "Well, the clouds are changing. What do you see now?"

"A chariot. Yes, that's what it is. I've seen a few in the streets in Rome. Sir, do you think a chariot came and took my family to heaven when the fire came?"

Paulus was at a complete loss for words. Stuttering, he asked, "Why do you think a chariot came for them?"

"Well, a chariot carried Elijah away. My parents were very good. I think they might have gone to heaven that way also."

Not knowing how to answer, Paulus asked a question instead. "Who is Elijah?"

"Oh," said Antonius, "he's a man from a long time ago. Look!

That cloud is a woman with long hair like Miss Philippa. I know a secret about her."

"What kind of secret?" asked Paulus with great interest.

"You must promise not to tell her I told you."

"I promise," said Paulus.

"She really likes you a lot!" said Antonius.

"Did she tell you that?"

"No, not exactly." Coming close to Paulus, Antonius whispered, "She prays for you a lot. One day, I heard her say, 'Please God, take care of Paulus. I love him so much!'"

"You shouldn't listen to her prayers, Antonius. They are private."

"I know. It was an accident, and I won't do it again. Oh look, that cloud looks like a fish."

"We'll just have to let that fish swim in the sky the rest of the day. I'm hungry, and we need to go back to the house."

As they walked, Paulus thought to himself, "Philippa loves me!" He could hardly contain his feelings of joy. As they entered the atrium, Antonius said, "Would you like to see my chest of 'treasures' someday soon?"

"I would indeed. Perhaps you can show them to me this afternoon."

"I'd like that, Father." It was the first time Antonius had called him Father without his name attached. He felt very moved. "What a strange few days it has been," thought Paulus. "First, there was that long conversation with Philippa about her religion, then Antonius and he had 'visited the clouds', and finally Antonius had said that Philippa loved him. Oh, and who is this Elijah that went to heaven in a chariot?"

After they ate, Paulus had to check some supplies he had received. When he passed Philippa in the kitchen, he asked casually, "Do you know anything about an Elijah in a chariot?"

As if in shock she hesitated, and then said, "Why, yes sir. I do know the story."

"Well, tell me the story if you know it," said Paulus a bit sharply.

"Antonius wonders if his family went to heaven in a chariot like Elijah. And also where is this heaven? Is it like our Elysian Fields where our gods live?" asked Paulus.

"I don't know where heaven is sir, but I know it's where I'll go when I die. It's why I'm not afraid to die. I know that even if I'm executed as a Christian, I'll go to heaven, where I'll be with Jesus and my family again," answered Philippa.

"Philippa, you mustn't talk openly with other people about your beliefs in this Jesus. Someone could tell the authorities that you are a Christian. I, I don't think I could bear losing you."

Philippa looked at Paulus for a moment and then suddenly whispered, "I love you sir." Then she ran out the door.

Completely unsure as to what he should do or say, he just stood there. He now knew that Antonius was right. She did love him, and by Jupiter, he loved her as well. While he was pondering the problems a relationship or marriage to Philippa would cause, Antonius appeared. Looking hopefully at Paulus, he said "Father, I have my chest. Do you want me to show you my 'treasures' now?"

Recovering from his dilemma about Philippa, Paulus replied, "I would be honored to finally see your 'treasures'."

"Let's go outside and sit in the sunshine so you can see them really well," said Antonius.

"That's a good idea. We can sit in the garden. They walked outside and sat on a bench among the flowers. Antonius clutched his chest of "treasures" to his body protectively.

Paulus began, "I remember the rock from your chest that you showed me earlier. It was very nice."

"It **is** a special rock, but my other things are special too." He then opened the little chest and took out a long feather. Handing it to Paulus, he said, "I found this the first day I came to live with my 'cousin'. I liked its colors, and when I looked at it, I dreamed I could fly away like a bird and be with my family again. Every time I see it, I think of them."

Paulus found himself so overcome with emotion that he had to fight back tears. He handed the feather back to Antonius. Antonius then took out a shell and gave it to Paulus. I found this shell by the docks. It's really special too. It reminds me of the sea and the places I might go someday. But more importantly, I found it on the day I first met you. Every time my cousin hit me I would go look in my chest. I would see my shell, and somehow I knew that you would be at the pier to talk with me again."

By now Paulus could no longer speak. Antonius then took out the last item from the chest. "Father, it's time for me to tell you my secret now." With this statement, he handed Paulus a twig which was shaped exactly like a cross.

"My parents were 'Christ followers' sir, and I am one too. This cross is how my Savior Jesus Christ died, and I will always want it with me to remind me of Him. That's my big secret, Father."

Paulus took the twig in his hands. Tears were now running down his face. As he held the twig, a beam of sunlight shone down brightly on the piece of wood in his hand, making it gleam as if it were gold. He could almost hear Paul's words, "The light will come to you, Paulus."

Putting his arms around the little boy, he bowed his head and in a trembling voice said, "Oh my Lord, I believe! I believe!"

Glossary of Terms

adrogatio—the adoption ceremony for a child who had no parents

Arelate—Arles, a city in southeastern France

Britannia—Ancient Rome's name for Great Britain

bulla—type of locket placed around a Roman's baby's neck to ward off evil spirits. A Roman boy at 16 (when he officially became a Roman citizen) removed his *bulla*. A girl would continue wearing her *bulla* until her marriage.

Campus Martius—a large (490 acres) area of ancient Rome located just outside the city walls along the Tiber river. It was a vast military complex that also contained many important Roman temples and monuments including the famed Pantheon.

chariot races—races held in honor of the gods and very popular with all classes of Romans. The races began with great ceremony involving parades and music. The charioteers wore colors of red, white, green, or blue. The "Blues" represented the aristocracy.

Circus Maximus—oldest and largest racetrack/arena in ancient Rome

cohort—military division consisting of three *maniples* (600 men). There were 10 *cohorts* in a legion (6,000 soldiers).

colonia—territory usually settled by retired Roman soldiers

Colosse—town on the Lycus River in Asia Minor. An early Christian church was established there by someone other than Paul. A man named Epaphras brought news to Paul that some of the people in Colosse were attacking the divinity of Christ and teaching other false doctrines. Paul wrote a letter to the Colossians to counter these heresies.

Comitia Curiata—main assembly of the people in ancient Rome. Commoners could participate but only the patricians could vote.

Corinth—ancient Greek commercial city known for its wickedness. The Temple of Aphrodite with its 1000 sacred prostitutes was located there.

Domus Aurea—golden palace of Emperor Nero, built after the fire destroyed the area of Rome where it was later located. It was begun in 64 A.D. and finished about four years later. There were pavilions, gardens, and even a lake built around the palace.

Ephesus—city in Asia Minor (now Turkey). It was a commercial center and contained the pagan temple to the roman goddess Diana. Paul preached there for 3 years. He wrote a letter to them to expand their depth of understanding of God's grace, and he called for unity within their church.

Esquiline Hill—one of the famous 7 hills of Rome. Many wealthy Romans had villas there.

Elysian Fields—where the gods dwelled in ancient Greece and Rome. Mortals could go there in the afterlife if they were heroic or linked to the gods.

Forum—huge complex of public buildings, temples, triumphal arches, and colonnades lined with shops and restaurants. The house of the Roman Senate called the *Curia* was located in the Forum.

Gallia Narbonensis—Roman province in the southeast coast of France

Gaul—an ancient European region including France and Belgium

gladius—sword

impluvium—shallow pool in the center of the atrium where rainwater came in through the funneled hole in the roof

insulae—large apartment buildings in ancient Rome. They were sometimes as tall as 6 stories and covered an entire city block.

lectica—litter carried on the shoulders of slaves. Since mule carts were not allowed from sunrise until 4:00pm, the lectica was used by wealthy Romans for transportation during the daytime.

Livia Prima, Livia Secunda, Livia Tertia—A Roman woman was named after the feminine form of her father's family. If there were several daughters, they were often numbered (Prima, Secunda, etc).

maniple—a military division of 200 men

Mare Nostrum—Roman name for the Mediterranean Sea

Massalia—Marseille, France

numina—divine spirits in everything (objects, animals, even ideas)

Ostia—ancient seaport not far from Rome

palla—shawl worn by Roman women over a *stola*

patricians—aristocrats or nobles of ancient Rome

papyrus—plant from which strips were used to make a type of paper

Pax Romana—ancient Rome's "peace" imposed on all its territories

Philemon—book of the Bible which was actually a personal letter written by Paul from prison to a man named Philemon. The letter was about a slave named Onesimus, who apparently ran away and was in Rome during Paul's imprisonment. Onesimus had become a Christian and one of Paul's close companions.

Philippi—a prosperous city in Macedonia. Paul wrote a letter to the Philippians in which he wanted to strengthen their desire to press onward even in times of trials. It is known as the letter of joy (Joy is found 16 times in the letter).

Pompey—Roman general and statesman (106-48 B.C.)

Pontifex Maximus—high priest of the Roman gods

Praetor—elected magistrate. *Praetors* often presided as judges in criminal court.

public baths—social and community centers of ancient Rome. They included parks, gardens, art pavilions, music and lecture halls, shops, restaurants, exercise rooms, libraries, and swimming pools. Of course, the most important things were the cold, warm, and hot baths (*frigidaria, tepidaria,* and *caldaria*).

Regia—building located in the complex of the Forum. It was said to have been the King of Rome's residence at one time, but it became the headquarters of the priests and the *Pontifex Maximus*.

Rhone—river flowing from the Alps into the Mediterranean Sea

sagum—short cloak worn by soldiers

shema—most important Jewish commandment

spelt cake—unleavened wafer or bread shared by the bride and groom at a Roman wedding *stola*—garment covering the body from neck to ankle. It had a high-waisted belt and clasps at the shoulders and was worn by a Roman woman over her *tunica*.

taberna—a type of Roman "bar and grill"

tablinum—office in a Roman house where death masks of ancestors were kept

Titus Livy—ancient Roman historian who lived from 59B.C. –17A.D.

Torah—Jewish Books of the Law or the first 5 books of the Old Testament in a Christian <u>Bible</u>

tunica—tunic

Vestal virgins—6 virgins who tended the sacred fires of ancient Rome in the House of Vesta. The girls were chosen at the ages of 6-10 and trained extensively for their duties. They served 30 years and were put to death if they broke the vows of chastity or let the fires go out. It was considered a great honor to have a family member chosen to serve.

vigili—firemen

Special Notes to My Readers

In writing this book, I have tried to follow the facts about Roman history and the stories of the *Bible*. For instance, the Great Fire of Rome and the problems with pirates in the Mediterranean Sea are well-documented. The persecution of Christians (which is so essential to this story) during the reign of Emperor Nero is also recorded by several different sources. I have also attempted to accurately use information about Paul as stated in his "prison epistles" as well as the stories in the book of *Acts*.

However, there are many areas where little is known about Paul. For instance, tradition has it that both Peter and Paul died in Rome, but there is no recorded information about their trials or executions. In this book, I have written a fictionalized account of events of those last days where no information is known. I have also made up other scenarios such as why Paul and his father had Roman citizenship. I do not want anyone to be misguided by my fictionalized account.

I pray that anyone who reads this story will know that I have written it with prayful consideration and respect for God and his Word.

Brenda Clemens